"Cindy Sproles is a beloved public speaker who focuses on matters of faith. Now, she writes of the Appalachians and its people with sensitivity and devotion. This labor of love is Cindy's opus. Cindy writes from the heart about the people she knows, in the place where she lives, all on journeys of faith and ultimately redemption." —**Adriana Trigiani**, *New York Times* best-selling author of *Big Stone Gap* and *Big Cherry Holler*

"At once chilling and compelling in its honest portrayal of nineteenth-century mountain life, *Mercy's Rain* is a beautifully written story of man's depravity and God's mercy. Its pages are filled with memorable characters and gripping scenes, and at its heart is a message you won't soon forget." —**Ann Tatlock**, Christy Award winner and author of *Promises to Keep*

"Cindy Sproles writes an authentic Appalachian tale of grit and mercy. Her voice is lovely, her story captivating. Cindy Sproles is an author to watch." —**Gina Holmes**, best-selling and award-winning author of *Crossing Oceans* and *Dry as Rain*

"Like Francine Rivers's *Redeeming Love*, *Mercy's Rain* is a story of betrayal and suffering and a woman-child's anger facing the world as a means of survival. It is a story of one man's use of the Word of God to damage and distort, and another man's expression of God's love and grace and, yes, mercy beyond measure. Don't let the hardness of Mercy Roller's life stop you; read to find the hope at the end." —**Jane Kirkpatrick**, best-selling author of *A Light in the Wilderness*

"I was blown away by *Mercy's Rain*. There are two things I look for in a good story: unique, interesting characters I come to care about and an author's ability to transport me to the time and location of the story. Cindy Sproles achieves both. Her prose is fresh and captivating, the kind you want to take your time with and savor. And the characters she's created come to life and hang around in your head long after you've finished reading. I'll definitely be looking for more from her." —**Mike Dellosso**, author of *Darkness Follows*, *Darlington Woods*, *Scream*, and *The Hunted*

"Author Cindy Sproles takes the concept of Mercy and crafts an unforgettable story. Her authentic Appalachian voice rings with simplicity and sincerity, as she explores issues as relevant to today's readers as those of yesteryear." —**Edie Melson**, codirector of the Blue Ridge Mountains Christian Writers Conference and author of *Fighting Fear*

"Like the Maker's great grace, *Mercy's Rain* never stops falling, not even at the book's end. Sproles's rich historical is a balm for the rent soul and a testament to the animating power of His great, all-consuming mercy." —**W. C. Bauers**, author of *Unbreakable*, book one in the Chronicles of Promise Paen

Mercy's
Rain

An Appalachian Novel

MERCY'S RAIN

CINDY K. SPROLES

Kregel
Publications

Mercy's Rain: An Appalachian Novel
© 2015 by Cindy K. Sproles

Published by Kregel Publications, a division of Kregel, Inc.,
2450 Oak Industrial Dr. NE, Grand Rapids, MI 49505.

Scripture quotations are from the King James Version.

Library of Congress Cataloging-in-Publication Data
Sproles, Cindy.
    Mercy's Rain : an Appalachian novel / Cindy K. Sproles.
    pages ; cm
1. Fathers and daughters—Fiction. 2. Young women—Crimes
against—Fiction. 3. Man-woman relationships—Fiction. I.
Title.
PS3619.P775M47   2015   813'.6—dc23   2014038906

ISBN 978-0-8254-4361-9

Printed in the United States of America
15 16 17 18 19 / 5 4 3 2 1

*Dedicated to my dad, Sherman C. Frady
and my niece, Erin Frady Thomas*

ONE

MARRIED AND WIDOWED at thirteen, a mother and childless at fifteen. Ain't nobody should have to learn life like I did. No soul should have to claw their way back from the bowels of hell, scared and scraped up like I was. I hate these memories.

"What don't kill ya will make you better." I reckon them was the only words from the Pastor that stuck. "Don't you make your Momma late to the river. Don't look right for the Pastor's wife to be late to a baptizin'." My arms weighed down from the pile of kindling the Pastor stacked on them.

"Yes, Pastor." I turned and walked fast to the porch, daring not to drop nary a piece of wood. "We'll be on time with a basket lunch." Nothing had changed since I was a youngin. Even as a woman, I still cowered at the sound of his voice. But I was never the same after the morning Pastor took on judge, jury, and Jesus.

Life ain't much different on the mountain than it is in the valley. A man's lucky to have a horse and wagon, lucky to have a shack with a tin roof. There are sinners on the summit and sinners in the foothills and I reckon Pastor Roller planned on washing every sin from every man.

They was no washing my sin away. I made a mighty harsh decision. One I'd grow to regret. One I'd have to live with.

I spread a blanket over a stand of grass and brushed down the wrinkles. "Over here, Momma. Bring that basket over here. I got us a spot laid out." Momma carried an apple pie in one hand and a basket full of chicken in the other.

"There you are, Mercy." She lifted the basket and wiggled her fingers in a half wave.

The aroma spun in the breeze, meshing with Mrs. Taylor's fresh sourdough bread. "It couldn't be a prettier day for a man to repent and then go down to the river for baptizing, is they, Momma? Ain't it a wonderful mornin'?"

I turned my face to the sky and let the sun draw out the mess that seemed to fill my mind. Best I can remember, I was happy for once.

I knew Stanley Farmer and what he lived with. When he mustered the courage to go to the Pastor and ask to be forgiven of his sin, be cleansed, I began to understand what forgiveness meant. It took a big man to fall on his knees before the Pastor instead of beating the tar out of him. Especially knowing what Stanley knew.

The Pastor scowled when he stepped into the water. He yanked Stanley to his side, raised his hand into the air, and started to preach on the sins buried in his soul.

"Pastor, be careful. Stanley's legs ain't strong. That cold water will wash more from him than sin," I said. I tinkered with the pages of Pastor's Bible. The rough edges of worn leather snagged the flesh on my fingers.

"I'll be up on the rocks when you get settled. Come on up." Maddie's hair flailed in the breeze like a sheet hangin' on the line. She'd been my friend for years. She stayed my friend, even though.

"I'll catch up in a bit." I winked at Maddie as she headed toward the rocks that jutted like fingers over the river. We spent a fair amount of time on them rocks tellin' secrets. She knew things not another soul knew.

"In the name of the Lord, I baptize you." The Pastor's voice boomed over the noise of the river water. He dunked Stanley Farmer by the forehead deep beneath the icy waters of the Indian River . . . held him under the rushing wash, all the time shouting for God Almighty to bring the man redemption. "Sin will kill a man. Take the soul right out of him.

Even the sins a man ain't got the guts to name." The Pastor growled the words like a grizzly bear on the hunt.

My stomach turned and the feeling in my gut forced me closer to the river's edge. "Let him up, Pastor," I shouted. "Let him up." Elsi Farmer, Stanley's wife, stood on the bank crying for Stanley's salvation and when the Pastor finally let Stanley catch a breath, he had the fear of God written all over his face. As fast as Stanley caught a gulp of air, the Pastor shoved him under the water again.

Stanley's hands stretched from beneath the cold wash, knuckles tight and bent. He grabbed for anything to save him.

"You ain't cleansed of your sin yet. Hell awaits your soul. I offer you back to the water and back into the hands of the Savior."

I raced to the edge of the riverbank. My shoes sucked into the mud and held me tight. "Stop, Pastor. You've done baptized him. Let him up. It's not for you to pass judgment." I grabbed my knee and tugged my leg. The mud popped when my foot pulled free. "Stop, Pastor. Stop. Let him go." The Pastor shot a glare at me that stopped me dead in my tracks.

"I'm the Lord's servant. Here to serve. Don't take neary another step. I'm doin' the good Lord's biddin'." He yanked Stanley up by the collar. Stanley coughed and gasped for a precious breath and before I could get close and into the water, the Pastor commenced to press Stanley down again.

Stanley dropped to his knees in the river, clasped his hands around the Pastor's wrist and pleaded not to be dunked again. "Good Lord has forgive me. He has. Don't put me back under, Pastor. I'm a changed man. I can't take the water again." His legs, weak from polio, couldn't hold his weight and once he got chilled in the Indian River, all he could do was plead for his life.

"Let Stanley up. God in heaven, don't let the Pastor kill him." The men on the bank splashed into the water to help.

Pastor Roller grabbed Stanley by the hair, yanked him backward, and placed his knee in the middle of Stanley's chest. "A weak body is a weak soul. Come out of this man, demon. God save his soul."

"Oh Lord, no!" shouted Elsi. "He's gonna drown Stanley." She dropped her Bible and lunged into the water with me. I fought at the current of the river surging against me. "He's changed, Pastor. Let him up." Her four children screamed in terror from the bank.

Stanley's feet and arms thrashed around—but Pastor Roller wouldn't give in and by the time me and Peyton Simmons got to the man, his body had stilled. A man riddled with polio wasn't strong enough to fight the cold water and the Pastor. Peyton shoved the Pastor off Stanley and pulled him from the clutches of the river. He tossed Stanley over his shoulder and carried him to the bank while Charlie Macon and Tom Boy Ralston dragged Pastor Roller out of the water.

I looked square into the Pastor's eyes and said, "What have you done in the name of God this time?" I lifted my hand to slap him but he caught my wrist mid-swing.

Tom Boy grasped both arms around the Pastor in a bear hug. "I never know'd you to be a murderer, Pastor." Tom Boy gritted his teeth as he fought to get the Pastor to the riverbank and tie his hands. "But you just outright slaughtered a man and a sick man at that. They ain't no mercy for that."

Maddie stood on the rocks, her hand over her mouth. "Mercy, stop. Wait for me." Maddie was always my redeeming grace. Any time I was ready to do something foolish, she was the voice that reasoned with me. Not this time.

"Not this time," I shouted. She come tearing down the hill toward me, pushing her way through the crowd hunkered around Stanley.

I looked into the eyes of my momma and saw fear. My past fell into place and she saw that it did.

I was just nineteen years old when Pastor murdered Stanley Farmer, and every one of them years I bore the Pastor's pain and righteous indignation. All the shouting, all the condemning—the punishments in the name of the Lord—all came together. It's funny how it takes a spell for a body to figure what's happening. But when it sunk in, when I finally figured out what was going on, my redemption went to hell in a rush and come back with a fury.

A blue tinge stained the outline of Stanley's lips. His face a slate grey, tinted with red. His eyes were wide open, his stare empty. Water pooled in the dimple of his chin and his jet-black hair lay strung across his face. Elsi bellowed like a cow giving birth and Momma pulled her away from Stanley's lifeless body.

"Help me, Mercy," Momma said.

"Help you? What about Elsi and these youngins? What about poor Stanley?" How could Momma ask me to help her? I'd helped the Pastor far too many times and now my eyes were as wide open as Stanley's.

"He was saved, Pastor. You killed my husband." Elsi fought to lay across the dead man's body. "Murderer." She sobbed into Stanley's chest.

"A weak body is a weak soul. The man was dammed to perish," shouted the Pastor. "It's the will of God Almighty."

Pastor Roller lifted his hands into the air and claimed the good Lord ripped the soul out of a sinful man. "What's done is done. Some men can't be saved. God have mercy on his soul."

I heard my name. Mercy. *Mercy on his soul,* and I wondered why Momma gave me that name. My guess, it was her cry to the good Lord to have mercy on her.

Mercy. Mercy! I heard my name echo through the angry crowd.

I was ashamed as I watched those four little girls smack at their daddy and cry for him to wake up. I was ashamed that this man of God . . . this pastor, was *my* daddy. He never was a father. He was a monster clothed in a high-collared white shirt that hid behind the Bible and served up his justice. Justice in the name of God.

Between the screams of Elsi, her girls, and the numb realization they'd just witnessed the murder of their father, the men in the crowd riled in a hurry. Justice on the mountain is quick. It's like a tornado, swirling and ripping a man's desire to make things right, pressing his anger to a point of no return—leaving a trail of twisted righteousness in its path.

Up here, men live by a code. They protect their own and when somebody takes a life, especially in front of a slew of witnesses—it isn't long before theirs is took away in return. It's just the way of the mountain folk. We see no need to drag things out. *Just hang the devil and pray for his soul later.* Charlie Macon and Tom Boy were hotheads anyway so justice would be served swift and heavy on the Pastor for outright killing a man who sought forgiveness.

The mighty stirring winds of revenge began. It swirled and whipped like a tornado tearing its way through the valley. The angry crowd only took a split second to accuse, convict, and serve the sentence.

The Pastor struggled to get free and when he couldn't he hauled off and belted Charlie in the face with his head.

"Let me go. Hell hath no fury like the wrath the Lord will bring down!"

Tom Boy winched the Pastor's hands tight behind his back. I knew what was coming. So did everybody else and not one of us took a step to climb into a storm shelter and let the tornado pass. We all stood headlong into the turmoil.

"Mercy, bring me God's Word. Bring me my Bible," the Pastor shouted as the men dropped a rope around his neck then tossed the other end over the limb of the giant elm tree.

"Mercy," the Pastor shouted. But the cries of Elsi and her youngins nearly drowned him out. Momma stood behind me, handkerchief clutched against her mouth while the Pastor spouted Scripture verse after Scripture verse.

"Mercy, you have to stop this. Don't let them hang your daddy," Momma screamed.

The men heaved the Pastor onto the back of Stanley's horse. Their shouts of revenge for an innocent and deformed man but loved by his family, stirred a vengeance in the crowd.

Edom Strong, a colored man who found his way up the mountain after becoming a free slave, raised one hand to quiet the crowd. "Don't you think we's oughta think this through? Takin' a man's life don't seem right, no matter what the crime."

Tom Boy shoved Edom backward. "Git on outta here if you don't agree. This here is a cold-blooded killer."

Folks knew Elsi looked past the draw in Stanley's face and the limp in his walk. She looked deep into his heart and though she'd admit to anyone who'd listen he needed to get his soul right, snuffing his life out like a candle was not what she had in mind.

There he lay, soaked to the bone in his ragged overalls and worn boots. Stanley had given it all.

"Mercy, stop them. Stop them. Don't let them do this."

Momma's screams faded into the background and at that very moment, my heart grew colder than the river. "It ends here . . . today."

Maddie run alongside me, grabbing at my arm. "Listen to me. This ain't the way to handle things. Mercy, please." I slapped her hand off my arm. The look in my eyes was louder than words.

"Mercy, I'm beggin' you. Let's go up on the rock. Ain't nothing you can do here. Come on."

"Git outta my way, Maddie. If you call me your friend, git outta my way." I regretted them words as soon as they come out of my mouth 'cause Maddie dropped her hands to her side and walked away.

"Mercy. You bring me my Bible. Read to me before these men commit a sin. Read the part where Jesus cried from the cross, 'Forgive them.' Mercy, now. Bring it, now. You people ain't to judge that which cannot be judged."

"Pastor, you done been the judge of Stanley. You sayin' you're God?" Tom Boy spit amber juice at the Pastor's feet. "Seems like cockeyed thinkin' to me."

My hand shook as I bent and picked up the Pastor's Bible. Mercy was the last thing he deserved. After all the wicked things the Pastor done to me, it was almost funny he'd call to me for help. Ask me, of all people, to read from his Bible. I felt the blood drain from my face and my cheeks turn icy. So did my heart. So did what little feeling I had for the Pastor. Suddenly the veil of naivety dropped from my eyes and I realized, like Elsi, all I'd lost at my daddy's hands.

The Pastor's Bible was worn. Its leather cover frayed and the edges tattered. Yellowed pages were dog-eared and ink smudges blurred some of the words. I looked at the Pastor. Looked at the men and their rage. Glanced at Elsi and her children. Remembered the bruises and slaps I'd taken over the years . . . all in the name of God. Memories of hearing Momma plead for leniency from her sin just before the Pastor beat her with a horse whip. Her cries . . . my cries as he carted off my innocent infant. From that minute on, I wasn't his daughter. He was nothing to me.

"What kind of man are you?" I shouted. "You call yourself a pastor? You claim to be a man of God. What kind of God do you serve?"

The Pastor glared at me, rope tight beneath his chin. "I serve a righteous

God who punishes sinners. Now read to me out of my Bible, girl." My
eyes drew into a squint, the sun glared behind the Pastor, turning him
into a black outline, faceless and empty.

Even now, his tone never changed. He never seemed sorry he'd drowned
Stanley. He just kept shouting for me to bring him his Bible.

I licked the end of my thumb and pressed it against the dingy pages,
turning them to Exodus. My rage boiled. "You want me to read to you?" I
scanned the words, then closed the book on my finger and held it high in
the air. At that moment, *I* was judge and jury. The crowd quieted.

"You want me to read to you? How 'bout I read your favorite Scripture.
How about this one, Pastor. *An eye for an eye.*"

I stuffed the Bible under my arm.

The Pastor opened his mouth, but no words came out this time. I
didn't let them.

I drew back and slapped my hand, hard, against the rear of Stanley's
horse. I watched the animal bolt.

The Pastor slipped off the horse's back and I heard the sickening crack
of bone snapping above my head. I stared into his lifeless face, an expression of disbelief froze into place. Somewhere in the breeze, the scent of
honeysuckle floated by.

The Pastor's feet dangled inches above the ground. There was silence
all around me.

"An eye for an eye," I said. "An eye for an eye."

TWO

I DIDN'T BIND the Pastor's hands behind his back or drop the noose over his head, but I was the one who drew it tight. I was the one that killed the man.

Stanley Farmer wasn't the first person the Pastor condemned to hell in his ungodly judgments. There was a bunch. When I was seven, he made me carry his leather saddlebag to the Widow Starling's house.

The old woman was half dead and nearly starved because she was too weak to get out of bed when Reburta Owens come to visit her. Reburta found her naked and lying in a puddle of her own vomit, a bottle of hooch clutched tight to her chest. The Pastor slammed open the door, yanked the Widow Starling up, and began to rant.

"The Lord has sent me to teach you His wrath. You're a disgrace to womankind and a drunk. Your tongue is evil."

"Girl," he demanded. His forefinger crooked as he pointed toward me. "Stoke that fire. Hang me a pot of coffee to heat." I inched to the fireplace and pulled the cast iron hook toward me. I pumped the billows and the fire roared. The smell of hot ash twisted and curled into the air and I coughed when I sucked in the suet. I was horrified at the sight of the Widow. She muttered things like, "Pastor, your hands are unclean. You ought not touch the goodness of a woman." The Pastor slapped her across the mouth and when the coffee was nearly to a boil, he commenced to pour the scalding liquid down her throat.

"Dear Lord in heaven," she cried. "Save me from this man." Blisters bulged on her lips as she pleaded.

There wasn't a thing I could do except run onto the porch and huddle against the side of the cabin. Her screams echoed through the valley and through my hands pressed against my ears. Her cries for mercy taunted me. The sound of a battle raged inside the cabin as the Widow kicked and clawed. Dishes fell to the cabin floor and chairs thumped across the room. She fought hard to escape the messenger who delivered a deadly message. "You'll be the one burning in hell," she screamed.

"For every kind of beasts, and of birds, and of serpents, and of things in the sea, is tamed, and hath been tamed of mankind: but the tongue can no man tame; it is an unruly evil, full of deadly poison." The Pastor spouted Scripture at the old woman. "Your tongue is your sin." The Widow gurgled for the Pastor to stop. I pressed my hands tighter against my ears and my legs began to quiver with fear. A puddle formed between my ankles.

The Pastor preached his hell-fire and brimstone message, all the time pouring hot coffee down the old woman's throat until finally her house was silent.

I heard the taps on his boots clank against the rough cabin floor. A thump rang out as he kicked a chair into the wall. The latch on the door jiggled and clicked.

"Mercy," the Pastor said opening the cabin door. "Get in here and clean up this woman. Put her in her Sunday best and I'll fetch the undertaker. The good Lord has took her."

"Yes, sir. Is she . . ."

"Dead?" He grabbed my arm and tossed me toward the cabin door. "I told you, child, the good Lord took her. Now, clean up the mess. All of it. Start with the floor, then the old woman." He shoved me into the cabin and slammed the door. Dishes were strewn in every direction. Both cane-bottom chairs toppled. I picked up a tin cup from the floor and walked the edge of the room trying not to step in the pools of coffee mixed with blood. The fire, embers now, barely shed enough light to see. Widow Starling laid long-ways across the bed, naked—her skin glowed as red as hot coals and a huge handprint was burned into her neck. It was like the Pastor's hands were hotter than the coals, but I knew it was where he held her down. I pulled a blanket over her body and tried not to look at the horrible twisted expression on her face.

Even at seven years old, I knew what the Pastor had done. Terrible things he didn't want told. I knew the old woman got loose-lipped when she got moonshine in her and the Pastor didn't like his antics being spread across the mountain. I wasn't stupid. I knew and I was horrified it could have been me. So I kept quiet about what I'd seen and what I'd heard. Still, in the back of my mind, I was storing up these things. One day I'd put the pieces together.

A peck come at the door and startled me. "Mercy. Mercy, you in there?" It was Maddie.

"Go home Maddie. Go home before the Pastor comes back."

"Won't do no sucha thang. Open the door."

I did as she asked. When the door swung to the outside, I fell into the arms of my best friend, my only friend. I felt her shiver as she looked at the Widow, but she never whimpered.

"I'll help you. Get the old woman's dress off the line."

And I did. The two of us dressed the Widow then cleaned up the cabin and when we was done Maddie twisted a strand of my hair around her finger. "Just remember to be better than this. My daddy always says to be better than what's bad." Maddie squeezed my hands then took off toward the ridge.

Be better than what's bad. Be better than what's bad. I sat on the porch step and closed my eyes. *Be better than what's bad.*

————

The roar of the river was as loud as the cheers of the crowd while the Pastor wallowed like a fish on a hook. His feet jerked and that same gurgle came from his throat, what come from the Widow Starling all them years earlier. Justice was served for the Widow. And it was served for Stanley too.

Momma wouldn't look at me when I passed her. I dropped the Pastor's Bible at her side then leaned and kissed her head. She never flinched. Never spoke. Never acknowledged me. Her way, I guess, of showing the people around her, she was disgusted at my actions and theirs.

There must have been twenty congregants at the river to see Stanley baptized. Twenty folks who witnessed the Pastor murder an innocent man. I stared at the palm of my hand, still red from the slap. No one seemed to care it was me that sent the Pastor to his death. All that mattered was the sound of a rope creaking against a tree limb while it sawed an impression of death into the branch. All that counted was the crack of my hand against the horse's rear and the wild flailing of the Pastor as his body jolted and bounced in the wind. When there's a crowd of angry men, it doesn't matter who fuels the rage just so it gets stoked. But I knew. I'd figured out the sickness the Pastor had. That didn't excuse his actions, and for the time, I was content with the peace I'd felt with the justice I'd served.

Elsi Farmer cradled her girls, one on each knee, and one under each arm. The least, was Bet. Her long black curls twisted and fell around her shoulders. They plastered tight with tears to her cheeks. I wrapped my arms around Bet and brushed her hair from her face. "It's alright, baby girl. It's alright." Elsi pulled Bet by the dress tail away from me. Three of the men crossed Stanley's arms over his chest. It must have been an hour before they sliced the rope that held the Pastor. His body dropped limp and twisted to the ground. Ben and Tom Boy grabbed an arm and a leg and tossed him into the back of a wagon.

"I ain't usin' my last quarter to press his eyelids shut," one man argued. "Money is too hard to come by. It ain't worth wastin' on a murderer."

Jess Macon, Charlie's boy and the town tattletale, ran down the mountain path to tell Undertaker Whaley. Stanley would remain laid out in the back of the wagon for three days while the neighbors kept watch shooing away vultures and wild animals.

I hated wakes. Never saw the point in watching a dead man rot before shoving him in a hole. But it would give Peyton time to build a pine box sturdy enough to hold Stanley.

I stopped at the river's edge and stared at the water washing over the boulders. In our parts, boulders are bigger than ten men put together and the water pushes so hard across the rocks that you can walk beneath the spray without getting doused. The Indian River was a thing of beauty; I could see where the Pastor thought it might wash away a man's sin. I put my hand up to shade my eyes. The sun glared off the wash so bright it warmed my cheeks.

They say the Lord is a good and gracious God, but I just couldn't believe any God who was worth a hoot would stand for ripping a man's soul from his body. Especially one on his knees. I rolled my eyes to one side then to the other, never moving my head. I took in the scenes around me. Elsi loaded her children into Peyton's wagon. A few of the men prayed over the lifeless body of Pastor Roller. Tom Boy hauled off and spit at the Pastor's feet a second time. "Take that you lowlife."

Before long it was just me and Momma.

I walked toward her. She knelt on the ground sobbing into her hands. I wasn't sure if her tears were tears of sadness or tears of joy since I'd just set her free from her prison. Guess only her heart would know the truth. Momma might mourn on the outside, but my guess is, her insides rejoiced. "The devil's gone to hell," I said.

I couldn't bring myself to look at the jagged rope hanging from that elm tree. It was enough I'd been the cause, and enough I'd have to live with the slap of a hand the rest of my life.

"Momma," I shouted over the roar of the river. "Go home. Start a new life. You ain't sayin' nothin', but I know what you're thinking. I'm thinking the same thing."

"You can't know what I'm thinkin'. You can't know what I'm feelin.' I lost my whole family today."

"No, Momma. You're wrong. You didn't lose your family today. You gained your freedom at the hand of your daughter."

"Oh Lord, forgive Mercy, she don't know what she's sayin'."

"No Momma, there ain't no need to plead for mercy. I am Mercy, and you've been set free." I knew as sure as the words left my mouth, I was the Pastor's daughter.

I was wrong and I knew it, but I didn't care.

I kicked at a stone then stepped on to a boulder. The river's water curled and rolled in front of me. "Tell me something, Momma. Ever wonder where the river begins? Ever thing has a beginning. I wish I knew mine, 'cuz up to now, it's all been a lie. A lie!"

My voice faded into the white noise of the water and when I turned Momma was gone. Buzzards circled the carcass of the devil on earth, and I knew what they wanted. I glanced over my shoulder at the Pastor's twisted body hanging half in the wagon.

I spit and walked away.

Three

After Undertaker Whaley hauled the Widow down the mountain, I knew the Pastor wouldn't be home. Once he'd give out his idea of the Lord's righteousness he'd go away for days. "It's when I pray for that soul that died. It's when I rassle with God." My best guess was he rassled with a bottle of hooch.

They was times I remember good things. Times I felt the warmth of the mountain sun against my face. And oh, the times I smelled them daisies blowin' back and forth in the wind. Maddie Holmes stayed my friend too. Even when the Pastor was hateful to her.

"Let's sneak up to the woods behind the shack. Think we could balance some of them hooch bottles on that elm branch and bust them with rocks?" Maddie loved to throw rocks. She'd lean back and let out a giggle that would make a dead man grin. "Come on Mercybug. Let's grab them bottles and sneak off tonight. The Pastor will be gone and we know your momma won't pay no mind."

"I get first sling."

"First sling? No fair. It was my idea."

"Might be your idea, but it's my bottles. We'll throw them rocks so hard, they'll sail clean to Chattanooga."

That night after Momma went to sleep, I crept out of the cabin, crawled under the porch, and got out the Pastor's empty liquor bottles. I could hear Maddie snickerin' as I pulled myself from under the porch.

"How many you got?"

"Enough. Can't take too many. The Pastor will get wise."

"Chicken," Maddie whispered. She grabbed the bottles and took toward the woods.

We climbed the side of that mountain, gatherin' all the rocks we could tote in our pockets. Maddie balanced the bottles on a low, long limb of the big elm tree. I drew back and spun a stone that would have skipped the length of the river had it hit water. It cracked against the side of the tree. Me and Maddie laughed and giggled until we about wet our pants.

"I thought you was a good shot." She dug her hand deep into her pouch.

"I am. But it's dark, you idiot. Let's see what you can do in the dark." Maddie pulled a candle from her pouch.

"Hey, wait a minute. That's what I call sneaky."

She grinned, her tongue slipped through a hole in the front of her mouth. She clicked the flint stones together and lit the light. "Now it's my turn."

She drew back and flung a smooth flat stone with all her might. It hit with a thud. "What in the Sam hill?" A voiced boomed from nearby the tree. "Who's there?"

Maddie squealed and I hollered. We high-tailed it down the hill. I don't reckon we ever figured out who was sleepin' near that elm, but the not knowin' gave us lots to pretend about.

Yeah, I remember good times. They was few, but I remember them. So when Maddie dropped her head and walked away from me at the river . . . when she looked at me with eyes that welled of sadness, I knew my friend had give up on me. And I become lost.

The wind whipped through the mountain pass and howled like a hound on a hunt. Black Rock Mountain sat on the eastern side of the Appalachians and winds from the south managed to work their way into the valley and tear up jack. Wadalow Mountain was square in the middle of the pass; about three miles as the crow flies. Burying day in the gap was no different and the wind had no sympathy on a family who'd lost its daddy. Instead, the draft just danced around folks, piercing them with a wicked chill.

Elsi Farmer pulled the tail of her black dress between her legs and squeezed it tight with her knees to maintain a shred of decency. Her daughters, all dressed in black, huddled close to their mother. The Colton boys had dug a hole beneath a weeping cherry tree that would hold Stanley until the good Lord come to take him home, and there I stood. Wondering why on earth Elsi Farmer would ask me, of all people, to say a few words over poor Stanley. It seemed to be just another twisted sort of blame. Intentional but unintentional. Make the daughter of the monster preach a funeral. Or, maybe it was Elsi's way of showin' me she didn't hold no grudge against me. Deep down she knew what I'd lived through. Either way, I'd guessed we were kindred spirits, each knowing what the other had suffered at the hand of the Pastor, and neither saying a word.

There wasn't no peace in holding the Word of God in my hands and speakin' over a dead man. The Bible seemed to burn the palm I'd hit that horse with. I know it was all in my head. Maybe it was an ounce of guilt. I ain't rightly sure. But all I knew was that book was like holding hot coals.

My finger held its place on a verse in Hebrews—the one about running the good race. I figured since Stanley was crippled from childhood by polio, it might be appropriate to remind folks that running a race ain't necessarily a physical race. And even though he'd run to the river to be saved and died, didn't mean he'd lost the race. Stanley was the winner and his win was our celebration.

The pages of the Pastor's Bible flipped in the wind, and I pressed my palm into the center of the page to settle them so I could read.

"I ain't no pastor," I said. "I'm just a friend. And Stanley Farmer was a good man and Elsi is a forgivin' woman. She ain't blamin' me for the devil's doing. Thank you, Miss Elsi."

The wind twisted my hair in circles, then shoved it into my mouth. I felt like a hungry rat with its jaws stuffed full of corn. That or God Himself was trying to choke the words back down my throat. I slipped my finger between my cheek and hair then pushed the mess of strands behind my ear. Elsi *was* a forgiving woman. Most folks would have hated me for the wrongs of my father, but not her. It was Elsi who pressed her hands against my face and smiled as a tear trailed down hers. She took time in her own grief, to comfort the daughter of the man who killed her husband.

"You've lost your father too. I'm so sorry," Elsi said.

That got the best of me. I struggled to look Elsi in the eye, much less speak over poor dead Stanley. *God, is this my punishment or the Pastor's?*

"Every man has his day. And Stanley had his. He went to his knees pleading for mercy and God Almighty, being the God He is, offered him that grace." I fought the wind to keep the pages of the Bible from turning, but the fingers of the breeze won out and opened my Bible to Ezekiel. I nearly lost my breath when I read:

> *The soul that sinneth, it shall die. The son shall not bear the iniquity of the father, neither shall the father bear the iniquity of the son: the righteousness of the righteous shall be upon him, and the wickedness of the wicked shall be upon him.*

It was like God Himself tried to comfort me. Thing was . . . I didn't want comfort, and I didn't want God—not now anyway. I wanted to be left alone in my fury. I made up my mind, right there over Stanley Farmer's grave, that I'd make things right. Where the Pastor failed, I'd succeed. I'd fix it. Somehow. I'd teach the sins of the father were not the sins of the son or the daughter, and it could be different if the son understood.

Elsi dabbed her handkerchief against her eyes then swiped it under her nose. "Hallelujah, Lord, he was saved," she whispered. "Praise the Lord."

"I can't speak for the Pastor, but I can, I think, say the good Lord forgave Stanley for whatever iniquities he might have had, and my guess is, he's walking on air today."

To one side of Stanley Farmer's grave was a fresh mound of red clay . . . a cross jabbed upside down into the dirt covering the Pastor—some kid's joke protesting the Pastor was hung out to dry, and too good to be buried with the cross turned the right way. I couldn't disagree. And I can't lie. I'd wished the old man's death 'cause he was the furthest thing from holy that a man could be.

The Colton boys lifted Elsi's girls into the wagon. Bet's tiny fist wallowed her eyes as she tried to dry the tears. How could a tyke like that understand what was happening? Stanley had his share of problems . . . being crippled and whatnot. He had a weakness of a short temper, but he was a good father. It was not uncommon to see him toting one or two of those girls at a time, even when he could hardly walk himself.

I remember when me and Momma helped Elsi deliver Bet. Stanley had come running to the cabin, as best that Stanley could run, early one Saturday morning to fetch Momma. "Reba, it's Elsi. She's been driving at havin' that baby since up in the night and it just ain't comin'. Can you help her?"

Everybody has gifts and Momma's gift was helping to nurse those who were sick. She had helped a slew of the women on the mountain birth their babies. It was only natural for Stanley to run to her, despite what he knew. That, and the fact we were the closest neighbors to their homestead. Momma didn't hesitate. She grabbed her shawl and a handful of rags then roused me out of bed. "Mercy, get up. Elsi's havin' her baby and things ain't goin' right."

The Pastor dropped his feet over the edge of the bed and slid one foot into his boot. "Youngin' ain't born after this long . . . usually means Elsi's bearing some sin she won't let go of. I'll go."

"You'll do no such-a thing. Babies come when they're ready and sin's got nothing to do with it. You'll keep your distance and let the women do their work this time."

"I'm the Pastor. It's my job to bless a newborn, to pray over the mother." He towered over Momma, but she put her finger in his chest and shoved.

"I done told you. This ain't none of your business. Stanley didn't come to get you. He came and roused me. Now, Elsi's in distress, and I'll thank you to get outta my way so I can go to her."

I can't remember many times Momma stood up to the Pastor, but when she put her foot down, she meant it. She'd pay a price later, and that didn't seem to matter to her. After all, it wasn't her fault—the things the Pastor did. Her eyes were set on the need of the person, not the beatin' she'd get when she got home, and she certainly never thought of the whipping I'd get by going with her.

The Pastor's hot breath bellowed over me and Momma. The smell carried the scent of something dead. He took a step closer to her and jutted his chest like a rooster, but Momma stood her ground. She dug her heels into the crevice of the wooden slatted floor, then shoved him to the side.

"Elsi needs me. Get outta my way. You can do what you need to do later." Momma took me by the shoulder and guided me past the massive man. Her hands trembled in mine. "Mercy, run down the path and get Pactol and Edom. They can get us down to Elsi in a snap."

I hung my head and looked at the cabin floor as I slipped past the Pastor. His toe tapped against the wood. Momma pushed open the door and I run like a mad person down to Edom's. I couldn't remember a time I'd run so hard, and when I stepped up onto their one-room shack's porch, I fell face-first, my palms smacked flat against the door.

The door opened and I dropped inside. Edom picked me up while Pactol brushed away my tears. "Momma needs help. Elsi Farmer is birthin' her baby and it won't come. Stanley come running to get Momma to help, but the Pastor won't let her come." I gasped for a full breath to fill my lungs.

Edom pressed his hat over his head, and headed out the door. He dropped the yoke over his horse and latched it to the wagon. Pactol and me loaded into the back as Edom rolled past. In minutes we were in front of the cabin. Momma stood in the yard while the Pastor blistered her with his words. "The Good Book says, 'Wives, submit yourselves unto your own husbands.' I'm tellin' you it's not you who needs to be going to Elsi."

Edom pulled the wagon between Momma and the Pastor. He didn't say a word. He just motioned to Momma to get in. Stanley stood at the side of the cabin bent over, trying to catch a breath. Pactol slipped her shoulder under his arm and helped him to the wagon. All the time the Pastor was screaming Scripture about obedience and submission. Edom nodded to the Pastor, then smacked the reins against the horse.

I ain't never seen nobody tame the Pastor like Edom. And he did it without saying a word. "Thank you, Edom. Thank you for getting me out so I can help Miss Elsi," Momma said.

"Find forgiveness, Missy Roller. Just find forgiveness." Edom didn't utter another word about the Pastor. Though I could see his disapproval in the Pastor's ways, he managed to find something good to hold on to—something I'd not found when it come to the Pastor.

Edom dropped us at Stanley's, and him and Pactol gathered up the

Farmer youngins. "Stanley, these kids will be with us. You and Missy Roller do what you need to do for Miss Elsi." They loaded the Farmer girls into the wagon and left.

"Oh Lord in heaven, bring this baby. It's killin' me," Elsi cried. Sweat beaded on her brow and a single tear slipped down her cheek. She grabbed Momma's arm and her eyes spoke louder than the thunder in a storm. Momma knew. I knew too. It was that unspoken secret about the Pastor. One we was either too scared to speak of, or too ashamed.

"I'm sorry, Reba." Elsi gritted her teeth through a pain, but Momma kept quiet.

Momma and me spent six more hours working on Miss Elsi. Momma took spoons and held open the exit for that baby while I pressed against Elsi's stomach. My stomach ached with every pain of Miss Elsi's. I knew her hurt. I understood the work of pushin' and not seeing no return for the labor.

"Push, Miss Elsi. We gotta force this wee one out. Push." When the little thing's head plunged into the world, Momma gently twisted it to the side. The child's nose was mashed flat, and its eyes were swelled. I started swiping gunk from its face, trying to clear the youngin's mouth and nose for a breath. But there was nothing.

"Elsi, you gotta push this little one out. It ain't breathin' and I can't help it if it's still lodged in your belly." Momma's voice was calm, but stern. Perspiration formed on her forehead, and I braced my knees behind Elsi so she had some leverage.

"Push. Hard." Momma patted Elsi's knees. "Let me hold this baby in my arms."

The blood vessels in Elsi's face bugled, and I thought of that Scripture the Pastor used to preach about Jesus sweating blood. Elsi strained. Her fingers dug into the flesh of my arms as I cradled her. That baby dropped from her body, and Elsi fell limp against my chest.

Momma prayed the whole time Elsi pushed that she wouldn't break the baby's neck pulling her free. We worked until we got that little thing a breath of air, then Momma gave the credit to the good Lord—I wasn't so sure He deserved any credit when Elsi did all the work.

"What a glorious sound," Elsi whispered as Momma laid the infant on her chest. "Listen to her cry." Tears welled as I stared into the eyes of that little one.

My baby mighta looked like that.

Momma looked at me and smiled. "You be strong now. You be strong." There it was again . . . that unspoken understanding that all this mess tied back to the Pastor. Still no one uttered the words. It was just a glance, a look, an understanding between the women. The Pastor's secrets weren't really secrets at all, and little Bet, she had dark curly hair, just like his.

Elsi thought Momma was talking to her, telling her to be strong, and she was, but she was mostly talking to me. We both knew what waited for us when we got home. Vengeance.

That was the beginning of a weeklong penance. The pastor made Momma cook his meals and then forced her to fast and pray while he ate in front of her. He wouldn't just ask her to cook regular vittles, he'd insist on smoked turkey . . . something with a mouth-watering scent. I followed Momma out to the coop as she kicked open the flimsy door, grabbed a turkey, and loped off its head.

"How'd you learn to do this, Momma?"

"Do what? Survive?"

"No, kill a turkey."

Momma smiled. "Granny Dodge taught me and her granny taught her, and so on. Now keep quiet. The less is said, the less we pay. Stay away. Outta sight."

She plucked that turkey's feathers, dressed it, and built a stone-lined pit that had to be stoked all day with hickory wood. Worst part was, the sun beat down on that pit with a vengeance. Water dripped off Momma's nose and her neck shined with perspiration. The Pastor wouldn't let her drink any water, either. But Momma kept at it. She held her head high.

"Momma," I whispered from behind an old oak tree. "Pssst. Momma." She wouldn't look up for fear the Pastor would see her talking and accuse her of speaking in evil tongues. She walked toward a stack of wood, knelt down, then answered.

"I hear you."

"They's a wet cloth behind that stack of wood. I soaked it heavy. You suck the water out of it then bury it back under the stack. I'll get it when I bring you a new haul of wood."

Momma smiled. "Mercy. Sweet, sweet Mercy."

"Just do it, Momma."

The next several hours I split more hickory wood and carried it to the stack. I hid the soaked cloth under a slab of wood. Momma sucked on the rag a little, covered it, then loaded her arms full of kindling until the Pastor noticed she wasn't drawing weaker as the day closed.

When he caught me rinsing the rag out by the pump, the last thing I remembered was Momma pleading to him. Screaming.

"Don't you hurt her. Don't you hurt my baby."

I could hear her screams with my head shoved deep into the trough of water by the pump. I didn't even fight him. I'd learned a long time before, fighting him just made dying harder.

"Leave her be. Pastor, she's your daughter."

"She's disobedient and I won't have a child who disobeys me." The Pastor's voice was muddled—distant.

My lungs burned for a taste of humid mountain air, and as the Pastor's hand pressed against my cheek, I pushed floating hair away from my eyes. If I died, I wanted him to see my face when he brought me up out of the water.

FOUR

I'M NOT SURE WHY, but I stuffed the Pastor's Bible along with my knife into my bag. I guess it held the only inklin' of a decent memory of the Pastor . . . Daddy. When he was in a good state, he'd sit me on his lap and teach me the Psalms.

"*The Lord is my shepherd.* That means the good Lord will always tend to you. Now say it after me. *The Lord . . .*"

I mouthed the words behind the Pastor. "*The Lord is my shepherd.*"

The Pastor pushed my hair behind my ear. They was times the Pastor seemed sorry for being meaner than a snake, and it would make my heart bleed. I was just a little girl but I could see the guilt he lived with. Tears filled his eyes as he run his fingers over the black and blue spots on my arms. "Oh Mercybug. Daddy is sorry." He'd lift my arms and kiss the skin.

Daddy. His words struck deep in my heart. I wanted to believe he was a good father. I wanted to believe he was sorry, but mostly, I just wanted the symbol of a man to love me.

I guess I could see where Momma would feel for him. He was a lot like King David. When he was sorry, he was genuinely sorry. His pleas would bust your heart right open. Them was the times I tried to hold to as a child. The moments were few, but precious. They were, after all, just memories. I threw my bag over my shoulder. Momma turned her back on me as I stepped onto the porch.

"Momma?" I touched her shoulder. She pulled away. "Momma, please."

"Don't *please* me, Mercy Roller. You do realize what you've done? Has it even sunk in that thick skull of yours that you are as bad as that devil?"

"I . . ."

"You what? You saved me?" Momma's nose flared as she shoved her

31

finger into my face. "I don't regret the death of the Pastor. I'd almost say it was an answer to prayer. But what you did. That's what I'm havin' a hard time swallowin'. You not only killed your daddy, but you took on his same ways."

I dropped my head and stared at the splintered floor. A gentle breeze pushed the rocker on the porch. For a minute, I wondered if the Pastor was sitting in that chair, leaned back like a proud peacock flitting its tail.

"I know what I did. And I'd like to tell you I was sorry. But I ain't. That devil deserved to die. For what he did to Stanley, and Elsi. And to my baby."

Momma drew back and slapped my face. "Don't you mention that baby," she said. "Not ever again."

"Why?" I dabbed a trickle of blood from my lip. "If I don't mention the child, then the meanness never happened?"

Momma pushed open the cabin door. The scent of fresh green beans and fatback floated across the room. Despite her anger or frustration, whatever it was, she never lost her ability to fix a good meal. I glanced toward the small room beneath the loft where Momma and the Pastor slept. She had already cleared the two long-tailed black coats and three white-collared shirts from the tiny dresser. His pipe lay neatly on the stack, and the socks she'd darned a week ago were rolled into a ball and stuffed into his work shoes.

"Face it. I had a baby, or I would have had one until the Pastor decided I needed to have the pagan ripped outta me."

Momma covered her ears and begun to sing "Amazing Grace."

"I would have had a husband, but the Pastor killed him too. That devil never wanted either of us to have any joy. Not you and certainly not me."

"Stop it. Stop it. Can't you see I've lost my family? Can't you mourn with me? Can't you . . ."

Mourning for the Pastor was the last thing on my heart and I couldn't understand why she wasn't grateful, because he'd have surely killed her too, before long.

I walked to the stack of clothes and fingered the long thin bowtie. Momma sobbed silently into her palms. "You want me to take those things to Macon's? They might fit him." On the mountain, clothes like the Pastor's were a luxury. She wheeled around and eyed me. One brow lifted.

"You don't grasp what you've done, do you? You don't understand my tears of mourning are not for the Pastor, but for you. Mercy, they's for you."

I guess I'd shoved my anger beneath the surface for so many years, that for the time being—I was content. Nary a regret. So when Momma pointed for me to get out, I really didn't care. All I could think was, *Ungrateful wench.* I'd saved her, saved me, and saved the other Stanleys on the mountain from the wrath of a man who'd lost his sight of God and made his self one instead.

I saddled the horse Momma named Slouch, tied my bag to her saddle, and threw my leg over her back. Momma stood on the porch and watched. She never uttered a word. Not sure she ever took her hand from her face. All I could see was the aged and wrinkled skin below her eyes swollen to a youthful tautness, washed in the tears of a grieving soul.

I guessed she'd get over it. She always did. Anytime the Pastor hurt her she showed this overwhelming forgiveness.

One thought stung my being as I headed Slouch toward the river. My momma hated me so bad she sent me away. I had nothing or nobody left.

"Ho horse." I clicked my cheeks. "Let's go."

Me and Slouch stood by the river for some time. I couldn't rightly say how long or when we started to walk, but when I woke up from my daydream I wasn't far from Stanley's grave. Or the Pastor's. The undertaker had done flattened the heaping mound of dirt on top of Stanley and pressed a neatly carved cross in the brittle red clay. A small pile of loose flowers lay at the foot of the cross and handprints were like names written all over the grave. My guess was, the undertaker patted down the dirt, signing his work like a rancher brands a steer. That cool breeze whipped through the valley and sent a chill down my arms.

Stanley didn't deserve this. I knelt at the grave and pressed the flower stems into the ground. They'd been pulled long enough that drooping was all they knew. A crow landed on a tiny wooden headstone above Stanley and called to his mate on the voice of the breeze.

I came to my feet and rushed at the bird.

"Git from here," I shouted. "Git away from my baby."

I'd not come to this spot in a long time. Hadn't visited Thomas since the day they buried him—my baby cradled in a quilt inside a box buried beside Thomas, covered deep beneath the earth in a blanket of rest. My fingers rubbed the letters on the tombstone:

THOMAS DAWSON 1873–1891

The stone beside his:

INFANT DAUGHTER

I never named her. Never could bring myself to give her one. If she had no name, then I had no child to call my own.

I went to my knees and wrapped my arms around the stone as the rage and hurt I'd managed to hide away bubbled to the surface. I couldn't cry. All I could do was wail away at the ground, screaming obscenities I never knew I could speak. And there, just feet away lay the Pastor. *This is all your fault. All of it.*

I picked up a good sized stone and lobbed it at the upside down cross on the Pastor's grave. My eye was good, and I struck that cross square in the middle, toppling it to its side.

"You devil," I screamed. "How could you do this to me? How can you stand in the shoes of God and take life in your own hands? You never gave my baby a chance." I stomped the mounds of loose dirt on his grave. "She was born out of your sickness, but that baby was innocent." My rage unleashed like the roll of a wrathful current. "You animal."

I glanced toward Thomas's grave, and more fury poured out of me. "And Thomas. That man never had a chance either. You took that too, you devil. Was it always your desire to make life a living hell for the rest of us?"

Then the tears I'd held back for years flooded like the Indian River in early spring. The kind after the first thaw on the mountain. I crawled to the Pastor's grave. It hit me square-on what I'd said. *How can you stand in the shoes of God and take life in your own hands.*

There I was, on all fours on top of the Pastor's grave, covered in red clay and faced with the reality that Momma was right. I'd taken on his ways.

"Grievin' ain't pretty, is it?" Maddie pressed her palms into the dirt she'd piled on top of the body.

"I reckon not. But it don't seem fair."

"What don't seem fair?" She swiped her nose with her sleeve then began to loop twine around the two crossed sticks.

"Death. This little thing didn't have a chance."

"Nope." A tear dripped off Maddie's nose.

I pushed her pigtails to her back and rubbed her shoulder. "There's gonna be another one. I'm sure."

Maddie smiled through her pain. "Yeah, I guess. It was just a kitten."

"No it wasn't. It was your kitten. Tiny as it was. You did all you could to save it. The good Lord will remember that." I found myself repeating what I'd heard the Pastor say at funerals. Still the truth was, there wasn't another kitten. This was the last of the litter and Maddie had attached herself to it like a momma bird.

Maddie stood. Red clay striped her nose and cheek. "Nope. Grievin' ain't no body's best. Let me go wash off in the stream and we can go play up on the ridge."

I stood there a little surprised Maddie wanted to hike the ridge to play. But then, that was Maddie. She splashed a handful of water on her face, then dried herself with the tail of her dress. She stood, straightened her shoulders, cleared her throat, and smiled. "Let's head on up the hill."

Just like that, Maddie did what most mountain folk was taught to do . . . attend to the moment, then shovel it over your shoulder and go on. She'd cried over that dead kitten, buried it, then washed her hands clean. Life went on.

I had every reason to do what I did. Every cause to justify my actions. The anger of the crowd was vented at the Pastor, and when I slapped that horse and the Pastor hanged from the elm at my hand, they cheered. They called me brave and righteous. When I dropped my hand on that horse . . . I'd handled things. Moved on.

Still, truth was, I was my daddy's daughter. Now that would be my own personal hell to endure.

FIVE

"GIVE THAT BACK to me,"

Jude Hawkins grinned while I screamed at him.

"That's mine," I said. I jumped up and down while Jude dangled the dainty white handkerchief above my head. We was just kids.

"Sissy. Sissy. Got a girly cloth," he chanted.

"You bullheaded idiot. Of course it's girly. I'm a girl. Or did yer pappy not teach you what a girl is?"

"Come on sissy girl. Jump. Git your prissy little cloth."

The sound of Jude's voice faded into a chomping noise at my ear. I come up off the ground, fists tight and swinging. It was just a dream. I'd grown to hate memories, and mine seemed to haunt me in my dreams.

Slouch stood over where I'd laid, gnawing away on my handkerchief. She'd pulled it from my pocket while pilfering for carrots.

"Give that to me, stupid horse. That's mine." I snatched the tiny handkerchief from the side of the mare's mouth then swiped the slobber off on my trousers. "I ain't got no carrots and besides, you sniffin' my pockets out like some rat after corn shells ain't getting you fed any sooner. What's a matter with you?"

Slouch slapped her head from side to side, lifted her nose to my nose, then sputtered in my face.

"Awe. You nasty thang."

I shoved her head to one side, but she nuzzled her head under my arm. I rubbed my fingers over the tatted lace sewn to the white muslin. Momma had embroidered a tiny green leaf on one corner. I'd had that handkerchief since I was a little tyke. It wasn't much, but Momma had give it to me for my birthday. She managed to hide it away while she worked on the embroidery, and when the Pastor took one of his trips to the coal mines to preach, she brought it out.

"Mercy, ever little girl needs a hanky. It's a sign you're a growin' up. So hold on to it. It'll serve you well." Momma folded the kerchief and stashed it neatly in my pocket. "There," she'd said. "Just for you."

I dropped my head and meandered down a darkened path cut into the woods. Slouch tagged along groping my pocket for any sign of food.

It seemed the biggest part of my life, what there's been of it, someone's always been taking something away from me. "It's high time I began to find what was rightfully mine. Don't you think, Slouch?"

I stared at the rushing swirls of the Indian River. The roar of its voice nearly drowned my thoughts. My eyes followed the bed of the river as it twisted in front of me, winding out of sight near the bluff. My mind wandered.

They was a time me and Maddie would rock hop across the boulders. We'd hop from one to the next following the river until we'd drop down worn out. "River ain't got no beginning." Maddie giggled. "We can run after it, but God just keeps moving it. I bet by the time we find the end, we'll be right back where we started." She laid her arm across her eyes and laughed.

"You most likely right. It's like a giant game to the good Lord. He's standing at the pearly gates hee-hawing at us whilst we try to run down the source of the water. I bet he calls us—"

"Idiots! Silly youngins." Maddie's belly bounced up and down as she giggled. She jumped to her feet and pressed her hands to her hips. "You odd children. Can't you see I'm foolin' with you? You know that's what the good Lord is sayin'."

"Where do you begin?" I spoke, but the river didn't answer. That was something I'd wondered since childhood. If I could just find the beginning, I might find the answers. Things like how does the sun rise and set, and what holds the moon in the sky.

I stretched my hand, snagged the reins on Slouch's bridle and pulled her next to me, patting the white diamond just above her eyes with the flat of my hand. "We got no place to go, girl. I killed a man." I let those words settle in the air just a minute. My eyes never left the bend in the river. Finally I sighed. "Momma has disowned me. All I got is the Pastor's Bible and you. And these memories opened up from the locked chest they was hid in."

I wrapped my arms around the mare's neck. Her hot breath dampened my back. A horrible memory raised its head to haunt me.

"If you so much as whimper, I'll cut the air off from your nose." His hand pressed tight against my mouth. "You just remember that what I do, I do to save your soul. We have to cleanse you and replace the flood of blood with the seed of God."

Momma and me had been washing clothes in the creek when I first saw the trail of red swirl over the smooth scrubbing stones. My right of passage. Womanhood.

"Mercy, Mercy. You've just become a woman." And Momma sat me down on the creek bank and explained how I'd suddenly gone from a child washing clothes to a woman in a matter of seconds. I never dreamed she'd tell the Pastor of my right of passage. I never imagined that I'd never dream again—not after that night.

"This cleansin' has to be done in the quiet. You keep your silence." The Pastor's breath against my neck combined with his drool horrified me. "You keep quiet girl and this will be soon done."

His hand climbed my thigh and with each thrust he whispered some God-forsaken blessing. "Save her soul Almighty God," he said. "Take your seed and fill her." I felt the vomit rise from my gut, and when it seeped from between his fingers he drew back and slapped me.

I was twelve. Twelve. And though I didn't think that the good Lord was in this deed . . . I didn't know no better either. But I grew to expect visits from the Pastor to be *cleansed.*

Momma knew. At least I think she knew because the Pastor would excuse me from chores the next day. He'd tinker with my long dark hair. Kiss my cheek. Then things would go back to the same old ways. My *reward* of no chores would come back tenfold.

Slouch nudged at my shoulder to remind me she was hungry.

"Come on girl," I said. "Let's work our way up the ridge to Jude's house. I got nothin' left but to figure where the river begins. Maybe he'll give us a place to bed down for the night. Then we'll commence at first light. Travel 'til we find it." I climbed on the mare, then ducked as we walked beneath the stand of weeping willows.

I shut my eyes and all I could see in my mind was the Pastor jiggling from that rope. *He deserved it. After all he's done. He deserved it.* It surprised me that days later his hanging would still bother me. But it did. It ate away at my soul. Then there was the look on Maddie's face. Worse than the look on Momma's. I knew right that second . . . I was alone for the long haul.

I remembered those four little girls of Stanley's, and just how pretty they was. It galled me to think of them youngins growin' up with the memory of watching their daddy die. I wondered, if by some chance, the Pastor thought Stanley would spill his ugly secret. Thing was, the Pastor's secrets really weren't secrets at all. People like the Widow Starling and Elsi and Stanley all knew, but they kept quiet. They was afraid . . . afraid they'd go to hell if they spoke about these things. How could the good Lord allow such terrible things to happen? I felt my mouth tighten and my teeth grind.

"I ain't so sure, Slouch," I said as I patted her neck, "that they is sucha thing as a *good* Lord."

Slouch kept a slow, steady pace, and I pulled the Pastor's Bible from my bag, along with a knife-sharpened pencil. Bet set me to thinking about them four youngins. Four daughters. I scratched their names on a piece of paper the Pastor had folded between the pages of Deuteronomy.

For some reason unbeknownst to me, these people from the past seeped to the front and writing them down drew me a picture I wasn't expecting. Was I making up this connection because I hated the Pastor so bad? I've not always been the fattest hen in the roost, but I was seeing something I didn't like on that sheet of paper. Stanley was dead and he had *four* daughters. The Widow Starling was dead and she had *three* daughters, and *three* granddaughters. They all had daughters . . . daughters that somehow tied back to the Pastor.

I needed to ponder on this. And ponder I did, all the way to Jude's homestead. I'd not spoken to Jude in three years, not since his Mary died. That was a sad sort of ways. Miss Mary grew sick with the plague she got from a tick. She dropped weight like a logger dropping a tree, and it wasn't no time until Mary was nothing but skin draped over bone.

When we were kids, Jude was the school-yard bully, but when Nat Muller jumped him and beat the tar out of him in front of his buddies, Jude took on a new side. The Pastor got wind of the flailing and called both boys to neutral ground. I remember peering from behind the wood-shed and waiting to see what the Pastor would do. He set them boys down side by side and told them the story of Daniel, and how he was bullied by men. Then he tied their wrists together on one side and made them stack hay. They wrestled around for a spell, then before long, they were working together. I reckon they become good friends after that.

"One good deed outta thousands of bad." I scratched Slouch's ears. "Even the devil deserves his dues."

Slouch turned the bend onto Jude's homestead. The squeals of little girls echoed up the rugged trail. The sound of metal against wood bounced off the summit as Jude split logs. That old Bluetick Coonhound lumbered down the path toward me and Slouch and let out one gruff rumble.

"Jude. Jude Hawkins. That you?" I hollered.

I threw my hand into the air and waved. Jude stood his axe on the head and leaned it against his knee. His hand slid into his back trouser pocket and pulled out a red cloth. He swiped his forehead with the rag, then yanked that axe off the ground. Jude wound his arm back, and sank the axe into the middle of a log twice the size of both my legs.

Slouch eased to a halt, and Jude's kids ducked behind him. "Whaddya want here, Mercy?"

I was taken back by his anger. "I was looking for a place to bed down for the night. Wondered if I could stay in your barn, get a meal?"

"Ain't no place in my barn for you. Not you, or none like you."

"Why, Jude? What's got your hackles up? I ain't seen you in a coon's age."

"And it's a good thing, too. I got no use for anybody with dealin's to the Pastor. So you git that horse turned, and head on outta here."

I did the opposite. I slid off the saddle and walked toe to toe with Jude. "What dealin's? You can't punish me for something the Pastor done. Least you can do is tell me what he did and why you're blaming me."

Jude was still a handsome man even though manning a homestead, tilling, planting, and caring for his daughters had taken its toll. His blond hair dripped off his head like strands of gold. The lines around his mouth had turned to age, and the smile I remembered, mean as it was, had faded.

"It ain't what the Pastor did. It's what he didn't do. When Mary was flushed with the fever he come here to pray with us—to see if they was somethin' he could do to help."

"So what didn't he do?" I asked.

"Well, he prayed over Mary. She was so sick she couldn't lift her head off the piller, and her eyes was sunk in her head. I'd gone to town to fetch Doc Adams and left him to tend Mary and the girls. When I got home Mary was just barely hangin' on, and there he set, rared back in the rocker. The devil just sat starin' at Mary. My baby girls sobbed for their momma, and he just stared." Jude's voice began to quiver. "Mary was pleadin' for water. 'Just a taste of water,' she'd say. And the Pastor just set there smilin', waiting for Mary to die. He never once offered her a drink. He let her die."

I dropped my head in shame. "But I didn't do nothing to you and Mary."

"You're his flesh and blood. The fruit don't fall far from the tree."

"That ain't fair, Jude. You know the Pastor's dead?"

A smile slowly parsed his lips. I turned and scooped the reigns in my hand.

"Come on, horse." I brushed my dark hair back, twisted it, and shoved it into the neck of my shirt. My anger built like a fire grabbing at underbrush.

"Mercy?" Jude called.

"Yeah." I slipped my foot into the stirrup and lifted myself onto Slouch.

"How'd the old man die?"

I hesitated, then tapped the horse's rear with a gentle pop. "By my hand." Slouch swayed to one side, then stepped off.

"I'll be. They really is a God." He laughed. "There's room in the loft of the barn. You can bed down for a few days if you is willin' to help spilt wood. You willin'?"

"I'm willin'. But let me think on this. Leave the barn open. I might be back later."

The axe slammed another log, and the crack of the wood breaking sounded like the tension on that elm tree by the river. Funny I never noticed how a tree groans when it's pressed with weight. And right now, I had the weight of the world.

Six

I slapped Slouch and she kicked her back feet like I'd stabbed her with a hot anvil. Can't say that I blamed her, the smack of my palm against her skin sent chills through me. I could have sworn my hand stung like fire.

Like before.

I rubbed the flat of my palm against my trousers, then blew on it, but the stinging didn't stop. Ahead on the trail, I saw what looked to be a shadow sitting on a tree limb. I'd never been afraid of the mountain or any of its trails in the past. Didn't know why I felt squeamish this time.

Slouch slung her head from side to side and snorted. Her blubbering echoed along the path. Birds flew up from the brush, spooking Slouch. She wrenched, then stood on her hind legs.

"Easy, girl. Easy. It's just some old buzzards pickin' at a meal." She stepped to the side, then straightened. Her ears perked forward, and her nose flared. "Easy, now," I said. "Ain't nothin' here to spook you."

The trail narrowed and seeds of the sun faded behind the heavy canopy of the forest. To my left, the rumble of the rapids over the rocks. "I shoulda took Jude Hawkins up on that barn for the night."

Up the trail, the shadows of the night dripped off the trees, and a cold breeze wisped around like the breath of death. I neared a stand of laurel trees, and the scent of their white blooms filled my nose. A rabbit sat frozen by the edge of a downed trunk. I reached to the saddlebag, quiet like, and pulled my knife from its sheath. With one swift motion I hurled the blade, nailing the rabbit in the gut.

"Supper," I said. I threw my leg over the saddle and dropped to the ground. I hated killing animals, hated killing anything. Or I thought I did. The memory of the Pastor hanging 'til he stopped wiggling didn't seem to bother me too bad.

I pulled my knife from the rabbit, and my mind wandered back to the barn at home.

"You're gonna learn that killing is the way of the mountain. A man's got to survive, gotta eat." The Pastor yanked me by the arm, and dragged me behind the barn.

"I can't kill no deer, Pastor. I can't." Tears streamed down my cheeks.

The Pastor pulled my hand from behind my back and slapped the butcher knife against my palm. He'd snagged a doe and tied her by the neck between two trees. She reared to her hind legs and pawed at the air. Her brown eyes pleaded for freedom.

"Tag her, girl," the Pastor shouted.

"No. I can't."

"You can hit a target at thirty paces. I taught you well. Tag her." The Pastor's hand slipped under my hair and wrapped tight in my locks. He pulled my head to one side. "Mercy, tag her."

"Please, Pastor. Please stop. I can't do this." Yellow eyes stared at me from the edge of the woods, and I caught a glimpse of a fawn. "I can't slaughter a momma in front of her baby."

The Pastor pressed my hand tight around the blade then swiftly pulled. I felt the hot singe of the metal slice my palm and the warmth of my blood drip down my arm.

"I told you. Tag her. Tag her or I'll slice the other hand."

"Daddy, please. We ain't hungry. Why are you doin' this?"

The Pastor's face hardened, and his eyes squinted. He pried my other hand from behind my back and slapped the blade into my palm. I kicked his leg, and bit his arm. The rage in the Pastor grew.

"You're just like your momma. You're a weak woman. Only interested in what women do." He rammed his hand into my chest and shoved me down. I screamed as hard as I could scream as he dragged me across the ground. He wrapped the end of a rope around my feet then tossed it over the tree limb, and hoisted me into the air. The deer and I were side by side, both fighting, both tied . . . both helpless.

"I told you, girl, to tag her. The good Lord tells us to teach our children.

He says 'Foolishness is bound in the heart of a child; but the rod of correction shall drive it far from him.'" The Pastor shouted, "My God in heaven. Bless me as I discipline this unruly child. Just like you disciplined the Israelites, so shall I hand down your wrath."

The blood rushed to my head as I dangled upside down. He drew back and spit at me. Then he wheeled around and sliced into the side of the deer. She shrieked.

I screamed. In a second slice, he rammed the knife deep into the stomach of the doe and tore her open. Blood splashed on my face and I saw the animal fall to the ground.

"No, Pastor, please. Let me down. Please let me down."

Momma heard my screams and come running. She dropped her rag on the ground and called to God. "Lord, Almighty. Have mercy. Pastor, stop. She's a child." Momma grabbed at the Pastor's arm. He turned in his fury and kicked her in the stomach. She fell to the ground and gasped for air.

The Pastor pulled my hair into a tight tail in his palm, then took that knife and laid it against the top of my head. "I give you to the Lord," he shouted and without hesitation he ripped the knife through my hair. The last thing I remember was the Pastor slicing the rope that held me off the ground. I fell into the belly of the deer.

—————

Daybreak come and the sun peered through the trees. My face warmed as morning dried the dew from my skin. The fire was nothing but embers, and the bones of a half-eaten rabbit lay on a hot stone. Every time I closed my eyes, things I thought I'd long since forgot, haunted me. Poked at me. Dug in deep under my skin. They seeped out in my dreams, leaving me little room to rest.

Old Edom used to say, "Betwixt guilt and regret, a body can lose what's left of their mind." Up to now, I'd never really understood that. If this was guilt, it was like a rattler rearing up, and striking over and over. With every hit the fangs sunk into the flesh, and the venom stung like fire.

I run my fingers through my hair and remembered how long it had took for the length to grow back. I remembered the bonnet Momma made to cover the bald spot on top of my head.

"Lord," I said. "If you're real, tell me why you let these things happen. How could you let a man . . . a man of the cloth . . . be such a devil?"

I walked to the edge of the river, knelt on one knee, and scooped some water into my mouth. I scrubbed my knuckle against my teeth, swished another mouthful of water, then spit. "Ugh. I hate the taste of last night's supper." I spit again, then snapped a laurel twig from a branch, and began to chew. The taste drew my mouth tight, but even that was better than the sourness I'd woke up with.

I rinsed the knife, dried it with my shirt, and slipped it into my boot. The rush of the water seemed to scream back at me. My reflection shined in the puddle between the rocks. My hair had grown back, long and lush, though the curls never returned. I took in a deep breath then vomited. Between the nightmares and the rabbit, I could hardly stomach anything.

"I'm thinkin' that they ain't no God," I said to the river.

"How can you be so sure?" A deep voice boomed over the river's roar. I gasped, and turned.

"Who are you?" I eased my hand toward my boot and slipped out the knife.

"Put that thing away. I got no plans to harm you." A tall, slender man stepped onto the boulder next to me. His eyes were as green as the grass in Cades Cove, and his skin as fair as the face of Stanley Farmer's Bet.

"I said, who are you?"

"And I said, put that knife down. I got no plans to harm you. I saw your horse and the end of a fire. Thought there might be a problem."

"You still ain't answered my question." I moved the knife from side to side. "I done killed one man. What's a second?"

He stepped back, then knelt for a drink of water. His hands were huge, fingers long, and his nails clean and groomed. A neatly trimmed beard lined his jawbone, and a thin blondish mustache rested on his upper lip.

"Samuel Stone. The name is Samuel Stone. I pastor the church in Indian Gap."

"Indian Gap? Have I made my way to Indian Gap?" I asked. I hadn't realized I'd traveled so far from home.

"No, no. You're close to Thunder Mountain. I was just tellin' you I started a church at the Gap, and I've been teaching the Cherokee how to read. Then there's the settlers there. God's work don't stop at the edge of town. Now, you gonna do me the honor of telling me your name?"

"Oh, Lord. I can't believe I'm here."

"Don't fret. You ain't lost. You're close to Thunder Mountain."

I twisted around looking for something familiar. Thunder Mountain was nowhere close to home.

Samuel Stone stepped toward me as I stared into his green eyes. He rested his hand on top of mine and gently loosened my fingers from around the knife. The scars of the past glared at him from my palms. "Looks like you lost the battle with your knife."

I stepped back. My nose flared, and my heart raced. "Them are scars from a cruel God."

"Really? Must not be the same God I know." Samuel bowed slightly and pointed his hat toward the path. Just the sight of another pastor made my skin crawl. Especially one that questioned me.

"I got some dried fatback and a loaf of sourdough bread. I'm happy to share it."

"Who are you?" I asked.

The man scratched his ear, and pressed his hat tight over his forehead. "Well, best I remember, I just told you that. Now you hungry or just stubborn?"

I walked to the embers of the fire and sat on a rock while Samuel unpacked his saddlebag. He smiled and laid a cloth on the ground. "Can I borrow that knife to cut the meat?" Pouring a splash of water on a hot rock, he cleaned a good place to warm the meat, then stoked the fire.

I couldn't talk. I was still trying to figure why I couldn't remember traveling this far, the better part of twenty miles. My mind must have been thousands of miles away. It frightened me that I could have come so far with no recollection, but when you're tired, and when you're twisted between mad and brokenhearted . . . I reckon a body might not remember a few things.

"You got a name, or do I just call you Girl?"

I jumped to my feet. "No. You don't call me Girl."

"Then what do I call you?"

"Mercy."

"It's not that hard. No need to beg for mercy."

"No, you idiot. My name is Mercy. Mercy Roller."

Samuel cocked his head to one side, then rubbed his forefinger over his whiskers. "You kin to the Pastor Roller?"

My heart sank. *Should I lie?* No. I never was a liar. "Why do you ask?"

"Word travels. I heard the Pastor passed. So I thought I'd head across the mountain to pay my respects."

"You don't owe no respect to the Pastor."

Samuel handed me a slice of meat and a piece of warmed bread. "Really? And so, if I don't owe no respect to the Pastor, am I to assume you're his family?"

"By name only." I shoved the bread into my mouth.

"So the Pastor *is* dead?"

"He is."

Samuel took my hands and twisted them palms up. "Those scars are the sign of righteous indignation?"

I eyed him and pulled them away.

"Them scars cover the skin of the woman who killed the Pastor."

Samuel wrapped my hands in his, then rubbed his finger across the scars. "You know, someone else had scars in His palms too. Scars put there by unrighteous men." I yanked my hands free. He had no right to touch me. No right to try and understand me.

I walked to Slouch and pulled the Pastor's Bible from the bag, then tossed it on the ground in front of Samuel. "I don't need no sermon on a crucified Christ. What I need is proof God is a man of His word." I kicked the Bible across the ground.

Samuel bent over and lifted the book from the coals. He brushed the cover clean and opened the pages.

"Forgive us our trespasses as we forgive those who trespass against us."

I pushed my hands into Samuel's face so he'd have a clear look. He took his fingers and pressed them into my scars. His touch startled me. It was gentle but I yanked my hands free. "What about the innocent who are trespassed against? What about, 'Blessed are the little children'?"

SEVEN

SAMUEL ROLLED THE piece of fatback into the cheesecloth, then tied the ends. He tore one last piece of bread from the loaf, folded the cloth over it, and stuffed it in his bag.

"Take this. You'll need it later in the day."

I stared at him wondering if I should slap the hand that offered me food. Instead I snapped the bread from his fingers.

"Thanks." I took a bite. "Where you headed to now, Preacher? Now that you know the Pastor is dead and they ain't no need to go pay your respects."

He pulled the cinch strap snug against his horse, and slipped his boot into the stirrup. His horse groaned as he lifted himself into the saddle. "What about your momma?" he asked.

"What about her?"

"You don't think she could use a visit from me?"

"No." *Momma's chosen her life and though I set her free from bondage, she picked her side and sent me on my way.*

Samuel leaned forward against the saddle horn and rested his arm across the horse's withers. He pushed his hat away from his brow. "Well, Mercy. Seems you're as bitter as a green persimmon."

"What do you know about bitter?"

"I know anger when I see it. So all I can say is, a young girl with the name Mercy, sure ain't got none."

I felt my anger rise. I wanted to take a run at that preacher and knock him off his horse, but I was smart enough to know the man might be right. I was angry. Had every reason to be. All them years of closing out the horrible things the Pastor did only served to make my fury burn like the fires of hell, and when I unleashed that fury, one could say, all hell broke loose.

Samuel eyed the fire. "I'm gatherin' you really *did* kill the Pastor. So having said that, I'll be on my way."

I came to my feet, and rested my hands on my hips. "That's it? You announce you believe I killed the Pastor, then you're just gonna be *on your way*? What kind of preacher are you?"

"At this moment, I'm a little confused. So why don't you tell me what it is you expect from me. Especially since I only just met you."

My face grew warm. I dropped my head. "Well, you could start by telling me where you're headed. Then you might act like you care. Show some compassion."

Samuel smiled. "I'm guessing you wouldn't know compassion if it slapped you between the eyes." He pointed to the bread he'd given me. "I showed you some. It went right over your head. I gave you a meal."

I couldn't find words to argue. He'd done just what he said.

"And like I said, since I'm not going to be welcome with your momma, then I reckon I'll head back across the gap. I got folks I can visit along the way. Terrance Johnson and his wife are working on their cabin on up the mountain. I'll stop there and help a bit. Isabella is ready to give birth any day. The extra hand will be needed around their homestead. Might even get to see that baby come into this world." Samuel tapped his horse. "Hup."

I kicked at the fire's embers, and stomped them into the dirt. "You'll hold up there, Preacher."

"I'll what?"

"I'll go with you to the Johnsons'. I've had experience bringin' babies into this world." I couldn't tell him I didn't want him to touch Isabella or her baby. I couldn't be sure he wasn't just like the Pastor, and I wasn't about to let another baby die, another mother suffer at the hands of a man who hid under the wings of the good Lord. No siree.

The preacher pulled the reins to the left and turned his horse nose to nose with Slouch. "You're coming with me?"

I grabbed my bag, stuffed the chunk of sourdough bread in my pocket, and threw my leg over Slouch.

"I didn't stutter, did I, Preacher? I'm a lot of things, but I do talk plain. Don't reckon I know anyone who can't understand what I say. Leastwise, you." I smacked Slouch. She nosed past the preacher's horse and kicked into a trot. "You best be gettin' in the lead, Preacher. I don't know the way and Slouch has got a spurt goin'."

I heard the preacher laugh, then click his lips. "Yo, horse, we got some catchin' up to do." Within moments, he galloped past me; his long black coattails flapped across the horse's rear. I wasn't sure about this man, but I knew for positive I wasn't about to let this lady Isabella have a baby in his presence. Somebody had to protect her and maybe this time, I might just earn some grace and mercy. I might just have a chance to do what the Pastor oughta done. Help.

The river pooled ahead and the horses were able to walk across. The river rock bottom turned to a settled silt, and the rapids quieted to a soft bubble. Slouch stopped midway across to drink. I leaned over her side and scooped a handful of water into my mouth.

Samuel hadn't looked back once. It was almost like I wasn't with him. I heard him occasionally break into song. *Bringing in the sheaves. Come, come, come to the church in the wildwood, oh come to the church in the vale.* His baritone voice echoed up the pass. Every once in a while, he'd snag a tree limb and break a twig, but he never turned around to see if I followed.

"Preacher. Don't you care if I'm trailin' behind you?"

I expected he'd turn and give me some big yarn about how glad he was to have me along, even if I didn't trust him. But he didn't. Samuel gave me a quick glance over his shoulder, then turned back to the trail ahead.

That just got in my craw. Made me a shade mad.

"Preacher?" I said. "You ever stood by a woman givin' birth?"

He lifted his hand and waved me off.

"What's a matter? Cat got your tongue?"

Not one ounce of attention come at me. The trail narrowed around the bluff to the point my leg scrapped the side of the hill. Dirt clumped and fell. What didn't drop into my boot sprinkled across my trousers. Maddie come to mind. She was forever throwing something. Rocks, dirt, sticks. A smile slowly tipped the edges of my mouth. I brushed my hand alongside the dirt wall of the mountain and broke myself a clot of red clay.

It had been a while since I'd thrown at a moving target, but I squinted my eye and took aim. "Preacher, I said, don't you care if I'm trailin' behind you?" I saw his shoulders lift as he shrugged. "I hate you feel that way, Preacher," I whispered, then drew back and let that clot fly. It landed square betwixt his shoulder blades with a loud thud. I pulled Slouch to a stop and waited.

"Ho there, horse."

The preacher halted his animal. He turned, smiled, and took off his coat. Next thing I knew he'd gently nudged the beast into a walk. I was stumped over that one. I'd guessed he'd snap back at me. But he didn't. He just smiled and went on.

I kicked Slouch into a trot to close the distance. "That's it?" I shouted. "That's all you're gonna do? Take off your coat. Keep goin'?"

"That's all I plan to do. What'd you expect?"

"I can't figure you, Preacher."

"Ain't nothin' to figure."

"You didn't seem to care I invited myself along."

"Nope. Isabella could use the help. Who am I to turn a provision into waste?"

They was something about this man that riled me. He drew my anger to the surface faster than lightning, but I liked him. The breeze whipped the hair around my face 'til I finally pulled a piece of twine from my pocket and tied it back. It had taken a good few years for the long strands to grow back after the Pastor butchered them. I never cut it again.

Momma parted my hair to one side, trying to cover the bald spot in the crown. As the nubs grew out, she'd try to trim the longer strands to even out the mess the Pastor had made when he chopped it. It come back, but not fast enough to keep youngins from firing jokes at me at school. On the days the Pastor would *let me* go to school, he'd bend me over so my hair hung over the top of my head then gently bunch what he could grab hold of into a bonnet Momma made me. He'd tie the straps under my chin, and lightly touch my nose. Some days the Pastor would even give me a gentle hug, and brush my cheek with his knuckles. Momma said it was his way of saying he was sorry.

"I think we'll bed down here for the night," Samuel said. He pointed to a small cave in the side of the mountain. "The pass is narrow around the side of the mountain and hard to see your way clear in the dark. So, if it's alright by you, I'll build a fire just outside the cave. You can bed down inside, and I'll toss my bedroll on the ground by the fire." Samuel slipped off his horse and draped the reins around a low-hanging branch.

"We can't make it to Johnsons' place before nightfall?"

"Lordy, no. We're still a good day's ride from the homestead. I promise I'm a gentleman."

"I didn't say you wasn't no gentleman. I just asked if we couldn't push on before nightfall. Or are you afraid of the dark?"

Samuel walked to my side and slipped his arm around Slouch's neck. Her head brushed against his shoulder as he slapped her sweaty hide. "Good girl." He pushed his hand into his pocket and pulled out a carrot.

I rolled my eyes. "You mean to tell me you carry carrots?"

"What good horse owner don't?" Slouch slapped her lips around the carrot and begin to grind at the vegetable.

"You gonna build a fire?" I asked.

"I said I was. But I'm waiting on you to get down off this horse so I can unsaddle her and wash her down. She stinks, and well . . ."

"Well, what?" I snapped. "You insinuatin' I need to bathe?"

The preacher shrugged as I climbed down from the saddle. "There's a stand of willows just around that bend, and a nice peaceful pool behind some boulders. You oughta find it private and since it ain't real deep, it might be a little warm."

"You're a pushy old goat, aren't you?"

"Well, no. I'm just an honest one, and I'm tellin' you the truth. You need to bathe. I bet you clean up mighty nice." He pulled the saddle from Slouch's back, then dunked it in the river, and scrubbed the underside. I found my way toward the pool. "Hold up there, Mercy."

Samuel rested the saddle on a boulder, then walked to his pack. He unhooked the latches and pulled out a shirt and trousers. "These are gonna be too big, but they'll do you 'til you can wash your clothes. They can dry by the fire." He tossed them, and I snagged 'em in the air. I must have stared for several minutes as he gathered wood for a fire.

"Mercy. Go. Git on over there."

In all my nineteen years, I'd never had anyone be so kind. Kindness didn't mean much though. The Pastor could be kind when he wanted to be. Like when he'd tie my bonnet on my head to cover the mess he'd made. I'd also seen him pull Momma close a time or two, and brush her blond hair away from her face. We just never knew how long his goodness would last. It was like he was two different men living in the same body.

My mind come back to the present, and I made my way to the pool to bathe. Even washed my hair and combed the rat tails out with my fingers. When Momma sent me on my way, I didn't bother to pack anything more than my knife and that blasted Bible. I sank into the water, and leaned my head against a rock. My toes poked through the clear ceiling, and waved at the sky. I could hear Samuel snapping branches with his feet, and before long I caught a whiff of hickory smoke.

My fingers grew numb from the chill of the river. I rolled to my knees, and crawled to the bank. I'd rinsed my trousers and shirt early on, and as the night air began to descend into the valley, I wasn't about to put on wet socks.

"Well, well. There you are." Samuel sloshed the hot liquid in his make-shift pot, and poured two tins full. The aroma of coffee twirled and danced around my nose. My stomach ached from hunger.

"I'm here," I said.

"I was beginning to wonder if you took off. You was gone so long."

"I wouldn't go nowhere dressed as the likes of you." I bent to roll the pant legs up to my ankles.

"You're lucky the Widow Elkins packs for an army. I got an extra blanket or two."

Despite my nasty attitude, he seemed to be a forgiving soul. I hung my clothes on the reins the preacher had strung between two trees. The warmth of the fire made my toes tingle. Samuel corralled the horses in the cave, and pulled up a bundle of dried brush for them to gnaw over. Before I know'd what was happen', he'd scooped a pile of leaves against the rock wall and folded a blanket over it.

"There, that oughta make your rest a little better." Samuel scrubbed his hands against his pants.

I eased around him and lay on the soft bed.

I turned my back to him, and pulled the blanket tight around my neck. It took a bit, but I felt the muscles in my back relax. My eyes closed as I took in a deep breath, filling my lungs with fresh mountain air. That's when I found out what kind of man the preacher really was.

Just as I was ready to drift off a wad of moss slapped me in the back of the head. I jumped to my feet and faced Samuel. He burst into laughter.

"The Good Book lends itself to this here thought. 'Love your neighbor as yourself.' Or payback is hell."

The preacher proved he had a sense of humor, and he knew just how to time his little attack. It didn't make me trust him, but it did make me respect him.

"Samuel Stone," I whispered as I snuggled back into my bed.

"Yes," he said. He stoked the fire with a log. Tiny flickers of ash sailed like fireflies.

"I'm much obliged."

Eight

I woke to Slouch huffing in my ear, her nose burrowing against my neck, her warm breath blowing against my skin as she nuzzled me. I raised my hand and scratched her jaw. Trees rustled in the morning breeze. A squirrel flitted about the saddles, sniffing the leather.

Samuel was gone.

His horse stood in the cave, but he'd already got a start on the day. His blanket was rolled and tied to the empty saddle.

I stood and brushed my fingers through my hair, then stretched my arms toward the sun. Its warmth relaxed the tense muscles in my shoulders. I twisted my neck from side to side, rolled my chin toward my chest, and yawned. I needed to find relief. Though our farm back home wasn't much, we at least had an outhouse.

Memories hit me square between the eyes. I looked toward a stand of pawpaw trees, and my heart stopped. The Pastor dangled beneath the trees, his head oddly bent to one side and his mouth covered with a white foamy slobber. I gasped and pushed my fists into my eyes, rubbing hard.

"Just a dream. It's just a dream," I said.

My clothes were stiff on the makeshift clothesline. The campfire blazed, as though the preacher'd never slept, but had kept the fire stoked through the night so my clothes, ragged as they were, would dry.

"Well, good mornin', Glory." Samuel's voice echoed off the side of the hill.

"Where you at?"

"Up here."

I wheeled around to see Samuel slipping down the leaf-covered bank. He held a squirrel by the back legs. "I never was good at huntin.' But my daddy taught me to survive." Samuel stumbled off the hill and landed against a mountain laurel. When his shoulder blades slammed against the tree trunk he let out a grunt.

"Seems to me you do pretty good," I said. "There might be a mouthful there." I pointed at the limp squirrel.

"I try to make the kill on the first blow. It's instinct that way. It's when I miss and injure a catch that makes wailing the life out of it hard." Samuel rubbed his hands on his trousers. "And it's enough for breakfast. Daddy always taught me the Lord provides what I need, not what I want." He smiled and dangled the dead animal. "You can cook it. Right?"

Samuel furrowed his brow. I yanked the thing out of his hand, and pulled my knife from inside my boot.

"Funny thing how a man can kill something so easy, but he leaves cleanin' up the mess to the women folk."

I nearly choked on my words. I'd not thought anything about striking the rear of that horse holding the Pastor. It never crossed my mind not to send the horse packing. I killed—just like the Pastor killed. Just like he did to the Widow and to . . . to my baby. My nose flared, and my jaw tightened. Tears filled the wrinkles lining my eyes. I'd killed the Pastor. Killed my father. *Killed.*

I skinned the animal and split it down the center. It only took a few minutes to clean and rinse it in the river. Samuel had whittled a point to a hickory stick so I could poke it through the meat. He'd stoked the fire till the flames burned blue.

"We want to cook the meat not burn it to embers."

"I know, but smell that hickory when it burns. Just what we needed to make eatin' in the wild pleasant." Samuel grabbed the end of a burning branch and pulled it away from the flame.

"Here. I've cleaned the mess. You cook it." I shoved the carcass at him. Samuel's green eyes reached out to me and I could sense his tenderness. I was beginning to hate that about him. That soft smile, those gentle eyes were so, so . . . condemning.

"You're mighty fine," he said. "This oughta cook real fast. You hungry?"

I was hungry, but I wasn't sure I could stomach the squirrel meat. Not after the guilt laid in. But I sat on a rock by the fire, and the sweet aroma of breakfast twisted its way around me, tickling my nose. My mouth started to water.

"Mercy?" Samuel said twirling the meat in circles through the flame. "We all make mistakes."

I laughed in his face. "What mistake you reckon I've made?"

"Well, I ain't quite sure. But somethin' is eatin' at you. And I guess for the lack of better conversation, I'd offer you that thought. We could start with your killing your daddy. Ever body makes mistakes."

"Didn't make no mistake," I said. I wasn't about to let on to Samuel there was a problem. "So stop your assumin'. You know what they say about assuming, right, Preacher? Assumin' makes an . . ."

Samuel interrupted. "Yeah, yeah, I know, you don't have to tell me. I just was trying to offer you some consolation. You've lost your father."

I came to my feet. "No, Preacher, I didn't lose my father. I killed a monster, just like you'd stomp a roach on the floor. I stomped out his life. I never lost no daddy. It's hard to lose what you don't got. He never was a daddy. You hear, me. He was a nasty son of a . . ."

"Mercy. Stop." Samuel laid the stick across two rocks. "Just stop. I'm not accusing you of anything. In fact, word travels in these parts and I'd done got wind of some of the things the Pastor had done. That's why I was coming across the mountain."

"You said you was comin' to pay your respects," I bellowed.

"I said," he reached to touch my arm, "I was coming to pay my respects. That's what I was doin'. I wasn't sure if the Pastor was dead. I'd only heard what folks was sayin.' I learned a long time ago, a man can't lay a lot of faith in what folks is sayin'. My intent was to just talk with him about the rumors."

I pulled my hand away. "Rumors. They was rumors?"

"There was. I'd gotten a few twisted tales from the mountain folk I visited. Figured I needed to seek out the truth. After all, that's what the good Lord tells us to do. Seek the truth."

"What kinda man are you, Preacher? What hell happened to drag you into bein' a man of the cloth?"

Samuel shook his head. I guess he was trying to regain what I'd just bit off.

"There was no hell to walk through. My mother and daddy are farmers. They've always known the graciousness of God. Guess it just rubbed off."

"I don't buy it," I snapped.

"Nothin' to buy. It's truth. Some of us was raised with loving parents. And me . . . well, I've always felt this nudge toward bein' a preacher. A callin'."

"Some of us was raised with loving parents? What kind of judgmental remark is that?"

"Mercy. Please. Sit down. Let's eat a nice breakfast. I didn't mean to get your hackles up. You gotta stop takin' ever thing I say like I'm poking at you. I don't know you. Ain't nothing to poke."

I covered my ears with my hands, and closed my eyes. *Mercy, mercy, mercy* echoed in my head. There was no mercy. Leastways, not this day.

NINE

SAMUEL SAT QUIET the rest of the meal.

He dug the toe of his boot into the fertile soil of the riverbank. I could tell he wanted to talk, but I was in no mood to spin idle tales just to make him feel comfortable. In the quiet, my mind drifted toward that woman who was having a baby.

Samuel seemed like a good soul, but I wasn't about to give him the opportunity to turn on me like the leaves in fall. I was gonna take it upon myself to make sure this Isabella and her baby would live a happy life. I didn't want her to suffer at the hand of another *man of God*.

Having a baby does something to your head. It's like something inside your body wakes up, and you see things you ain't never seen before. You can read people, read their heart, see their intention.

"It's the good Lord's way of stirring your senses. Preparing you to be a mother. Sharpenin' that thing inside you that makes you protect and care for the gift you carry." Momma rubbed my protruding tummy. "We'll take good care of this little one." The child inside me kicked and bounced Momma's hand away. She laughed. "That youngin's gonna be just like her momma." I was stupid to think Momma meant those things.

I thought Momma was a good woman but I could never see the line of where she loved me, and where she protected me, much less the line she walked with the Pastor. I think she loved him, or leastways, she loved living in fear. But when that wagon rolled up to our house and those two folks climbed out, I knew something wasn't right.

Momma greeted the man. His boots shined with a brass tip, and his long coat and tie told me he was someone important. I stepped beside the cabin and peered around the corner.

"I'm Jonathan Oats and this is my wife, Abigale. We came as soon as we got your message. How is she?"

The woman placed her glove-netted hand into her husband's and stepped out of the wagon. She brushed the wrinkles from her skirt tail.

"Yes, how is she?" I could tell from a distance the woman was frail—almost sickly.

Momma swiped her hands on her dress. "I'm nasty. Been diggin' taters in the garden." A bead of sweat trickled over her nose. "Mercy is fine. She's ready any time now."

The woman clasped her hands together and pulled them close to her heart. "I'm so happy. I've never been able to have a child. This is a dream come true."

Momma commenced to explain how the Pastor was traveling. "He's been gone since early spring and won't be home until early winter." Me and Momma rested while the Pastor was gone. For a few months there was not one ounce of strife. "He's across the mountain preaching to them coal miners. One of the miners come over the mountain and asked the Pastor to help them start a church, and find a preacher. We don't expect him back until the first snow."

"Mrs. Roller, are you telling me the Pastor doesn't know about his daughter's baby?"

The color drained from Momma's face. "No, no. And he can't never know. Mercy didn't have no belly when he was here, and if you get her gone before . . ." Momma's voice raised. "You have to understand, he can't never know. I've packed Mercy's clothes. She ain't got much, but if you'll give me a minute to talk to her."

The man stepped forward. "Wait, Mercy don't know? And we didn't expect to take the mother. Just the baby."

Momma began to fidget. "No sir, she don't know. She's a child, and I'll state what's best. What's safest for *my* baby."

"Mrs. Roller, I don't think we can take a baby what its momma don't know."

I couldn't believe my ears. Momma was giving me and my baby away.

Surely not. But surely so, because when Miss Abigale stepped forward and
her voice arced a pitch, I could see there was trouble on the rise. I kept
close to the side of the house trying to stop my knees from shaking. *This
couldn't be happening.*

Abigale dabbed her eyes with her handkerchief. "Jonathan, we can't
walk away from this baby. I want this baby. Jonathan? I don't care if the
mother comes. Let her. I just want this baby."

"She's right, Mr. Oats." Momma pushed her hair away from her face.
"We can't keep this baby. If I save my daughter's life, you have to take her
and the baby. It don't matter if she has a say. She's my child, and I won't
have her killed by the . . ." Momma caught herself before she uttered the
Pastor's name.

I came from my hiding spot. "You're giving me away?" I shouted.

Momma grabbed at my arms and pulled me close. "Mercy Amile, you
listen to me. You know what will happen if the Pastor finds you with a
child. He'll go crazy. He'll kill you, the baby, and any boy you've ever
talked to—you know that."

"What boy. This child is—" Momma pressed her hand over my mouth.
She was right, but that didn't matter to me. What mattered was she was
giving me away. Me and my baby. She was giving us to strangers.

"No," I screamed. "I ain't goin' give my baby away. I'll hide in the
mountains and live alone, but I ain't givin' my baby away."

Momma drew back and smacked me across the mouth. The Oats were
stunned. I pressed my palm against my lips.

"You listen to me. You have a chance at a new life, and this baby has
a chance to live past birth. You're going. I can make up a story to tell the
Pastor. And when you go, you don't never come back 'cause if you do, he'll
kill you on sight." She grabbed my bag and tossed it in the back of the
wagon. Momma turned to Mr. Oats.

"Go, please. Take her. You'll be saving her life."

That was when it hit me. It was the gosh awfulest pain. It felt like somebody had stabbed me in the back, pulled out the blade, and did it again.
There was a splash. Water poured down my legs leaving me in a puddle.

"Momma?" I cried. "Momma, what . . ."

"Good Lord, could this not have waited another few hours?" Momma grabbed me and led me into the house. "Mr. Oats, the well is right around the back. Would you draw me some water? And Miss Abigale, you wanna be a momma? This is the closest you'll come. Let's go have a baby."

Momma fingered a strand of my hair. "The labor will be bad," she said. She was right.

I was grateful it wasn't any worse than one of the Pastor's beatings.

Mr. Oats paced the front porch while Momma and Abigale praised every pain. And when it came time for that baby to stick its head through, all I could do was scream.

"Push hard, Mercy." Momma stroked my knees. "That baby's head is out. One more good push, and we'll see if you have a girl or a boy."

I sucked in a deep breath. Abigale helped me lean into the push. Just as I bore down, the cabin door flew open, and the Pastor bounded through.

"What's going on here?" His voice sounded like thunder.

"Get out," Momma screamed. "Get out."

"The gates of hell will open for this child of sin," the Pastor ranted.

Mr. Oats tried to escort the Pastor out, but the Pastor shoved him across the cabin. Mr. Oats landed on the small board table, tipping it to one side and dropping to the floor. Miss Abigale rushed to her husband. The Pastor elbowed Momma out of the way, then took the baby by the head and yanked.

I never heard her cry.

The pain was so horrible I lost consciousness. All I remember was the Pastor shouting it was a child of the devil. I couldn't argue that, since he was the devil himself.

When I woke up, I was in the barn. Mr. and Mrs. Oats were gone and Momma's face looked like she'd been horsewhipped. Her jaw drooped to one side and her chin shined a reddish-purple. Momma sat crying.

"Mercy. Lord, help Mercy. Lord have mercy."

"Where's my baby?"

Momma dabbed my forehead with a damp cloth. "She's gone to heaven. Heaven, Mercy. Edom laid her to rest."

I never heard my baby cry. Never saw her.

TEN

MADDIE SLIPPED DOWN the boulder and pressed her knees against my back.

"Hi there, Mercy Roller. Brought you a daisy." She pulled my hair behind my ear and slipped in the green stem of the daisy. "There. Perfect. It looks beautiful." There was one thing about Maddie. She always saw the bright side of things. Even when she saw the worst of what happened to me. I turned to face her, and she sighed. "Oh, Mercy." She gently dabbed my lip with her dress. "The Pastor go on a rant again?"

I nodded.

She pulled a tiny Bible from her pouch. "I don't go nowhere without my pouch."

"I know. I'd swear it was sewed to your dress."

A grin stretched across her face as she thumbed through the Bible. "Momma read this to me yesterday. She cleared her throat, and began to stumble through the words. 'And why take ye thought for raiment? Consider the lilies of the field, how they grow; they toil not, neither do they spin.'" She swayed back and forth on the rock while she read. "Now ain't that nice? Do not worry. That's what Momma said this means."

I wrapped my fingers through hers. In my darkest times, Maddie made me feel loved. She sat still for a spell, then let out a giggle. "Let's scour for honey out of the elm stump."

"Really? You think you can get a handful without getting stung?"

"'Course I can. I'll steal the honey, the bees'll chase you."

Samuel sat by the river. A breeze twisted his hair around his cheeks. I saw him scoot next to a boulder, and lean against it, Bible in hand. His lips moved, and he raised his finger into the air.

Crazy preacher, I thought. *Talking to himself.* Still I was curious.

"Whaddya doin'?" I asked. Samuel jumped.

"Mercy," he said, "you scared the tarnation out of me."

"So who you talkin' to?"

"I wasn't talking to no one. I was reading the Good Book. I was reading how God can give and take away."

I kicked at a pebble sending it sailing into the wash of the rapids. "I call that being an Indian giver."

Samuel stared at me, speechless. Or I thought he was speechless, but he was just pondering what to say. I had to give the man credit. He never just opened his mouth and spouted out Scripture. He thought things through.

"Ain't you gonna quote me some two-bit Scripture about how God provides our needs, or how I ain't supposed to worry 'cause He cares for even the lilies in the field? I ain't seen too much provision in my lifetime."

"Actually, I was just reading out of Job . . . 'the Lord gave, and the Lord hath taken away—'"

I grabbed the Bible from his hand and slapped it shut. "Least you can do, Preacher, is give it to me right." I straightened my shoulders, cleared my throat, and spouted in a deep voice, "'And said, naked came I out of my mother's womb, and naked shall I return thither: the Lord gave, and the Lord hath taken away; blessed be the name of the Lord.'"

"Well now, you impress me, Mercy. You know the Scripture."

"I grew up a pastor's daughter. What do you expect?"

"I'd expect a pastor's daughter to be a little less angry. Why are you so bitter, Mercy?"

"Why are you so nosey, Preacher?"

Samuel stood, took the Bible from me, and tucked it inside his jacket. He stepped behind me, and as he passed, his hand squeezed my shoulder. I could feel his pity, and it made me angry.

I stormed past him and yanked Slouch's reins out of the bush. "How much farther to the Johnsons'?" I stabbed my foot into the stirrup, and flung my leg across Slouch's back. The leather of the saddle popped and cracked as I twisted in the seat. I don't know why, but for some reason, the scent of leather comforted me. Maybe it was because of those times the Pastor locked me in the root cellar. All I had was the leather Bible Momma had stashed behind the potato bin—that, a lantern, and a piece of flint. She knew what it was like to be locked in the darkness alone. So she gave herself the only thing that brought her hope . . . a Bible. It brought me hope too. Or I thought it did. Now I figure it was just something to hold on to. Something to connect me to the world outside the cellar.

Samuel dropped in behind me on the trail. "It's about another half-day's ride. Not too bad. Miss Isabella oughta be about ready to have that baby. She was ripe when I came through last time."

"And you got plans to stay with them for how long?"

Samuel nudged his horse next to mine. He pushed his hat to the back of his head, swiped the sweat, and pulled the rim over his forehead enough to shade his eyes. "I told Terrance I'd stay a couple of months and do the chores so he could spend some good time with his wife and new baby."

I laughed out loud. "You sound like a mother hen. A couple of months?"

"No, not so. I just learned over the years those first few weeks are important. And things is hard in these mountains. Especially on Terrance. Babies struggle. I figure I can give a new family a little time together before life settles in. Let Terrance see if he can manage tending a baby."

"You make the man sound like he's some sort of an invalid."

Samuel smiled and said nothing. Slouch eased past as the dirt path narrowed.

I didn't want to like this preacher, and I fought the urge as best I could. But he seemed like the real thing. After my experience with the Pastor, I couldn't see there was anything real about preachers, or God for that fact. He certainly hadn't done me any favors. Despite it, Samuel seemed to be genuine.

The clop of the horses' hooves became more than I could stand. I didn't want to talk to Samuel, but at the same time, his silence was driving me mad. I looked over my shoulder at him, his nose pointed up sniffing the air like a hound. *Could anyone really be this content?*

"Job 1:21," I said.

"What?"

"That Scripture. It was Job 1:21."

The corner of his mouth angled upward, and the edges of his teeth shined. "Like I said, I'm impressed. How'd you memorize such Scripture?"

"Let's just say, when I was hid away I had plenty of time to read."

"You know Mercy, being a man of God ain't so bad."

"So you say, Preacher. It's being the child of a man of God that will carry your soul to hell and back."

"No Mercy. It's being the child of a cruel man that will carry you there and back. You need to figure on that for a while."

The trail turned and steepened. Slouch's hooves slipped on the loose rock as we topped the summit. A hawk circled then swooped toward the ground. Small trees jutted from the rocks and tiny yellow flowers tipped in the breeze. The valley below spread as far as the eye could see and clouds floated within an arm's reach.

"It's somethin', ain't it? Look at these clouds." Samuel leaned against the neck of his horse. "I don't never tire of it."

He was right, the view from the summit was breathtaking, but I wasn't about to let him know I thought so. "I don't know what they call clouds like this where you come from, but up here, Preacher, we call this fog."

"I call this the doorway to heaven. Can't get no closer to God than right here. No more land above you. You're on the good Lord's ground now."

The hills below rose and fell like a sheet blowing in the wind. There was one thing for certain, whether it was the good Lord, or something else that formed these mountains, they sure didn't forget to add in the peace. Up here, a body could see for miles, and the beauty would carry you away.

"Right, Preacher. The good Lord's next step is a long way down."

Samuel didn't flinch at my remark. He just sat there gazing across the land and smiling. Me, I looked for the river. I couldn't see it, but I could hear it. As beautiful as the sight was, I couldn't have cared less about the view. I just wanted to find where the river began. Maybe if I could find that spot, I could figure out how my life began . . . how it twisted and turned—how I'd survived the attacks. Anybody could climb the summit, but few could follow the river to its start, and if I could do that, I might just be strong enough to find the answers.

"You done gawking?" I asked at last.

"Blessed are they that mourn: for they shall be comforted," Samuel whispered. Again his bear-sized hand touched my shoulder. I bent away and his hand fell to his knee.

"No, Samuel. They ain't no comfort. What I want is righteousness. I want things right." I pulled at the reins and Slouch snorted. "What about 'Blessed are they which do hunger and thirst after righteousness: for they shall be filled'? What about that?" Tears clouded my sight.

"You got it wrong, Mercy. They's a difference in righteousness and revenge. You seem to have taken the revenge path. So you tell me, are you happy with that?"

His words stung like a swarm of bees. "I did what I had to do." My jaw ached from gritting my teeth.

"So you *had* to kill the Pastor?"

"If not me, one of the men in the crowd."

"But why you, Mercy? Why you? Look what you gained. More anger and hurt. And now guilt, too. Let me help you, Mercy."

I snatched my knife from my boot and pressed the tip against Samuel's throat. "I don't need your help, and I don't need you messin' inside my head. You understand me? You think you know, but you don't know nothing, Preacher."

Samuel's chin pointed upward as he swallowed. He spoke softly. "I don't need to know details, Mercy. I only need look in your eyes and see your misery. And you don't have to be this way. I can help. God can help."

I pushed the point of the knife into his flesh and a trickle of blood oozed down the shank. "Get this. You can't help me. Nobody can help me. What's done is done. Because of him, I've become the very thing I hated most. Thanks to the Pastor, I'll burn in hell. I think I've had enough help from men of God. Now turn that horse toward the Johnsons' and let's make haste."

I dropped the knife to my side and waited. I could see compassion in Samuel's eyes. He'd reached out with that same compassion, but I looked away. There was nothing he could say to comfort me—nothing he could do to block out the years of memories that rushed at me like a waterfall. He couldn't shut off the nightmares, or turn off the echo of the Pastor's voice. He couldn't take away the ache of a lost child, or the pain of the Pastor's fists. He couldn't erase the feel of the Pastor's naked body against my legs, or the stench in his breath as he pressed his lips against mine. No, there was no helping me, and even though the sting of my palm slapping that horse from underneath the Pastor still burned, it had to be me that did it.

For what it was worth, I had no regrets sending the Pastor's soul to hell, even if mine was attached.

ELEVEN

THE SUN DIPPED between the fingers of the mountaintops. Samuel had spoken little since we left the summit. That was fine by me. I wasn't in the mood to listen to his Scripture quoting, much less his attempt to *heal* me. I didn't need any more *men of God* in my life.

"Just up ahead. That's the Johnson farm."

Samuel slid his hat off, and brushed his hair from his face. I felt a twinge in my stomach. The preacher was handsome.

"Hey, Terrance." Samuel waved his hat in the air. "Got a youngin yet?"

The man returned the wave.

"You'll like Terrance. And I ain't met a person alive who don't love Isabella. They're real homefolks. Generous."

I didn't care who they were. My only aim was to make sure that woman gave birth in safety, and not in the clutches of a preacher.

Terrance Johnson stood at the end of a spilt rail fence, repairing a hole. Sweat covered his face like rain on a window and one sleeve of his shirt dangled to his side—void of an arm. I felt my face grow warm from embarrassment. I had no idea Terrance was missing an arm, or I'd never have called him an invalid. Still, he appeared to be working enough for two able-bodied men. He balanced a block of wood on the ground, and with one mighty swing, struck the axe against it. The wood cracked and tore in half. The split echoed across the valley like a lightning strike. Terrance had already built a fire as dusk approached. The yellow glow of the flames blended perfectly with the setting sun.

Samuel lifted his hand to his lips and whistled. "Terrance," he shouted. "How's the fence coming?"

Terrance leaned against his axe, and swiped his face with the loose sleeve. "Well, howdy, Preacher. You're back early. Must be a real glutton for hard labor."

"Bible says gluttony is wrong, but it speaks highly of those who work for the night is coming."

"I reckon you done made yourself a religious joke." Terrance leaned back and let out a loud guffaw.

"Can't you wait till you get closer?" I said to Samuel. "You yell like they ain't no tomorrow, and the man is just up the path." I pressed my finger in my ear.

"Well now, Miss Mercy, seems you ain't yet come to like me. That's all right. I'd like it better if I thought you liked the man and hated his ways, but I'll take what I can get from you in the way of conversation. Even if it is grouchy."

I rolled my eyes. "I'm just sayin' it's like a man to shout, when a few steps can give a body normal talk."

The preacher laughed. No, he turned a deaf ear. That's what Momma used to say when I paid her no mind. I wasn't too sure I appreciated being ignored, but then I wasn't along to please the preacher.

Samuel handed me his reins, threw his leg over the saddle, and stepped down. "How's Isabella?" He extended his hand to Terrance. The two shook, then butted shoulders.

"She's ripe, Preacher. Her ankles are swelled the size of melons, so I plumped up the feather bed and forced her to stay down today. She's miserable. I'm hoping that youngin' comes soon." Terrance wrapped his arm around Slouch's neck. "And who's this pretty thing you got taggin' alongside you?" When he smiled his tongue slipped through the hole of two missing teeth in the side of his mouth.

"I reckon they call the old nag by the name of Slouch." Samuel covered his mouth to hide the grin.

I sneered at the lame joke, while Terrance took to laughing.

Samuel took the reins, and I climbed down. "Terrance Johnson, meet Mercy Roller."

"Mercy Roller. That name has a ring to it."

"Maybe because folks in these parts wear it out saying, 'Lord, have mercy,'" I said.

"She's got a sense of humor, Preacher."

I glared at Terrance. "I'm standing right here. You don't have to talk around me."

Terrance laughed again.

"Well, Miss Mercy. Welcome to Thunder Mountain." He stuck his hand at me to shake. I stared for a minute before I took a firm grasp.

Samuel stepped up and broke the awkwardness of the moment. "Uh, Mercy here has offered to help Isabella. I met her on the road toward Wadalow Mountain. When I told her about Isabella, she insisted on coming to help."

"That's mighty good of you, Mercy. I was tickled just to have the preacher offer to help me out a little. Things have been tough since I lost my arm. Samuel here has been good to help me and Isabella adjust."

"Yeah, I hear he's good at sticking his nose in places it don't belong."

Terrance slapped my shoulder, and pulled me close. "You're a real wit. I like that. I hope you don't mind staying in the barn loft. I'll fix the preacher a bed in the lower stall, and we'll set you up in the loft. Isabella will be glad to have a woman's hand when she gives birth."

The barn loft. Just what I needed, more memories of a loft.

───── ∘◦◦∘ ─────

I don't recollect how long I was unconscious after my baby was born. I guess a day or two, but every time I opened my eyes, I saw through the cracks in the barn loft. I remember I bled a lot. Momma packed small buckets of cold water from the creek against my hips and between my legs. "Mercy, we have to stop the bleeding." That's what I remember . . . that and the pain of having my child yanked from my body. It was worse than any pain I ever can recall.

Momma sang to me while I lay bleeding to death in that loft. "Hush, little baby, don't say a word. Momma's gonna buy you a mocking bird . . ." Her voice was tender, soft, quiet. Just like her lips on my forehead when she kissed me. It took me days to get back on my feet, and when the sheriff came by to talk to the Pastor, Momma told him the Pastor had gone back across the mountain to the coal town.

"We don't expect him back till early winter." Momma twisted the tail of her apron between her fingers. She'd warned me to keep quiet. "Don't moan," she said. "I'll send him away."

"Word has it Mercy give birth to a baby, but the Pastor took its life and run. Any truth to that Reba?" The sheriff eyed Momma, waiting for an answer. He stared at her bruised cheek. "What happened to that jaw of yours?"

Momma rubbed her face. "Reckon it's just dirt. Anyway, The Pastor ain't set her up to meet any young men yet." She laughed. "Mercy's just a child herself."

"Mind if I check inside the cabin?" The sheriff stepped onto the porch. Momma pushed open the cabin door.

"No, come in. Mercy took the horse yesterday and carried some supplies up the mountain to the Thomas place. Maria has been ailing, and we take her some food every other day or so." He stuck his head in the door and peered around the two-room cabin.

There was one thing about living with the Pastor. A person learned to lie, and Momma could lie with the best of them. She hated being dishonest, but she did what she had to do to protect us. Her story about Maria was a half-truth. The part about taking supplies to Maria was true. It just wasn't true that day.

The sheriff paced the front porch looking around the edge of the cabin and out toward the pasture. He chewed on a twig. "Well, I reckon they must have had the wrong family."

"I reckon." Momma dabbed her brow with her apron. "Sure you won't sit and join me for some cider?"

"Much obliged, but I got a day's ride to the ridge. Sorry to have troubled you."

My stomach cramped like a cow had kicked me, and I bit down on a leather strap Momma had left me while the sheriff was at the house. I closed my eyes, and pulled my knees to my chest, tipping the buckets of water. The pain was too great and I cried out just as Momma climbed the loft ladder and put a clean blanket over some dry hay. "Come on, baby. Let momma help you outta these wet clothes."

"Is he coming back, Momma?"

"Who, honey?"

"The Pastor. Is the Pastor coming back?"

Momma hesitated. "I don't know, Mercy. He was mighty angry, and you know how he gets when he's in a rage."

I knew alright. I figured the Pastor was sitting hid behind some bushes waiting for darkness, figuring new ways to punish me and Momma. Right at that moment I didn't care. Between the pain and the loss, my heart felt cold and numb. I closed my eyes and prayed the good Lord would just let me bleed to death. Death would be better than suffering. But God being God Almighty, chose to remain silent.

———

"Mercy. Mercy?" Terrance waved his hand in front of my eyes.

"Oh, sorry. I was just admiring the view of the mountain from here."

Samuel dropped his head, and drew with his toe in the dirt. I could tell he knew more was going on than I let on.

"I hear the river. Where's it run from here?"

Terrance pointed behind the house. "Just over there. It's nice to lull a body to sleep at night." I reared to my toes to see if I could catch a glance. Maybe this side trip wouldn't slow me up, or leastways, that's what I hoped.

"You folks come on down to the house. I told Isabella to stay in bed, but she's stubborn. My guess is, she's done cooked up a mess of greens and fatback. How about some supper, Preacher?" Terrance scratched a dirt ring around his fire. "There. That oughta do 'til it burns down." He smacked his hands together, and a puff of dust wafted upward.

"Supper sounds good."

"Terrance worked hard to build a nice house for Isabella. He owns a traveling sawmill powered with steam, so he can cut nice flat planks. Makes for nice equal sizes." Samuel pointed down the path to the little homestead. The house had whitewashed boards, and glass in the windows instead of shutters. By most folk's standards on the mountain, that would make Terrance fairly well-to-do.

"Is Terrance rich?" I asked.

"Heavens no. But Terrance is good at horse tradin'. What he has ain't expensive, just well crafted, and hard earned by the sweat of his brow. Or it's traded for." Samuel chuckled. "Money is the last thing the man has."

Before we reached the porch, the smell of fresh sourdough bread permeated the air. My mouth began to water and my stomach tied into knots.

"Sure smells nice," I said.

Terrance shoved the door open and pointed his finger at Isabella. "If that youngin is half as stubborn as you, I'll have two mules instead of one." He leaned down and kissed his wife. "I told you to rest."

"Work don't stop just because I'm great with child." She smiled. "Howdy, Preacher. You really did show back up."

"Yes'm. And I brought a little extra help for you." Samuel took my arm and pulled me to the front. "Isabella, this is Mercy Roller."

Isabella stood head to my shoulder. Her arms weren't much bigger than a sapling limb, but her stomach hung to her knees from the baby she carried. Her hair dangled in a braid down her back, and her dress was split up the front of the skirt to accommodate her bulging tummy. Isabella had golden eyes. I won't never forget them. Ain't seen nothing like them before or since. Looking into her eyes was like looking at a sunset over the mountain. Dimples pressed deep against the corners of her mouth. Her hands, dainty as the pearl bracelet Grandma gave Momma on her wedding day. She pressed the heel of her palm against her back to support her stomach, then pointed to the table.

"Mercy, there is plates in that cupboard by the fireplace. If you don't mind, I ain't too proud to ask for help."

I slid a chair to one side so Isabella could sit. "Here, you sit. Let me do this." Isabella pressed her hand lightly against my cheek. "You're a dear."

I can't remember the last time I was ever touched with such gentleness. Momma's touch was pity. But Isabella's touch was sincere. So sincere, it burned against my cheek. There was a tenderness about her that warmed even my cold heart.

"It's a blessing you've come with Samuel. A real blessing. I think we're gonna be good friends."

We ate supper and when that was done, I helped Isabella wash off and get into bed. She rolled to her side, and let out a long groan. I'd heard that groan before. We'd gotten to the Johnsons just in time. I'd not sleep in the loft tonight. I'd dodged the nightmares again. This time I'd hold vigil while Miss Isabella pondered giving up this baby to the world. Terrance stretched out on the floor by the fireplace, and I sat by the bed, gently stroking Isabella's back.

"Your fingers . . . they feel rough against my clothes." Isabella touched my arm.

"What?"

"You've been through some hard times. They always show themselves by the touch of our fingers." My face grew warm. Isabella took my hand and gently rubbed the tips of my fingers. "Yep, these is tired fingers."

She made me uncomfortable. It was like she could see straight into my soul. "These is fingers that till the land. That's all." I pulled my hand away.

The fire spit embers into the chimney, and its voice crackled and sizzled. I took in a deep breath and felt a moment of peace. Staring out the window, I saw the lamp in the barn go out. Nothing lit the darkness outside but the moon and the stars. A cricket sang in the corner of the room. I leaned my head against the window and closed my eyes.

Was this peace? *Dear God, I hope so.*

TWELVE

THE NIGHT PASSED with an eerie silence.

I tried not to sleep, to keep a close watch on Miss Isabella, but I jolted awake every now and again when she moaned. My neck ached as my head hanged . . . my chin stretched to touch my chest. I twisted my head from side to side, the joints popped and cracked in my ears. I eased out of the rocker. Isabella labored to turn over in the puffy mattress of down. Her face contorted in discomfort, as she rubbed her side with her palm.

"Miss Isabella," I whispered. "Miss Isabella, let me stuff this pillow between your knees and take some pressure off that back."

Isabella opened her eyes. They shone like a cat in the darkness. A gentle smile tipped her lips.

"Slip your arm around my waist and let me pull you up a bit."

She draped her arms over my back, the bend of her elbow rested on my hip. I wrapped both arms around her, burrowed my knee into the mattress, and pulled her to a sitting position.

"You're so kind," Isabella murmured. "I'm so grateful the good Lord pressed your heart to come take care of a stranger."

I couldn't look her in the eye. The good Lord hadn't nudged me to my recollection. I just had no intentions of letting the same thing happen to her that happened to me. "It's my pleasure, Miss Isabella. I thought you'd have that baby tonight." I pushed a pillow between her knees.

"I'll be truthful. I thought the same. This child's not moved since yesterday."

"That's good. You rest. It's the quiet before the storm," I said.

I'd helped Momma bring five little ones into the world on the mountain. And every time, just before the child began to raise the fires of hell for birth, they'd quiet down. Get still. Rest. Judging from the looks of Isabella's stomach, the severe ache in her back, and now this silence, I figured it was about her time.

"This is our third baby." Isabella fingered circles on her belly.

I glanced up. "What?"

"The others poured outta my body like they were poison about halfway through my time. They just wasn't meant to be." Her lip quivered.

"Don't think about the past, Isabella. Just look to the future. Look what waits for you now." I patted her tummy. "Good things are in store. Would you like me to wake Terrance?"

"Heavens no. Let him sleep." Her voice remained a whisper. "Let him rest. He works so hard."

It took me a few minutes to situate Isabella where she could rest, and my curiosity was itchin' at me about Terrance's missing arm. Momma used to tell me I was always a nosey one and I'd paid the price for that a couple of times.

Like when Mabel Whaley gave birth to her child. The Pastor went on a rant. He paced the front porch, shouting Mabel was too old for another baby, and what with Asher, her husband, being sorta sickly and all, his loins could only produce evil.

Momma sent me to pump some water and get it boiling over the fire. Mabel moaned horrible sighs from inside the house, and when I came around the corner of the Whaley's cabin, and heard the Pastor carrying on, I knew something was up. I squatted at the edge of the cabin and listened while Momma tried to calm the Pastor. She'd take him by the arms and turn him away from Mabel's door, while her husband sat inside cussing.

"Go home, Pastor. Babies are God's gift to this world. You go home. I done told you that you ain't welcome here. Now git on home."

"This baby ain't no gift. It's born from sin. It's a blemish on the Lamb." He pushed Momma to one side, but she grabbed his coat.

"Pastor. What this baby comes from is not its fault. Lucky for you, God is a God of mercy."

Why would Momma say the Pastor was lucky God was a God of mercy?

Asher stormed from inside the cabin, his rifle squeezed between his arm and ribs. "Get off my porch, Pastor. Get off my land. Don't you never set foot here again." Momma stepped between the men.

"Stop this. Both of you. This ain't the time."

Asher stopped inches from the Pastor. "Get off my land, and God have mercy on your soul."

The Pastor stomped off the porch, mounted his horse, and as he pulled the mare toward the north, he spied me squatted at the edge of the cabin, listening. He eased the horse toward me, and motioned for me to stand. His eyes cried with sadness as he mouthed for me to come to him. I can't remember many times the Pastor was vulnerable or repentant, but this looked to be one. As I slowly stood, my back scrubbed the cabin. The Pastor smiled. "Mercy. Come here, honey. Don't you pay no mind to all that. Come here."

Honey. He called me honey. My gut told me to run, but my heart ached for the love of a father. And this looked like love. His monster hand dropped to his knee and patted it. "Come here."

Honey. The word echoed in my head. His fingers curled for me to come to him. My feet felt like big rocks were tied to the bottoms, and I struggled to lift one in front of the other.

"Come here, Daddy's girl. Come here."

I was touched by his tenderness. I stepped toward him, and he took my arm, then hoisted me onto his lap. His hand slipped under my hair, and he caressed the back of my neck and head. My hair fell between his fingers, and I felt him squeeze the lengths. I wanted my daddy. I needed him, and as he gently pulled my hair, tilting my head upward, I closed my eyes. His breath warmed my lips. Suddenly a panic shot through me.

This wasn't right. This wasn't a daddy's love. I grasped his wrist, then hauled off and spit in his face. The Pastor yanked my head by the hair and flung me to the ground. Sliding off his horse, he drew his foot back and lobbed it into my side.

"Nosey girl. Lurkin' around, sneakin' about. Watching to see and hear things that ain't your concern. You stick your nose where you got no business." He shouted at me and drew back his leg for a second swing.

Asher stepped around the edge of the house and cocked his rifle.

"I got a reason to kill you now, Pastor." He pointed the rifle and fired. The Pastor squalled, and grabbed his leg. "But killing you is too easy. This way you pay a price."

The Pastor pulled his horse around and tore down the dirt road while Asher Whaley reached his hand to me. "Help your momma."

"Mercy," Isabella whispered. "Mercy, you with me?"

I'd wandered off in my head. "Oh, I was just thinking. What were you saying?"

"I wasn't sayin' nothing. You were mumbling about the Pastor. If you need to go get Samuel, I'll be fine."

"Heavens no. I was daydreaming." I laughed an awkward laugh. "Didn't think you could daydream in the middle of the night, did you?"

Isabella smiled. "That's alright, honey. Come here. Sit." She patted the bed. "Come on. Come sit by me." I eased to the bed and sat next to her. Isabella pressed her hands tight around mine. Again, her touch brought me an instant calm. She gazed into my eyes, the yellow glow from the fire reflected off her porcelain skin.

"We all have memories. Some are good, others not so good. And sometimes the not-so-good rise up like ghosts, haunting us. I can't be sure what haunts you." Her fingers rubbed across my knuckles, tender and soft as a lamb's coat. "But whatever eats at your heart will only keep gnawing away bite by bite until you cast it out." Isabella pulled me forward and gently kissed my forehead. She wrapped her arms around me, and pressed my head against her chest, then sweetly began to rock me and hum.

"Amazing grace, how sweet the sound, that saved a wretch like me." Tears filled my eyes. Is this what love felt like? Love from a stranger. Honest love.

She must have rocked me for an hour as my tears wet her gown. The sun broke through a pinhole in the darkness and streaks of orange, lavender, and pink swirled through. That hour felt like an eternity, and one I didn't want to end. I knew that minute, I was bound by the good Lord to be here.

Isabella dropped into a restful sleep, and I brushed the loose strands of hair away from her face. I could never remember a time in my life when there was such peace. Stuffing the blanket around her waist, I turned into Terrance.

"Oh." I gasped. "You startled me."

"She has that effect on people." He smiled.

"What effect?"

"That sense of peace. When I got my arm cut off, she rocked me too. I felt like a failure. A broken man. Isabella spoke soft words of encouragement to me as she nursed me back. I'm glad you're here to help."

I pushed my hair behind my ear, and rubbed my cheeks dry. "If you'll stoke the fire, I'll rustle up some breakfast." I stepped around Terrance.

"There's bacon in the springhouse, and you can pick eggs outta the henhouse. There's a basket on the porch." Terrance leaned over his wife and kissed her tummy. "Reckon we'll have us a baby today?"

I shrugged and headed to the springhouse. I wanted to ask how Terrance lost his arm and what happened to the other two babies Isabella had lost. I wondered why them babies died before their time. I wanted to ask what it was about Isabella that made folks love her, and how she had an ability to read right into your soul. But now wasn't the time to be nosey. Now was the time to work and to help this woman who, for some unknown reason, trusted me with her care.

I pushed open the springhouse door and grabbed a slab of pork hanging from a rafter. Between the darkness of the springhouse and the cold river water rushing through, I could see my breath. I climbed the two dirt steps to the door. The cool dampness brought back a sweet memory. Momma always kept pork, salt rind pickles, and kraut makin' in her springhouse. My mouth watered thinking of the times I raced her to see who would be the first to dig to the bottom of the crock and snatch the cabbage stalk. I could almost taste the sour. And for a second, I smiled. The door slapped closed behind me. I hooked it shut, then headed to the house. Just as I got to the porch Terrance met me.

"Thank you." He extended his hand. "Thank you for stayin' up with Isabella. I'm obliged." There wasn't no need to thank me. What I was doin' didn't deserve thanks. But I reckon Terrance didn't know that.

I walked onto the porch and grabbed a basket from a table in the corner, then headed to the henhouse. The sun washed over the valley, and the grass leaned in the morning breeze. Apple trees bore beautiful blossoms that snipped off the branches and twisted in the wind. The smell of river hung in the air, and just below the springhouse, knelt down, was the preacher.

He went to all fours and dipped his head in the icy water of the stream. When he threw his head back, a trail of water flashed in the morning light. I watched him wash his face, then brush his fingers through his hair. When he turned to one side, I could see the stubble of a beard around his jaw. Samuel stood and shook his head like a dog after a swim.

Before I realized it, he'd caught my eye. His hand climbed into the air and he waved, tipped his hat as he planted it on his head.

I remembered the twinge of excitement I'd felt when I fell into the arms of my beloved, Thomas. I never took his name. Never was married to him long enough to know him. Never had a chance to be called his wife before a shot rang out and he dropped to the ground.

That night, my wedding night, started as a joyous lie.

Me and Thomas ran away. Judge Holt married us down in Chattanooga. I'd hinted to Momma I was going to Chattanooga, kissed her good-bye. She must have sensed it was a final good-bye. I'd be free of the Pastor and his nasty indiscretions. Indiscretions that hurt, punished, and killed.

"I'll slip up the holler behind Judson's Livery," Thomas said. "You be ready and we'll take off." So we did. Thomas snatched me onto the back of his horse. I wasn't afraid. I figured I'd be safe in the arms of the man I loved. Safe from the Pastor. Safe to never see the devil rear his head again.

I remember the joy I felt—the wind blowing through my hair, the deep breath of freedom from the slave master of Satan, and the comfort of my face buried deep into Thomas's back. Thomas didn't care about the Pastor, or Momma, or my past. He loved me. I was a kid, but I loved him too. I knew after Judge Holt pronounced us man and wife, my life would change. I just didn't expect it to change so sudden, so harsh.

How the Pastor found me was a mystery, but he did. I guess he beat it out of Momma. At times he could coax her with sweet talk she couldn't refuse, other times he played on her sympathy, apologizing for his meanness. Most times, he just beat the fool out of her. One way or the other, Momma would give in, telling him whatever he wanted to know.

"Momma, you can't tell the Pastor. You can't let him know where I'll be."

"I won't," she said. "I promise." Worthless words, empty meaning.

I don't think he knew me and Thomas were married. My guess was the Pastor thought I'd run away. Marriage would have been something he'd deny I could or would do.

Me and Thomas got a room over the general store in Chattanooga after the judge married us. He understood why I flinched when he touched me, so he was good to just kiss my forehead, and make hisself a bed on the floor. That was Thomas. Gentle and kind. "I can wait for you," he said. And he was willing to wait for me to give myself to him. Willing to build a trust.

I was sleeping sound, or least as sound as I could. Experience had taught me to never let my guard down. In the throes of my dreams, I heard a horse whinny outside. The stairs to our room come up from the outside of the building, and I heard the creak of the wood, and the click from taps on the heels of his boots.

You're dreaming, Mercy. You're safe. Remember, out of the mire and delivered from them that hate me. The Scripture from Psalms offered me some comfort.

The knob on the door twisted, and my eyes popped open. The Pastor slipped into my room, and just as he run his hands down my gown, Thomas come off the floor in a flash. I gasped.

The Pastor wasn't expecting the bear grasp of Thomas's hand. They brawled. The fighting sent the Pastor through the window, which sent Thomas clattering through the door after him. Thomas got in a few more good punches before the Pastor slithered back into the darkness, ranting I was his girl and vengeance was the Lord's. Nobody knew the Pastor's vengeance better than me. Not even the Lord.

I rushed to Thomas and helped him to stand. Blood trickled over his lip and down his chin. "You're bleeding."

"I'm fine."

I wrapped my arm around his waist. Thomas pulled me close, embraced me, and gave me the last kiss I'd ever have from his tender lips.

"It must be gettin' ready to rain," I murmured to him. "That sounded like thunder."

Then Thomas's knees folded.

His weight caved against my body.

Reality set in.

"No," I shouted. "Somebody help me! Somebody!" Thomas twisted and both of us fell to the ground. "No, Lord. No. Somebody help!"

It wasn't long before a lantern cast its glow across the ground. The store owner and his wife huddled on their knees next to Thomas. "Do something," I screamed. The man's wife ran to get the sheriff. But for me, time went into slow motion. The man I loved. The very one who actually loved me, lay dying in my arms.

No one had seen it happen. The sheriff had nothing to go on as to who might've killed him. I kept my mouth shut.

But I knew in my heart where the bullet came from, and to this day, I think it was meant for me.

I managed to get Asher Whaley to take Thomas back to Wadalow Mountain and bury him. And when everything was said and done, the only place left for me to go was back home. Back to the mother who'd betrayed me and the monster who held me in the mire.

THIRTEEN

THERE'S A SAYING ON the mountain: "What don't go away will crawl up your bed and bite you in the night." I don't remember much about Granny Roller, but I reckon she was the thing that wouldn't go away—the thing that bit the Pastor back.

I was just a little tyke, six or so when she passed, but I remember the Pastor never could look her in the eye. Every time she came to visit, he became like a young boy, falling over his feet, wallowing in his own pity.

"Momma. I've missed you," he'd say. She'd tease him. Sometimes showing me a hug. Other times a glare.

I wasn't sure where the Pastor got his meanness, but when Granny Roller came around I could imagine what his life was like as a boy. He'd shake all over. Sometimes he'd shake like he was chillin' . . . the way I'd shake when he'd go on a rampage at me and Momma. Then they was times he'd just kinda quiver in his boots, like a dog darin' you to touch his bone.

"They's history between Granny Roller and the Pastor. It's history best left unsaid." Momma would warn me before the Pastor would come around. "You're best to just mind your own beeswax. Keep your lips sewed tight." And I did.

"Oh, oh, oh. Such sweet, tender little legs. They're enough to make me want to chew on them." Granny Roller would hold me on her lap and gnaw on my ears, tickle my neck, and then start to pat my bare legs. Her touch started out gentle, but the more she patted the harder the strikes became, until the calves of my legs were bright pink and a purple outline of her boney fingers welled up.

If I cried, Momma would shush me. "Mercy, don't be a cry baby. Granny Roller is just giving you love pats." I wondered as I grew older, if Momma was as bad as the Pastor. She might as well been the one doing the hitting, to condone such behavior. Still, I'd fight back the tears, and count the hours until Granny Roller went home.

"Walk with me, son," she'd say to the Pastor.

I didn't feel sorry for him often, but it was clear Granny Roller was never very kind to her own boy. I'd watch him cower like a whipped animal when she'd speak to him. The Pastor feared Granny Roller, and when she was gone, then he'd take his vengeance out on me and Momma.

"Yes, Mother." The Pastor looked pitiful when Granny Roller called him. He'd take off his hat, shoulders slouched and hunkered down, walking alongside her. When they reached the big elm tree, he'd sit by her.

"You're such a good son. You love your mother, don't you?" She said pulling his head close and stroking his cheek.

"Yes, Mother. I love you, Mother. I'm your boy." I could see things wasn't just right.

I'd sit, hid in a bush, peering through the branches to see what happened.

Granny Roller was a beautiful woman. She didn't look anywhere near the age of a granny. I used to think I'd like to look like her when I grew up. Skin tight on her face, soft gentle curls of hair streaming down, lips the color of raspberries, and eyes a deep blue. She was a sight. Despite her beauty, what lay hid under the surface was pure evil.

I had mixed feelings about Granny Roller. I loved that she brought me trinkets when she came to visit, and that she'd tell me stories of her mischievous youth, but I hated her love pats and how she gnawed at my ears with her teeth. If I wiggled, her claw-like nails would push into the skin of my arm. "Granny Roller, folks say you eat flesh." I pulled her nails out of my arm.

"Folks say that, do they?"

"I told them you just eat bacon and eggs." She roared with laughter and kissed my cheek.

"Don't believe everything you hear."

I took her at her word and tried not to believe what folks said, but one night when Momma trimmed the Pastor's hair, I noticed the top edges of his ears was gone. I never asked the Pastor what happened. But as I grew older, I suspected there was more to the stories of Granny Roller than the Pastor let on.

"Mercy, run down to the barn and fill this sack with corn," Momma said. We'd picked the rows of stalks clean in the garden the week before and filled the giant bin to overflowing. Us, the horses, and the mice would eat well all winter. I took the bag Momma gave me and skipped across the field counting my hops to the barn.

"Jimmy crack corn and I don't care. Jimmy crack corn and I don't care." I sang as I spun the burlap bag round my head. "My master's gone away."

The latch on the door hung inches above my head, so I pulled a log close, stepped up, and freed the heavy wooden board from the looped rope that held it. The door creaked open. I grabbed the bag and skipped into the barn. Hay rained down from the loft above me, and a hateful voice echoed in the barn.

"You're a poor excuse for a man. I'm ashamed to call you my son." Granny Roller shouted at the Pastor.

"Mother, I'd never do nothin' to harm you."

"Get thee behind me, Satan," she scolded. "I plan to slice my throat right here in front of you. You'll live with my death on your hands."

"Stop, Mother. Don't do this. Let me have the knife," the Pastor pleaded.

I inched toward the ladder and placed the sole of my foot on the first rung. My legs were hardly long enough to reach the next step, but I managed. The Pastor's voice quivered as he begged. I pressed my shoulders against the drop door in the floor and pushed. I was shocked at what I saw. The Pastor stood whimpering as Granny Roller sliced her arms with a knife.

"I ain't crazy," she screamed.

"No, Mother, you're not crazy. Now let's go back to the house and let Reba fix them gashes."

Granny Roller was like a changing breeze. One minute she'd be sweeter than honey, the next, a horrible, nasty woman. I'd never really seen it until then. I was a child, but I was smart enough to understand Granny Roller wasn't quite right.

She looked up and caught a glimpse of me. A hideous laugh gurgled out of her throat as she drew the knife along her arm. Before I knew what hit me, the Pastor pounced on the drop door, slamming it shut. The framed edges of wood snagged my fingers and mashed them between the door and the floor.

I screamed, yanked my hands free, and fell into the bin of corn below. All I could remember was the thud of my body crashing into the bin. All the air rushed out of my mouth. When I woke it was four days later, they'd buried Granny Roller. Momma sat dipping a rag in cool water to dab my face.

"Mercy, honey. Wake up. Momma's here." I opened my eyes and Momma fell to her knees. "Thank you, Jesus. My baby is alive."

My hands were bandaged, and my fingers throbbed. Edom and Patcol sat to one side. They always seemed to turn up when I needed a breath of air—some peace.

Momma ran outside and hollered at the Pastor. "She's awake, Pastor. Her eyes are open."

"Miss Mercy." Edom's black hand gently brushed my cheek as he scooted close to whisper in my ear. "I promise they is hope here, wee one. It's hard to see. And at times we is the sacrifice. But they is hope. You hold on now. Edom don't make promises he can't keep. Hold on, sweet child."

Edom kissed my head. His eyes offered comfort. *If* I could do what he said, and hold to it.

Edom sidestepped the mess that had happened. He knew if I owned up to seeing anything Granny Roller had done, I'd pay a price. In his kind way, Edom tried to nudge me to lie.

Momma ran back to my side, and lifted my head to give me a sip of water.

"Drink, Mercy. Momma is right here. You fell in the barn. Do you remember?"

My eyes focused on Momma as I swallowed. I remembered. I knew what I saw, too. Blood rushin' down Granny Roller's arms, a puddle as round as a bucket at her feet. I remembered.

The Pastor rushed into the house and knelt on one knee by the side of the plank bed. His face twisted from fear. He hovered over me waving his hand in front of my eyes.

"Mercy, it's me, your daddy. Do you remember what happened? Why was you in the loft? You're not big enough to climb that old ladder. They was nothin' for you to see."

The Pastor seemed concerned, but I knew better. Even at a young age, I could read him. I knew the answers to all the Pastor's questions. As little as I was, I'd learned early when to play stupid. I rubbed my face with the thick roll of bandages on my hands. My fingers ached.

"Mercy," Momma said. "Answer your daddy. Do you remember what happened?"

Who'd forget seeing Granny Roller rip her arm open with that knife? My stomach turned, and my mouth filled with saliva. I looked into the Pastor's eyes and without a second thought, I lied.

Fourteen

Samuel wasted no time scarfing down the last of the bacon and eggs. I'd not thought to ask him how long he'd been traveling . . . living off fatback and bread. Though I did notice as he worked alongside Terrance, his ribs jutted out.

"Preacher, this young fawn you dragged along with you is a real good cook."

Samuel glanced at me and winked. "She's full of surprises. That's a fact."

"How'd you meet up with this charm?"

I buttered a slice of bread and poured a cup of coffee for Isabella. As I brushed past the preacher, I made sure my elbow pressed into his shoulder blades just enough to keep him from telling everything he knew. He squirmed and twisted in his chair.

"We met on the other side of the mountain. She was headed up Thunder Mountain and I was headed down. We got to talking and she was good enough to offer to come along and help with the baby. Mercy's helped deliver several little ones on her side of the mountain. She'll be a real help."

"Be a help?" Terrance reared back and laughed. "She is a help. Last night is the first night I've slept in months. She kept watch over Isabella. Usually Isabella spends the biggest part of the night eyeballing me whilst I eyeball her. Neither of us sleeps. But with Mercy watching over us, we both did. When I woke this mornin' Isabella looked rested."

"Well, good." Samuel wiped his mouth with the corner of the checkerboard tablecloth. "Now, what do you say we head out to finish that fence?"

Terrance followed me to Isabella's side. He pulled a small wooden table close to the bed, and helped Isabella slide to the edge. He kissed her head, then brushed his knuckles across her lips.

"I'll be down the lane with Samuel. I've moved the bell by the window. If you need me, just pull the rope and strike the bell."

"You worry too much." Isabella smiled and pressed his hand against her lips. "I'll be fine with Mercy here." Terrance placed his hand on my shoulder and gently squeezed.

"I worry about what's important, like gettin' that fence up before that storm brewin' over the summit gets here. She's in your hands, Miss Mercy. Let's see if you can keep her off her feet."

I wasn't too worried. Especially since Isabella could hardly stand, but something in my gut told me things weren't right with her. I couldn't let anything happen to this angel—this woman who seemed to know me without really knowing me.

"We'll be fine," I said as I handed Isabella a fork. "Eat slow, Miss Isabella. You want that bread to stay down, not come back on you."

Isabella sliced into the bread crust and slipped a taste into her mouth. "I think this baby will come today."

"Likewise," I said.

"It's just too quiet." Isabella twisted around on the edge of the bed. She stuck her feet into the air. "Besides, look at my feet. Much more and they'll bust clean open."

I knelt by the bed and lifted her foot onto my knees. Walking my fingers along the sides of her feet left dents in her skin. It reminded me of walking barefoot by the river pressing my feet into the black silt, leaving my print. It was like I signed the riverbank with my own name and made it mine.

Isabella sighed as I gently rubbed her toes. "They feel so tight," I said.

"I told you. Like they was gonna bust clean open."

The sun now peeked from behind a giant cotton-like cloud. One side fluffy and light—the other dingy grey. Behind that, a black low-hanging thunderhead. A deep rumble whispered in over the summit, and from the corner of my eye I caught a streak of lightning rip across the sky.

"That thunder?" Isabella asked.

A heavy breeze flipped the thin curtains over the window. "Yes'm. Guess this mountain is aptly named."

"Oh it is. I hate storms in this cove. It's like the wind drops off the ledge of the mountain and into our pasture, then runs from peak to peak, kicking and screaming like a mad youngin trying to escape. Tears up jack, too."

Another bolt of lightning cracked in the distance, and I saw the preacher look up and point across the ridge. The curtains on the window sucked to the outside of the house, and a surge of hot, humid air filled the room.

"That ain't a good sign, Miss Isabella. Cool air goin' hot. You got shelter for storms?"

"Out by the side of the house, there's a root cellar." Isabella's voice raised. "I hate storms."

Terrance took across the field to the barn, while the preacher grabbed up what tools he could and tossed them into the wagon bed. The horse stepped from side to side, its mane twisted in the wind.

"Looks like we're in for a summer storm. Rascal just cropped up over the mountain. Here. Let me prop your feet on this pillow."

Isabella patted me away as she struggled to stand. A second rumble of thunder echoed in the valley. "Where's Terrance?"

"He headed to the barn like a shot. The preacher hightailed it to the wagon, and he's nearly to the barn. You should sit yourself down. It's just a summer storm."

"That ain't just a storm." Isabella hobbled to the window. "That's a night cloud." She grasped her belly. "Oh, Lord. It's a night cloud." She doubled over, and then vomited.

"Oh law, here Isabella. Let me help you. Looks like this baby is coming."

"Terrance . . . where's Terrance?" Isabella grasped at her belly trying to stand.

"The men are coming. They're almost here. Don't panic."

Isabella wasn't panicked, but I was feeling it. I was raised in the mountains, and I only recall one time hearing Momma cry those two words— night cloud. It was the kind of cloud that covered the width of the valley, moved slow, and occasionally dropped its tail on the ground. It was horrible. Me and Momma was out in the back pasture when that storm hit. Edom had plowed a small garden in the field earlier and left two sets of leather reins hanging over the fence rail. "Get them reins. Quick. We can't make it back to the house before this storm hits." Momma grabbed one set while I snatched a second pair. She wrapped them tight around the poplar tree.

"Hug that tree and I'll knot these reins around our legs and the tree." She snugged them tight then looped the second set around our wrists and the trunk. Momma pressed the ends of the reins into my palms. "Whatever you do, don't turn loose of these. Pray to God the twister leaves the tree."

I did as Momma asked.

She'd tied us together with the reins, me on one side of the tree and her on the other. Her fingers grasped mine as the night cloud dropped its twisting tail along the riverbank. It pulled giant rocks out of the river and flung them across the pasture, its roar so loud my screams were silenced. Stuff was flying everywhere. Trees, rocks, pieces of the house, even the Pastor's plow whipped past us with a deadly force. I laid my face tight against the tree. Even through the noise of the wind, I could have sworn I heard that tree moan as its roots grasped tight into the ground. It bent to the left and then back, and when the top started to swirl I thought of how Momma taught me to pull carrots and onions in the garden.

"Grab the green tops. Twist and pull." It felt like the anger of the wind had grabbed ahold of that tree and twisted. I only hoped there'd be no pull. The roar of the wind sounded like the train comin' through the pass.

I thought me and Momma would split wide open while we hugged that tree. The rain that storm wailed at us turned to chunks of ice the size of my fist. My nose and forehead bled like a stuck pig from the pelting. Me and Momma buried our heads into our arms just to try and grasp a wisp of air as bits of the barn sailed past . . . including Momma's favorite milk cow. The old poplar tree twisted and popped, but its roots held firm. Minutes felt like hours. When the cloud swatted its tail over the mountain, all that was left standing was the back half of the barn, and Momma's kitchen table. The house was a pile of twigs. That's when the Pastor dug a root cellar whilst he rebuilt the house.

Here I was again, facing that same kind of storm. Terrance and the preacher bounded through the door.

"Twister."

The two of them scooped Isabella into their arms, and bolted out the door.

Samuel glanced over his shoulder and shouted, "Mercy. Don't just stand there. Get out here and unbolt the root cellar."

I rushed off the porch around the men.

Just to the north of the house lay a heavy wooden door built on a slight angle. I flipped the plank slat from the latch and pulled hard against the door. The wind grew a giant hand and pressed back against the door, refusing to let me open it.

"Mercy," shouted the preacher, "brace your foot against it and heave." Terrance's face was panicked as Isabella tilted her head to the sky and screamed. "Hurry."

I shoved my foot against the frame and took hold of the handle with both hands, grunting as I forced the door open. The men tromped five steps down and rested Isabella on a burlap sack of feed. When they turned back to help me, that angry wind lashed out at us, grabbing the door and shaking it with a vengeance. Terrance slid a second plank into the latch to secure it shut. Since the storm couldn't rip open the door, it thickened the air and made it like breathing in molasses.

"Lord, have mercy," Isabella cried. "Mercy. Mercy. My baby is coming."

I stood, stiff and stunned. Was it not enough we were in the middle of a storm? Was it not enough Terrance had to lose an arm, or that Isabella couldn't have the pleasure of giving birth in peace rather than the chaos of a storm? Was this God's way of punishing me?

And to boot all, my name again. Someone pleaded using my name. All I could do was stand helpless. In the daylight, it had been easy to take a life out this world, but here in the dark, I couldn't see enough to bring a life in.

I guess that goes to show we come into the world blurry or blinded— fightin' to find our way through the fog. But we go out . . . eyes wide open. I slapped that horse in the fog of my life. My eyes blinded by rage. I killed the Pastor without a second glance. Now here I stood, facin' a new baby headed into the world, and all of a sudden, I see the wrong I did big as life. How could somebody who killed a man think they was good enough to bring a life in?

Fifteen

THE ROAR OF THE storm stomped above us like a monster. I wondered what we'd open up to see when the torment silenced. Would life go on as usual, or would the storm leave a clean slate to draw on?

I felt my way across the tiny cellar and wrapped my arms around Isabella. She laid her head against my chest. With each labor pain I reached down and stroked her belly, hoping her baby would stay safe inside her a bit longer. Terrance and Samuel fought to keep the door on the cellar shut. When the anger of the storm finally gave up and left, the two of them dropped to the steps and rested.

"Dear Lord," Samuel prayed. "Your hand covered us, and we are grateful. They was no way the strength of two men could have kept out the violence of this storm. But through Your mighty strength we held on. Thank you, Sir, for Your hand of protection."

I wanted to kick dirt at Samuel.

Why would God Almighty save us, when as a child, He ignored me . . . let me suffer at the hands of a demon? He wouldn't. Still, I wouldn't say that just then. It wasn't the time. My time would come. I'd have a chance to tell the preacher what I thought of his God.

Isabella whimpered with the next contraction.

"Can you open up this hole and see if it's safe?" I said. "We don't want to deliver a baby in this filthy place."

Terrance pressed his ear against the door and listened.

"They ain't no sound. Either the world has ended or the storm has passed."

Samuel pulled one slat while Terrance banged a rock against the second plank lodged in the latch. The wood board loosened and Samuel nearly fell when it released. They pushed open the door and a stream of sunlight filled the cellar. It didn't seem right that the sky could hold an animal like that storm one minute, and the next boast sunshine. To me, just another twisted idea of a confusing God.

"World's still spinnin'," Terrance said. He poked his head through the opening and glanced around. "Lordy, Lordy. The barn is a shambles, but the house is untouched. What a miracle."

It was a miracle.

I hated barns and the lofts in barns, and the thought of poor Isabella giving birth in one sent chills down my back. She coughed and gasped as another labor pain struck.

"Get her out of here," I shouted.

Terrance lifted Isabella with his arm, and the preacher scooped her into his as well. Together they managed to carry her up the stairs.

The barn's wood lay splintered across the pasture, and trees were strewn down one side of the farmland. Oddly enough, Terrance's fence stood intact. A cow laying sprawled against the side of the house struggled to gain its footing and stand. Isabella's chickens scratched the ground for food. The house stood solid. Only one side of the porch hung to the ground.

We was lucky.

Terrance rushed ahead of the preacher and tested the porch by the door. Samuel carried Isabella into the house and laid her on the bed. Outside of things being turned upside down and rustled, the house suffered little damage. I stood staring out the window at what was once the barn, and for a minute, I wondered where I would sleep . . . where Samuel would lay his head. It looked like we'd bunk in the small shack. I shivered. That meant sharing the cramped space with him. A preacher man.

You've done it to me again. Some God.

Though Samuel seemed to be a gentleman, the thoughts of sharing a space with any man sent chills up my spine. If I was forced to stay in the same shack then at least it was with a man who appeared to have scruples.

I felt down my boot and wrapped the ends of my fingers around my knife. *I can split him from top to bottom before he knows what hit him if need be*, I told myself. Samuel extended his hand to help me over a toppled chair. I stared at him, took hold of the skirt Isabella gave me, and stepped over. I didn't need his hand.

Isabella let out a holler and a splash of water gushed from between her legs. Her face grew red as she strained against the pains of birth.

"Get me some water, Preacher. Terrance, see if you can restart the fire." All I knew to do was bark orders. I pushed a fallen cabinet over and pulled out a handful of quilts, spreading them under Isabella and covering her sprawled legs.

"Lord, Lord. The good Lord made this hard," Isabella shouted.

"Try to breathe." I pulled her dress up and spread her legs. I saw a circle of hair the size of a jar lid. "Isabella, I see your baby. When you get the next pain, push hard." Samuel poured water from the bucket into a pan, then wet the corner of a rag and wiped her face.

Isabella thrashed from side to side on the bed, and the preacher took one of her arms while Terrance took hold of the other. She grasped hold of their fists and cried as she pushed into the pain. Nothing.

Nothing happened.

What little bit of the baby's head I'd seen was sucked back inside her.

"Isabella, you need to push harder. Push."

Terrance lifted her into a sitting position and leaned against her back. "Come on, Isabella. Push this little thing out."

Isabella pressed down, blood shot from her body, and still no baby. I was at a loss.

Isabella ain't going to be able to push this youngin out. And I ain't about to let her die.

I balled up my fist and shook it at the Almighty. Her cries of pain screeched in my ears as I tried to slip my fingers inside her to help the baby out.

Again nothing. Something was wrong. Knew it early that morning.

Isabella had been trying to push this baby out for some time and with no luck.

Desperate times call for desperate actions.

I looked at the preacher, then motioned him to the door. "What do we do, Mercy?"

"We don't let that woman die. You hear me, Preacher? We don't let her die."

"I know. But what can we do?"

"You trust in that Bible, and you trust in a God you cannot see. Right now, I'm asking you to trust me. Do you trust me, Preacher?"

Samuel looked me straight in the eye, brushed my hair away from my mouth, and smiled. "I trust you."

"What we're gonna do ain't conventional. But you gotta help me get her outside and lean her over that hitchin' rail."

"What?"

"Trust me," I whispered.

Trust was not something I'd ever had. But Samuel didn't hesitate. He hardly knew me, yet without a second glance he put his faith in me. For an instant I wondered if that's how God must feel when folks put their trust in Him. I could see how it would make a body high and mighty.

Samuel rushed to Isabella and wrapped a blanket around her. In one yank, he threw her over his shoulder. Terrance commenced to cuss.

"What are you doin', Preacher?"

"I'm trusting Mercy."

I pressed my hand into Terrance's chest. "We're saving her life. Get all the covers you got in the house and bring them."

"What you goin' do?" Terrance shouted.

"Get her out to the hitchin' post by the porch." Samuel eased as best he could down the porch steps to the rail. Terrance came along right behind him, toting blankets.

The preacher stood Isabella on her weak legs, then leaned her face-first across the rail. I braced my foot against the log rail and wrapped my arms through Isabella's.

"When I say three, Preacher, you lean against her back and push her forward. Terrance, you get them blankets ready, and when you see that baby's head, you grab on with that one hand and don't let her body suck it back in."

I leaned against Isabella's head and whispered. "Honey, it's this or let you die. And you're gonna feel like you're dying, but we gotta get that child out. We're gonna force it out. You scream as hard as you want . . . you can hate me if you like. But I ain't gonna let you die."

I looked at the preacher, terror written on his face, then I tightened my grip on Isabella.

"One."

I pressed my foot against the railing.

"Two."

The preacher laid against Isabella's back.

I took a deep breath.

"Three."

I pulled against Isabella with all my might.

Samuel burst into tears as he pressed against her back. Isabella's scream was so hideous and long that it echoed off the summit of Thunder Mountain. Her body pulled across and over the railing, sending me flat of my back, her on top of me. Samuel hung by the waist over the rail and Terrance, on his knees, cradled a tiny infant, sac and all—a daughter.

"Get over here, Samuel," I shouted. "I need to get to that baby." The preacher leaped over the rail onto the ground, and rolled an unconscious Isabella to her back. I rushed to her feet, run my finger around the baby's mouth, then turned her upside down and whopped her rear. She took in a breath and squealed.

"Can you manage her with one arm?" I asked. Terrance nodded and wrapped her tight in the blanket, a tear trickled down his cheek. "She glorious, ain't she?" His face dropped. "Isabella. Lord, Isabella."

The preacher had picked Isabella up and started toward the stairs to the porch when she come around. She moaned, then panic struck.

"Mercy!" she hollered, "Mercy, Lord. I feel another one. I got the need to push again. They's another one comin'. Lord help me, they's another one."

Samuel laid her on the porch and Isabella began to push out another child. "Come on, Isabella. Push with all your might. Push."

The vessels in her forehead bulged and streaks of blue run the length of her face. I could see her heartbeat in her neck. Isabella's nose began to bleed, and her lips swelled from the force she put behind that baby.

"Push. Push," Terrance said, as he leaned close to her with the baby. And she did.

This baby came with a vengeance and when Isabella's body spit out the child, blood gushed from her. "It's a girl! A girl. Isabella, you have twins."

I tore a strip of fabric from the tail of Isabella's dress and tied it around the baby's life cord. "Give me your knife, Preacher." Samuel pulled his knife from the sheath and I cut the infant free from her momma.

Weak from losing blood, Isabella lifted her head to glance on her babies.

"Get her to the springhouse," I squalled at Samuel. "Set her in the stream. We have to stop the bleeding. Bury her up to her chin in the water."

Samuel didn't hesitate. He grasped Isabella up and headed to the springhouse, his knees buckled from exhaustion. Terrance hovered over me while I cleaned the girl's nose and throat, then held her up by the ankles.

"Breathe, little lady," I said. "Come on, take a breath."

The child hung lifeless in my hands, so I smacked her rear—once, twice, three times before she took in a gulp of air. I pulled open the blanket and laid a second crying infant in Terrance's lap, then ran to springhouse. My hands and arms were covered in dark red blood, but there was little time to think about that.

When I pushed open the door, Samuel sat holding a third infant. Isabella laid half in the cold stream and half out. The baby's chin quivered from the cold water.

"Looks like I trusted right," Samuel said. "But Isabella's in bad shape."

We cut that baby free from its momma and I handed him to Samuel. "Get that baby to the house, then get yourself back down here."

Samuel unbuttoned his shirt and pressed the baby against his chest. He pulled the shirt tight around them. "It's a boy. A little boy." With that he tore out of the springhouse.

I fell to my knees and slid my arms under Isabella's. I lifted her out of the water. Her lips were blue, and her face contorted from the pain. To one side lay the pouch that had cradled the last baby. "Isabella? Isabella, can you hear me?"

The lids of her eyes cracked open and part of a smile tipped her lips.

"You did it," she whispered. "You saved my baby."

I dipped the edge of my skirt into the water, and wiped the mixture of sweat and blood from her face.

"Isabella, listen to me." Her eyes rolled back in her head. "Isabella. You lost two babies before. But today? You gained those two plus one. You have triplets. Two girls and a boy."

Her head sagged toward her chest, and she lifted her hand from the icy waters of the stream.

"Lordy, lordy," she said. "Three babies. Huh."

Isabella's body went limp.

SIXTEEN

FIVE DAYS PASSED and Isabella was still so weak she could hardly hold her eyes open. I did what I could to rouse her, including using Momma's remedies. It was nasty, but I forced it down her.

"Come on, drink up. This will build your blood."

Isabella had bled like a stuck hog after them babies was born, and forcing her to drink mashed chicken livers was the best thing for her. Momma used to tell me they would get your blood back.

"Drink this," Momma said. She smashed livers into a pulp and shoved it at me. I hated what the Pastor had done to me—first making me with child, then ripping her away, nearly killing me. Now Momma sat cramming some gosh-awful mess down my throat saying, "It's gonna get your blood back. Make you strong." I didn't like it, but I had to give her credit. It worked.

Here I was, making the same mess of squished livers and hot water for Isabella. I lifted her head and braced her against my chest. The stench made me gag, but it was what she needed.

"Come on, Isabella, these babies need you. Drink up." I tilted the glass to her lips and dribbled the liquid into her mouth.

"Lord have mercy." Samuel sat cradling the baby boy by the fire, sweat steamed off his forehead. I shot him a stare. "I mean, mercy sakes alive." My stare sharpened while he dug a deeper hole. "I'm sorry, Mercy. I'm not making light of your name. I'm just about to burn up between this fire and the heat of the day."

My brow softened and a smile surfaced from the scowl. Though it was a little mean, it was fun to make the preacher squirm.

"This boy is still so cold, but I don't know how much more of this heat I can take." He smiled, and wiped his cheek against his shoulder. He tightened the blanket around the baby and laid him next to his sisters.

"Consider this your first experience of hell," I said. "Think of it as training. You can preach about the heat of Hades with good account."

"Funny. You're a real hoot. But despite your sour sense of humor, I gotta give the devil her dues. You pulled off a stunt that saved Isabella. She'd have died if that first youngin' hadn't come. I'm much obliged."

His words stung. *Give the devil* her *dues.* Is that how he saw me? How others saw me . . . as the devil? It was the Pastor who was the devil. Not me. I swallowed hard. "Desperation makes us do what we have to. Now we got to nurse her back to health, so she can take care of these babies."

Samuel nodded and lifted Isabella so I could attend her.

It didn't seem to matter how I poked at the preacher. He just brushed off the jabs. Thing about Samuel . . . the thing that just got my goat . . . the man was sincere. Even though I wasn't wanting to hear a kind word from him, he meant what he said. He appreciated my efforts. And more so, he had trusted me.

I tilted the glass against Isabella's mouth. "Please, Isabella. Help me out. If you don't snap outta this, Terrance won't never name these babies." She groaned and wretched. I dabbed her mouth, then dripped some cool water on her tongue. She lapped at it like a dog drinking from the river.

Terrance shoved the door open with his shoulder. He carried one baby pressed tight to his chest. "She looks like her momma. Don't you think?" Terrance walked to Isabella.

"Look, honey. She looks like you. What do you think we should call her?"

Isabella cracked her eyelids and tried to mouth a word, but fell back into a deep sleep.

"Terrance, we can't keep calling them kids by numbers. Isabella would want you to name them." Samuel pulled the wooden box of blankets close to the fire, and snuggled the boy in. I handed him the second daughter.

"Keep on rockin', Preacher. I'll get you a bottle of milk for this one."

Terrance laid the first daughter close to Isabella. "There little one. It's your ma."

I'd managed to find the leather sacks Isabella had sewn from deer hide for the baby to drink from. She'd have put them to breast, but no one imagined something like this would happen. Terrance kept the goat milked, and the liquid skimmed free of butter. All I seemed to get done was feed one baby, clean it, and feed another.

The first daughter, despite her being forced out of her momma, was a big baby. But she looked healthy, her skin a peachy pink, and a head of black, curly hair. The second daughter was weak and small, but when she was hungry she could kick up a fuss. She'd strengthen up. That boy, though. The last one born, struggled. His skin kept a pasty grey look to it, and his eyes were sunken. The baby's lips stayed a bluish-purple and no matter what we did, we couldn't seem to warm him up. Terrance made a wood box we stuffed with a blanket and lamb's wool. He stirred the fire, and kept the embers blazing, then scooted the boy as close as he could.

I thought about my baby girl. I never named her. She went to her grave with no name. For a long time I couldn't hardly stand to think about her, but the truth is, I felt worse that I'd let that little thing go nameless. It was enough I was a nobody with a name that haunted me, but that poor baby never had a fair shake. She was somebody with no name.

"Terrance. What do you think about *Melody*?" I asked.

"What?"

"Melody. How about we call this least daughter Melody. She snuggles right into you when you start to hum a lullaby. I think Isabella would like Melody."

Terrance furrowed his brow and turned away.

"You come right back here. These babies deserve names. Beautiful names to honor their beautiful momma. Now sit down and let's talk this through." I kicked a table chair toward him. He pulled the chair next to the fireplace and tinkered with the boy.

"Melody. It does sound sweet."

I picked up the baby and held her close so Terrance could look her over. His gruff face turned soft at the sight of his daughter. He pressed her blanket under her chin, and swiped away a drop of drool from her lip.

"Yea, I reckon Mercy is right, little girl. We'll call you Melody Faith.

'Cuz I have faith your momma will pull through this." He leaned back. "Isabella talked about Amelia Claire if she'd had a girl. She just didn't count on two. So it's only fittin' to give that name to the firstborn daughter. Amelia and Melody. I like it."

"What about you, Preacher?" I asked. "You got a suggestion for a boy?"

Samuel tucked the blanket tight around the boy. "I do. I tried to think of a name I thought would be a proud name. One the boy would be pleased to have. How about Braden Seth?"

Terrance looked toward the preacher. Tears filled his eyes. "Braden was my father, and Seth is my middle name."

Samuel smiled. "I know. A name any boy would be proud to have." The preacher patted Terrance on the knee.

"I hate to break up such a tender moment, but we're all hungry," I said. I looked at Terrance. "Anyone here care to rustle us up some meat? Maybe clean one of those chickens you killed for the livers, and get it started cooking? And Preacher, I need diapers washed."

Samuel's face lost the color. "You want me to clean . . . uh . . . wash . . ."

"You got it, Preacher. Like I said. Consider it your experience in hell." I let out a cackle that startled all three babies. Samuel picked up the basket of diapers and headed to the creek.

I was touched by the preacher's willingness to do such a dirty job. If there was one thing for sure, washing messy diapers would humble any man, and any man willing to do a woman's job might actually be a decent person. Samuel earned a little bit more of my respect that day.

"Preacher," I shouted from the window. He turned. "You really are a'going to the river to cleanse." I burst out laughing a second time. Samuel lifted his hand to his forehead and saluted me. He turned and walked toward the creek.

It was an amazing thing to watch Samuel carry them diapers down to the river. I wondered about his momma. What kind of woman she must have been to raise her son with enough humility to do this kind of thing. Either that, or he harbored his own guilt he was trying to rectify. Somehow, though, I thought Samuel must have been honest in his ways. Gentle. Kind.

Isabella rustled a bit. I picked up the glass of liver and water, and poured the liquid into her mouth. "Miss Isabella," I said. "These babies need you. You can hate me later." I kissed her forehead.

Isabella lifted her hand and pressed it to my lips. "Shhh. It's fine." She whispered. Tender and sweet, a tear oozed from the corner of her eye. And I knew without a doubt, I'd felt the real love of a family.

SEVENTEEN

I PULLED THE BRAID tight against my head and poked a piece of carved cedar through the bun. A twig of hair curled from my forehead. Sweat soaked the roots at the scalp, and I'd begun to wonder if we'd have any relief from the early spring heat.

"Ha. Got ya, you no good—" Terrance caught himself mid-sentence.

"Let's hold our tongue. The good Lord has blessed you with three babies. You don't want them growing up with curse words burning in their ears." The preacher laughed. "Need some help?"

Terrance drew his arm back and launched his hatchet, landing it dead center in the back of a chicken. "Naw. I'm much obliged you wanna help, Preacher, but I've learned to manage with one arm. Sometimes it takes me a couple of tries with these blessed chickens scattering, but I usually nail one pretty quick."

I watched from the window while Terrance braced the carcass with his knee and commenced to yank the feathers free.

"Isabella," I said, rolling her to one side and propping her there with a pillow. "I don't know how you and Terrance will manage with three babies. You sick and him with one arm and all." I raised her shirt and laid Amelia against her chest. "Here you go littlun. Take your momma's breast and eat."

Eight days and still Isabella was in and out of consciousness. I kept talking to her, pressing them babies to the breast hoping her milk would drop, and the youngins would eat. Amelia puckered her lips, suckling before her mouth touched her mother's skin. She cooed and latched onto her momma like there was no tomorrow.

When Elsi Farmer had little Bet she was deathly sick. Momma kept squeezing the milk from Elsi's breasts to feed the baby. "This baby needs its momma's milk. Can't let her dry up."

Five days passed before Elsi's fever broke and she was able to hold Bet. Momma kept that milk pouring from Elsi's breasts by hand. She was good at caring for the sick. I helped Momma that whole week before Elsi finally came around.

Edom and Pactol kept dropping by, bringing the rest of Elsi's youngins to visit. Even when I had foul things to say about the Pastor, Edom was always quick to remind me of what was right. "Forgive seven times seventy. Care for others as you want to be cared for. That's my own version of the golden rule," Edom would say. I guessed he was right, though I wasn't sure how come.

It never sunk in why Stanley was so mad at the Pastor—outside the fact that he kept the Pastor from kicking my teeth out of my head. But he stewed for days after Elsi told him the Pastor has shamed her into having his way with her so he could cleanse her of her sin . . . cleanse her of Stanley's sin. Stanley held onto that indiscretion until it was eating him alive inside.

"It ain't never gonna be the same after what the Pastor did," Stanley ranted. Momma nabbed his arm and twisted him toward her.

"You keep your voice down. You got other youngins. And you got Elsi. I didn't say what he did was right. But—"

"They ain't no *but* to it. No man of God just has his way with another man's wife."

Momma pointed her finger in Stanley's face. "We don't speak about this. We don't never speak about this. Not for the Pastor, but for Elsi and certainly not for that little baby. Somethings is best left alone."

"Reba, did you know about the Pastor having his way with Elsi?" Stanley broke into a stare that would turn a body to stone.

Momma stood silent. Then she spoke. "Not really. I suspected. But I wasn't sure. But I could tell when Elsi quit comin' to the house to can jelly, somethin' was wrong. Then she come up pregnant. I put the pieces together."

"Well, she told me. She told me ever detail. She cried. Sobbed in my arms, and it made me want to kill him."

"I don't need to know them details. All that matters is Elsi." Momma turned away, then stopped. "And what the Pastor does ain't my fault. You best keep quiet. Let this ride. The Pastor is sly. He'll get even by the hand of God."

"Reba, you gotta live with what you pretend not to know. It'll get up with you one day. It'll get up."

Momma tried to make excuses for the Pastor, but there was no real reason to try and explain his ways. He was what he was. I slipped into the house and whispered to Elsi, "What did the Pastor do to you, Miss Elsi?"

Tears welled in her eyes. "I went to him to ask for repentance. I'd told a lie." She turned her head and brushed her fingers over her baby's head.

"Go on," I said.

"He read me some Scripture about giving myself to the Lord then he . . . he . . . took me in the name of Jesus. Said he would plant the seeds of righteousness in me, and I'd be forgiven. When I come up pregnant with Bet, I just figured the Lord had forgiven me. But I know in my heart this wasn't right."

I was such an idiot. Never putting together the evil the Pastor did. I guess I was just blinded, but when the Pastor drowned Stanley, I understood why. And Elsi knew why. So did Momma.

Stanley begged the Lord to help him forgive the Pastor, let him get on with his life. Out in the river, Stanley was about to confess to the entire mountain about his anger toward what the Pastor had done—unforgivable things to Elsi, and the Pastor couldn't let that happen. Stanley wanted forgiveness. In the name of God, the Pastor drowned a man seeking help—murdered the man that could have give out his own sin. I hated him for that. Hated him for Elsi. Hated him for little Bet, and hated him for Momma.

Then there was Momma—knowin', but never admittin'. Stanley was right. One day it would get up with her.

My nose flared and I felt the rage build inside me. My stomach turned and I leaned my head onto my knees. The cries of Elsi and those girls

echoed in my head. I covered my ears but that didn't block out the memories of Momma screaming for me to do something to stop the hanging
of the Pastor, and the anger, the rush of knowledge that hit me.

"The demon deserved to die, and if I had it to do over, I'd not change
a thing. Except that *I* might drop the noose over his head this time," I
muttered.

Samuel placed his hand on my shoulder. I come clean out of the chair.
"Keep your hands off me," I snapped.

"I didn't mean to give you a start. I was just . . ."

I backed toward the fireplace. Horrible memories bubbled to the surface. "You just keep to yourself."

"Look, Mercy. I know something mighty terrible has happened to you.
And I ain't real bright, but I ain't stupid either. I understand just by the
hate, Pastor Roller wasn't good to you. Let me help you get past this."

Samuel stepped toward me. I pulled the chair between us.

"This ain't none of your business. You hear? None of your business." I
felt my voice raise a pitch. The babies started to rouse. "I got work to do.
You go on and help Terrance."

"Look." A muffled whisper seeped from Isabella. "My baby."

"Isabella. You're awake."

"Praise God," said the preacher. "I'll fetch Terrance."

"You do that, Preacher." I glared at him.

"We'll finish this conversation later."

"Ain't nothing to finish." I picked Braden out of the makeshift crib
and scooped Melody into the bend of my other arm. "Isabella, I have a
surprise for you."

She laid stroking Amelia's head, a tear dripped onto the baby's cheek.
"I have a baby."

"Lord woman, you've been unconscious for days. Don't you remember?
You ain't got one baby. You got three." I lined them little ones side by side.
"Two girls and this here little feller."

A look of shock settled on her face. "Triplets?"

"Yes'm. This here is Amelia, Melody, and Braden." I tapped each baby's
head gently as I introduced them to their mother.

"Oh my Lord." Isabella coughed and tried to raise herself in the bed.

The door flew open. Terrance dropped to his knees and crawled across the rough wooden-planked floor.

"Lord, God, you are almighty to hear a simple man's prayers, much less answer them. Thank you. Thank you Lord for bringin' my Isabella back to me." By the time he'd finished his prayers, his head was buried in Isabella's stomach. He blubbered like one of the babies.

"The Lord is good," Samuel said.

Good my foot, I thought. *I ain't so sure You're all that mighty.* And in my silence, I hoped God had heard me.

We were in church in Cold Creek Run one Sunday when Salem Olsen said, "I pray but the Lord don't answer. I ain't so sure He's all that good."

The Pastor stepped down from the pulpit, walked toe-to-toe with Salem, drew back his fist, and hit him square between the eyes. "How dare you question the Lord's goodness?"

After the service folks could hear the Pastor rantin' at Salem, telling him he was goin' to hell unless he repented. "The Lord sent Abraham up the mountain to sacrifice his son, but Abraham proved his faithfulness. I say, offer up your own daughter and see if the Lord accepts your repentance."

The next day, Sara, Salem's youngest daughter, come limping to our cabin, her face swollen on one side, and her eye cut to the temple. "The Pastor told me I had to come here today to show him Papa had handed down my discipline. I ain't sure what I did, but Daddy whooped me till I couldn't stand."

Momma pulled Sara close and kissed her head. "Child, you ain't done nothin'. You're innocent in this unjust act."

Sara stood on the porch beat to a pulp and trying to understand why the sins of the father fell upon her for punishment.

The Pastor was good at delvin' out punishment to suit his needs. He'd take the things that meant the most to a person, then force a man's guilt. Salem questioned his teachin' and that riled the Pastor. He'd make Salem choose. Punish the thing he loved the most or go to hell.

A weak man wouldn't stand his ground against a man of God, especially after he'd just listened to one of the Pastor's hellfire and damnation sermons. Salem would do what he had to do if he thought it would keep hisself or his daughter from the gates of hell.

"Sara, did you come here on your own?"

"I come 'cuz I was afraid if I didn't get here, Daddy'd go to hell. That's what the Pastor told him. I don't want Daddy to go to hell."

"Oh you poor child. He ain't gonna go to hell. And the only place you are goin' is home. Now git on home." Moments later the Pastor bounded through the door.

"You call yourself a man of God?" Momma kicked at him. "Look at this child. Look what you pushed Salem into doin'."

The Pastor yanked a leather strap off the porch and headed toward Sara. "Looks like the Lord didn't accept Salem's repentance. I need to whip her again and pray for God to accept this punished child as penance."

Momma pushed Sara behind her. "You'll do no sucha thing."

"Pastor," I screamed. "I'll take her punishment. Let me be the atonement for the sin." As soon as the words left my mouth I regretted them.

"You think you can take the punishment for Salem's sin of the mouth?" The Pastor hovered over me.

"I don't know, Pastor. Sometimes I think you are crazy. Punishing children for things their daddy's done."

He drew back his hand and slapped me across the mouth. In an instant, the Pastor shoved Momma and Sara to the side, yanked me off the floor, and dragged me to the barn.

Oh Lord, I prayed. *Don't let him hurt me. Please, Lord, save me. Don't let him beat me to death.*

But the *good* Lord didn't answer. And by the time the Pastor had got done hittin' me with that strap and hollerin' for the Lord to accept me as the sacrifice, I could hardly stand.

"Get up," he squalled as he wiped the sweat from his face. "Get up. Let me see if the good Lord has accepted you."

"I can't stand, Pastor. How can you know if the Lord accepts me? I can't stand."

Tears run as fast down my face as the blood ran down my arms and back. He jerked me off the ground, tossed me over his shoulder like a bag of wheat, and he didn't stop until he'd dropped me in the river. His fingers twisted around my dress and he bobbed me up and down in that water until there was no fight left in me. When I quit wiggling, the Pastor dropped me and walked back to shore. I floated on my back a good mile downstream. Dazed.

I reckon I paid the price for Sara and for Salem. When I floated onto a large rock, I asked God, "Why didn't you save me?"

He didn't answer.

Where was the goodness of the Almighty then?

Old man Wilton spied me lodged on the rock in the middle of the river. I reckon he was my savior that day. His wife bathed me, soaked me in a hot tub of water to ease the pain in my joints. Days later Momma come to their homestead looking for me. Mrs. Wilton pleaded with her husband to hide me so Momma couldn't take me home, but he said it was a lie and lying to a man of God would do nothing but bring wrath on his family. Mr. Wilton loaded me in the wagon with Momma. Mrs. Wilton sobbed on the porch of their cabin.

"Mercy, forgive me. Forgive me," she cried.

My jaw hung to one side, broke, preventing me from speaking, but it didn't stop me from crying. Momma slapped the reins on Slouch's rear. The horse jumped forward, groaning as he pulled the wagon down the trench-filled road.

"Just as I am without one plea . . ." Momma began to sing.

I knew at that moment, Momma was as crazy as the Pastor, and I was stuck between them.

I watched Isabella cry over her youngins.

Terrance and the preacher prayed over Isabella and the babies. I couldn't take it anymore. They were giving praise and adoration to a cruel God. So I walked across the field to the river. Memories flooded my mind. I untied my shoes, pulled my feet free, and stepped into the water. The Indian River was quiet by the Johnsons' homestead. Its ripples gently rolled across small river rock whispering its soft song as it made its way past. I waded up to my waist. I don't recall taking a breath before I laid face-first into the water.

My eyes focused on the colored sandstones, tiny pebbles, and roots on the bottom. The cedar stick that held my hair loosened, and the current twisted the locks around my face. My arms floated to the surface, and for the first time in years, I prayed again.

Just let me die.

My chest burned and ached for air, but my mind repeated a Scripture I'd learned as a child. "Whom shall I send . . . Send me." I couldn't take the memories anymore, so I sucked in a mouth full of water and thought, *Here I am Lord, take me.*

An arm wrapped around my waist and rolled me over. Samuel leaned me across his knees and beat on my back until the water spit from my lungs.

I didn't ask to be saved this time. Why didn't He take me? I wondered. *Why? God just take me. Let me die. Let me die.*

But He didn't. He made me live . . . again.

Eighteen

When I came around, Samuel sat holding me in his arms. I cracked open my eyes and saw his were closed. He mouthed words, but no sound was uttered. I just know I felt safe.

"Samuel," I whispered.

"Thank you, Lord. Thank you." He pulled me close to his chest, his hand caressed my face, and he rocked me there on the bank. "Just keep your mouth shut," he said. "Don't you say a word. Don't you fight me. Don't you cuss me. Just lay still. You owe me that much." His hand trembled against my face.

"Don't be mad Samuel. I just can't see the light of day no more."

"I told you hush. Can't you just be quiet for one minute? You scared the living fool out of me. I wanted to think you tripped and fell into the water, but when I saw them boots on the bank . . . I knew better." Samuel kissed my head. "Please, Mercy. Don't never do this again."

I blinked away a tear.

"You did an amazing thing getting them babies here. I ain't a man who believes in consequence either. God put you here so you could save them babies. I could never have done that. Don't you see? Don't you get it? There's good in you. Look at them babies. They'd have died without you. Shoot, Isabella would have died."

The more the preacher talked, the tighter he held me, and the harder he rocked. His voice cracked and I could tell he was fighting back the hurt. It never occurred to me I could hurt him. He was just another man of God. Another man not to be trusted . . . just waiting to be strung up like the Pastor. Still, I was quiet like he asked.

"I've come to know one thing. And that's this. Together we are goin' to help this family survive, and together we're goin' to become friends, whether you like it or not. I'm gonna keep at you like a mouse on cheese until you spill what eats at you. And when you do, I'm gonna help you past it. The Pastor is dead, and so is the evil he did. You can't fix what he did. More so, you ain't him. And it's high time you figure out, I ain't him either."

My teeth chattered as a cool evening breeze stirred. "Can I talk now?"

Samuel smiled. He kissed his finger and touched my nose. "Yes, I reckon."

"The Pastor. He was the father of my baby girl. And when she was born, he tore her outta my body. He killed her. I never saw her face. Never touched her. Never named her. There. You wanted to know. There you have it."

Samuel wiped his hand over his mouth and forehead. He said nothing at first, figuring it all in his head. Finally, he took me by the arm and lifted me to my feet.

"Where are we goin'?"

"To the base of the mountain."

"Why?"

"To name your baby. To bury her."

My feet grew heavy and my knees weak. The bile in my stomach rolled until I vomited.

"Come on, Mercy. It starts now."

Samuel pulled me along, my feet scraping the ground until he gathered me in his arms and carried me—across the knee-high grassy field, down the lane, and along the path to the foot of Thunder Mountain. His wet clothes dried tight to his back, and the new dampness that seeped through the cloth was his sweat. I pushed away from him and vomited again.

"I can't do this, Preacher. Why you doing this?"

"You can, Mercy. And you know why."

Samuel knelt beside me and pulled my hair away from the stench that fell from my mouth.

"I can't begin to imagine how you feel," he said, "but I'm telling you, none of that was your fault. None of it. And you can't keep carrying the blame."

Samuel gathered an armful of mountain laurel blooms and daisies and laid them by my side. He took a sturdy, flat rock and pawed at the ground until he finally had a hole knee deep. Dirt pooled in the wrinkles of his forehead and with every scrape of the rock he prayed.

"Why you doing this?" I said again.

"Because I saw you try to take your own soul . . . a soul filled with goodness and fight, but buried beneath bitterness and pain." The preacher pulled himself out of the hole. "Now you sit here. Take these flowers and weave them together. Make me a purty ground cover. I'll be back in a few minutes. And while I'm gone, you spend time naming your girl." He pointed his finger at me and dared me to move. "You stay here. You understand? Name that baby girl. I mean it, Mercy. That child deserves a name and you deserve to give it."

I glanced at the flowers, their scent filled my lungs, and when I looked up, he was gone.

"Momma," I said after the Pastor took my baby. "Momma, was it a girl or a boy?"

Momma's lip quivered. "A baby girl."

"Could you see her face?"

"Mercy, stop this."

"No, Momma. Could you see her face?"

"I did not." She hung her head and I knew right that second Momma had lied. "She's buried. Gone. She was dead when she come."

"Momma, that ain't true." I burst into tears. My voice bounced from sob to sob. "It ain't so."

Momma pulled me straight up from the bed of hay. "You listen to me. She was dead. That's all you need to know. Put her out of your head. She was dead."

She eased me back into the hay and wiped my face. "Don't never mention her again." And I didn't. Not even when Maddie asked me when I had her. "You're crazy," I said to Maddie. "I ain't never had no baby."

I sat by the pile of dirt Samuel had dug. Tears dripped off my nose. I'd cried, bellowed, cursed . . . I guess I mourned the child I'd never held.

In my innocence, I didn't know for a long time I was carrying an infant, but when that little thing kicked inside me the first time, instinct took over and I knew. I knew she was breathing when she come too. At least until the Pastor snapped her neck. I didn't know no better about the Pastor 'til that day. Well, I reckon I knew, I just didn't want to admit it. Things was too horrible to imagine. I didn't want to know. It was my way of keepin' my sanity. But that day, the scales dropped off my eyes, just like they did in the Bible when Saul was healed. From then on, I faced the Pastor, eyes wide open. Bits of reality started to creep in. Just like I'd eat one of them apples from the Tree of Knowledge in the Garden. With every moment of understanding, I hated him more.

Down the lane a rise of dust flew about. A wagon. I squinted to see who it was. Terrance, the preacher, and to my surprise, bedded down in the back, was Isabella and the babies. The horses came to a halt, Slouch headed the team. Everything that was anything to me stood at that hole in the ground—Isabella, Terrance, the babies, and yes, the preacher.

Samuel stepped down from the wagon and Terrance pulled it about so Isabella could see.

"We're gathered here in this place of quiet and solitude, to give back a precious soul." Samuel eyed me, waiting for me to cough up a name. I stood silent, numb, unable to speak.

"Mercy, your baby. What's her name?"

Pent up tears rushed over my cheeks and into the corners of my mouth. "I . . . I . . ."

"Yes. Go ahead. Give us her name."

"Angel. Angel Grace Roller."

Samuel pressed his hand against my shoulder. Terrance wrapped his arm around me. Isabella cried.

"Angel of mercy," Samuel said.

I froze in place. Time, for a moment, stopped. I'd never heard my name used in any other way except to plead for mercy. *Angel, my baby. Angel of Mercy*, I thought. *Perfect.*

"O Lord, take this little one into your arms. Set her soul free and allow her to know only your peace and joy." Samuel motioned for me to drop the wreath of flowers into the hole.

What woman wants to say good-bye to her offspring? My heart ripped and for a few moments, I held those flowers, smelled the soft scent, and felt as though I held my infant. I caressed the flowers and closed my eyes.

In an instant, I felt the joy of being a mother. I brushed my daughter's hair, told her about life on the mountain. Taught her how to care. I sang to her . . . *Amazing Grace . . . how sweet the sound.* For a few moments, every ounce of my being sensed my child. Years of memories for her whirled around my head. I imagined her grown, having her own children, and kissing me as I lay dying to my age.

"Why couldn't I hold her?" Sobs of guilt echoed across the mountain. "I'm sorry, baby girl. I'm sorry, Angel Grace. But I have never stopped wondering what it would be like to hold you. And I ain't never forgotten how much I love you."

Terrance steadied me and Samuel lifted his hand toward a wispy cloud. Braden commenced to cry and then, Amelia, and after her, Melody. Their voices rang through me like a sword set afire to refine.

I knelt and gently laid the flowers into the hole. My tears offered them their last taste of water. Samuel pulled a shovel from the wagon, and gingerly covered them. Terrance held a small wooden cross lashed from two sticks, while Samuel tapped it into the ground.

The breeze danced around me, playing with my hair, teasing, twisting it about my face. Momma always said, God is loudest in the silence.

I climbed into the wagon and took hold of Braden. Isabella's weak hand opened and clasped around mine.

All this was nice. It gave me some peace, but it also served to fuel the fire of hate for the Pastor. My best guess was he was in hell . . . waiting patiently for me.

NINETEEN

FOR SEVERAL DAYS I found myself walking across the field to the foot of the mountain. I'd go just to visit the makeshift grave for my Angel. There were hard moments. Times when I wished I'd never laid eyes on Samuel. Times I hated him for forcing me to bury a dream, and times I wish what had been buried was me. But I suppose in the bigger picture there was a plan.

Some of us was made to suffer while others never skip a beat. I reckon I was one chose to suffer.

"You goin' back down the mountain?" Isabella laid Braden across her knees and gently patted his back.

"Maybe. I got chores here first."

I lifted Braden from her knees and laid him on the bed while Isabella reached into the crib for Amelia. I brushed my fingers through Amelia's hair. The tiny ringlets unwound softly around her head. "She looks like you. All that dark hair. And she's got her momma's pouty lip."

"Pouty lip?" Isabella poked her bottom lip out and made it quiver. She let out a laugh that could have rattled the plates right off the shelves. I was glad to hear her laugh. It reminded me how precious her life was to us all.

"You're looking so much better. Getting some color back in your face. No more sunken eyes." I handed her a plate of hot fried chicken livers. "You developed a taste for these things yet?"

Isabella wrinkled her nose. "I'm afraid not. But your momma taught you right. These nasty things have helped me."

"They ought to help you. Terrance has bartered work for chickens for the last two weeks. I'm about as tired of chicken and dumplins', fried chicken, chicken potpie, chicken and vegetables. Boiled chicken, chicken soup . . ."

Isabella cackled. "A good piece of pork loin might be pretty tasty."

"Hmm. Maybe I'll convince Terrance to work off a good pig next week. I saw you had plenty of salt in the springhouse. We can salt it down and have meat for a month."

"I owe you my life, Mercy. I haven't thanked you."

"You don't owe me nothing," I said. "Just being here to see these little beauties into the world is pay enough."

I unpinned Braden's diaper. It was dry. The baby hadn't wet for two days. Even I knew that wasn't a good sign. Isabella would put him to breast and he'd gag. I spent hours dribbling water and milk into his tiny mouth just to get something in him.

"Isabella, I think Terrance needs to get Doc Mosley up here. Let him look over Braden. This baby still ain't peed." I pinned his diaper snug around the tiny waist and bundled him tight. "He's still cold as a cucumber. And we can't heat this house any more. The rest of you will die of heat exhaustion."

"Terrance talked to Doc day before yesterday. He said he'd be along this week. I know the child is weak. I try to feed him, but I can't force the baby to eat. He gags and chokes." She stretched her arm toward him and patted his rump. "He's so frail. All else I know to do is pray for his little soul."

Frail wasn't even a good description. I was surprised the little thing had lived to be three weeks old, but he was fading and I could see that. I took to carrying Braden with me to the shack at night. Isabella and Terrance could handle the girls. At least they would sleep steady. "I got you a make-shift crib in the shack." Samuel stuck out his chest like a proud peacock. "It's not my ideal of the best place to sleep at night, but it'll have to do until me and Terrance get the barn up."

"And just how much longer on that little task?" I teased.

"Pushy, ain't ya? But I'm guessing by the end of the month. Terrance has a barn raisin' planned. When the neighbors get this direction, we ought to have it up in a day. Then I can get the men to help me add a room to the shack and a fireplace. So three days or so."

"I hope it's soon. I ain't sure that damp shack is the place for an already frail child."

Isabella reached for Braden and laid him to breast."Come, baby. Eat just a little."

All I could do was shake my head in worry. The little feller just wasn't thriving. I kept a small fire built in Isabella's copper apple butter pot at night. Between that and the spring heat, the shack stayed warm but damp. Still, Braden was lifeless. His lips still carried that blue tint, and his eyes rarely opened. I can only recall him crying one or two times, and the amount of food I could get down him wasn't enough to keep a bird alive.

I hardly slept through the nights for fear he'd stop breathing. I'd find myself pacing the cramped quarters, snuggling the baby close and humming to him. I'd sing, *All night, all day, Angels watchin' over me my lord. All night, all day. Angels watchin' over me.* And I had to believe my "Angel" was doing just that. She had to be in heaven, nowhere close to the Pastor.

Momma used to sing that same song after the Pastor made his monthly visit to me. She'd bathe me in a warm tub of water out behind the shed, wash my hair, and sing to me. Her way of trying to make up to me for letting the Pastor have his way. Her way of trying to wash away his filth and her guilt.

I wasn't sure how Isabella would react if something happened to her little man, but things weren't looking good. Doc Mosley didn't seem to be in any hurry to get to our side of the mountain, so I did what we mountain women do. Made do. Did the best I could to feed the baby, care for him. He'd at least know he was loved.

"Mercy, can I come over to your side of the shack? Read the Word to Braden. Pray over him." I'd scrubbed a line onto the floor with my boot to divide the shack. I didn't want the preacher crossing over the barrier. He was to stay on his side, and I'd stay on mine.

Samuel prayed every night for Braden and his coming never seemed to be from habit, rather out of true concern and love for the little feller. And I think for me too. He'd ask if he could come across to my side, say his prayers, and I'd let him come. Samuel never stopped believing Braden would pull through, but I think even Isabella was preparing for the worst. Mothers just know these things. Even the instinct of a momma dog over a weakling puppy tells her to let it die. Why we don't listen to our instincts, I suppose, is what sets us apart from the dogs. That and the infernal desire for hope.

"Little man," I said to Braden, "you're certainly a determined little feller, but you're going to have to do more for Miss Mercy than barely eat. You're gonna have to gobble down some food. Get strong."

Days turned into weeks, and I drew closer to Braden. Maybe because him and me had something in common. Both of us pitiful. Both of us sick—me sick on the inside, sick in my heart, sick of my life, and him just plain sick. I just know every time I held him in my arms it was like holding Angel Grace.

Is this what you would have felt like?

"It's a real job splittin' my time between three youngins. But I love it." Isabella dropped a dirty diaper outside the window into the bucket on the porch. She'd began standing a little each day. It wasn't long before she was easing outside to feed the chickens and messing in the garden. I could see her strength growing. She'd insist on always having one or two of them babies strapped to her. Toting those girls was enough to strengthen anyone.

"How 'bout we have collard greens and bacon for supper?" Isabella tee-tered to one side as she stood. I took her arm and steadied her. Isabella did what she did best—pressed a tender palm against my cheek, and thanked me with her golden eyes.

"I hope the men soon get that barn up. I know it's hard on you sharin' the shack."

"Isabella, you have babies to worry about. I ain't your problem, and I ain't here because I'm forced. I'm here because I want to be. Terrance pulls that sawmill across the pass and splits lumber for that new coal camp once a month. Not to mention fixin' that porch that got damaged by the storm the day them babies came. He's the one you need to worry over. The man hardly rests."

"He is a hard worker. But life ain't easy on the mountain. A man does what he has to do to care for his family. Terrance ain't no quitter. He works harder since he lost that arm." Isabella leaned against the table.

I glanced out the window in time to see the preacher step onto the porch and snag the bucket under the window. I never had to ask him again to wash the diapers. Twice a day he'd make a trip to the river, scrub them with lye soap, and hang them on the line to dry. That said something for him.

It got so I couldn't seem to take my eyes off Samuel. Despite the fact he was a preacher, he was still a man and a handsome one at that.

Isabella held the broom out to me. "You know, he's a nice man."

"Who?"

She laughed. "Who? You're asking me who? Samuel is who. I think you have eyes for the preacher."

I snatched the broom from her hand and commenced to sweep the clay dirt between the cracks in the slat floor.

"Mercy, it's all right if you have a little hankerin' for the pastor."

I snapped when she said *pastor*.

"Isabella, first of all, he ain't no pastor. I ain't sure what the difference is between a preacher and a pastor, except that one travels from place to place, but he ain't no pastor."

I knew there was probably some sort of official difference, but I understood about a pastor. Leastways the one that raised me, and I wouldn't begin to insult Samuel with that title. If I was going to imagine what a real man of God was, then I'd suppose Samuel would be that man. "Trust me"—I pressed the broom deep into the crevice of the floor—"Samuel ain't no pastor."

Isabella stared at me, a blank look across her face.

"And furthermore, I ain't got no eyes for the preeeaaacher. I'm a married woman."

Isabella's mouth cracked open, and a slight gasp eased out. "You are? Married, I mean?"

I grabbed a chair and slid it under Isabella. "You may as well sit down before you fall down."

"You're married?"

"Well, I was. My husband is dead. He was shot by a bullet meant for me."

The water over the fire began to boil. I scraped some butter into the pot, added some salt, and dumped the mess of greens into the rush of bubbles.

"And before you ask, I'll tell you. My daddy was a pastor. He did wrong things to me. Things that ought never be done." The color left Isabella's face. "That's how come I know Samuel ain't no pastor."

"Lord, have mercy."

"And that's another thing. Everybody calls my name next to the Lord's." I dug the bristles of the broom into the corner by the hearth. "Lordy Mercy. Lawsy Mercy. Mercy, Mercy, Lord have Mercy." My head swayed back and forth with each swish of the broom.

"He ain't kept me safe, ain't offered me no mercy from a man of the cloth, and He certainly didn't stop the Pastor from firing that rifle."

I took hold of the metal handle on the pot and turned loose as fast. "Lordy. Lordy." I pulled my palm away from the pot handle leaving the hide. Blisters bubbled immediately.

Anger climbed up my stomach and into my throat. The rage wrapped itself around me and squeezed tight. I'd tried not to bring my feelings out, but they gurgled up in me faster than a hungry fire. Pulling the tail of my dress around my hand I tried to lift the heavy pot from the fire hook. The weight was more than I could hold on a freshly burned hand. The pot dropped, sending collard greens, boiling water, and new onions across the floor.

"Oh my god," I shouted.

"He is that for sure." Samuel grasped my shoulders and pulled me toward him while Isabella soaked a rag in cold water.

"He who? What are you talking about?" I snapped.

"You said, 'oh my god.' I agreed. He is your God."

I jerked my shoulders free of the preacher's grasp. "Let go of me. Don't never touch me again." Panic overwhelmed me.

"Mercy, calm down." Isabella tried to press the rag around my palm.

"Calm down. Calm down. You people want me to calm down. You pester the stuffin' outta me about having eyes for the preacher. You both keep telling me how to feel when you got no idea why I refuse to feel. And God. Well, I ain't right sure He's nothing more than a—"

"That's enough," Samuel snapped. "Enough, I said."

He pulled a chair in front of me and pushed me into the soft cane bottom.

"I can see we've touched a nerve here. And you ain't goin' nowhere until you fill in the blanks." Samuel knelt at my feet as I kicked at his stomach. His hands wrapped snuggly around my ankles. "You drop hints, Mercy. Like a kid dropping bread crumbs, giving us just enough about yourself to keep us wondering—refusing to let us know you." The preacher's hands around my ankles felt like iron shackles. "Well, I got news for you. Today you finish one story."

Isabella swiped a tear from her cheek. "Mercy, I'm sorry. I'd never upset you."

Suddenly, I was ashamed. It was a different kind of shame than I'd ever felt before. Not the kind that comes from someone doing something horrible to you, but the kind that comes when you've done something you know is wrong. And I was wrong. Isabella had been nothing short of wonderful to me. She'd done nothing but show me her love and acceptance for who I was.

The babies began to cry. I'd startled the precious souls with my shouting. I tried to stand and go to Braden, but Samuel held tight to my ankles. "Them babies will be fine. They got their momma. Now finish the story."

Isabella patted my shoulder and rushed to the cribs.

"Go on. Finish the story. Say the words. Until you say them, they won't never be no peace on your soul."

I pressed my knuckles into my eyes. My voice cracked and broke as I uttered the words. Between sobs I conceded.

"I run off and married Thomas Dawson. I was thirteen. He was a good man. The Pastor had been gone for a spell from the house, and as my bad luck would have it, he'd return the day after Thomas and me went off to get hitched. He . . . he . . ."

"Go on. He what?"

Tears rushed down my cheeks, and the pain I felt was like someone had sliced open my chest and snatched out my heart by the roots.

"I was in Chattanooga. Somehow the devil found me, and when he slunk into our room in the dark and run his nasty hands over my body, he wasn't expecting to find Thomas. The Pastor felt the grip of someone much stronger than me. Thomas shoved him away and the Pastor went to shouting and preaching about the sin of fornication. Them two went to wallerin' all over the room. Thomas was wailin' the tar outta the Pastor, when Thomas managed to land a swing that sent the Pastor through the window.

"He called me nothing. 'Nothing but trash. Nothing but an abomination. Best off dead.' Ever word sailed through the broken window and pierced me like an arrow. Thomas shoved the Pastor again. This time he slammed against the horse that stood, head down, gnawing at the grass. The Pastor mounted the horse and took off. I rushed to Thomas. Blood dripped off his chin. He wrapped his arms around me and whispered everything would be fine. He kissed me—then I heard the gunfire."

Samuel loosened his grip as Isabella pushed between us. She wrapped her arms around me and pressed my head against her chest. "Oh my sweet girl. My sweet girl. Mercy, it wasn't your fault."

I can't remember ever hearing real compassion and I certainly never remember anyone telling me this wasn't my fault. But the caress of someone who loved me opened up a wound that bled for days. What bled out of the wound wasn't blood, but anger and hate. What healed it was love.

Samuel, once again, scooped me into his arms and walked. He carried me across the field, to the base of the mountain then back again—never once stumbling a step. When he finally laid me on the bed of hay in the shack, he said, "The good Lord carried our burdens just like I carry yours."

He never uttered another word that night. Instead, he sat on his side of the shack, hands clasped and fingers twined, praying.

Samuel, by his example, proved what a real man of God was. And if anything would soften my anger toward God Almighty, it would be the servant who carried my burden.

TWENTY

Summer 1897

"ALL I CAN SAY, ISABELLA, is you're really coming along. And that's wonderful."

"I feel much better. My strength is back and I want to walk with you to Angel's grave."

I stuffed the kitchen towel between the band of my apron and dress. "You're crazy. You're improving, but you ain't up to a walk."

The smile on her face dropped. "We can take the wagon."

"What about the babies?"

Isabella pointed toward the river and Samuel. "I bet the preacher would watch them for a bit."

I let out a guffaw. "I imagine he'd love anything that gets him outta diaper washing."

Isabella got tickled. She grabbed her stomach, grimaced and laughed at the same time. "He's been such a sweet man. I mean, he's left his duties at the church across the mountain to help us."

"Yeah," I grumbled. "That's what preachers do. Stuff to show humility."

Isabella took my arm and twisted me toward her. Her smile turned sour and her brow furrowed. "You listen to me. The things that man has done was not for his own gain. He didn't have to come here. He didn't have to drag you along. But he did and he did it out of love, friendship, and humility. I've grown to love you, Mercy. But don't you rile me, 'cause they is a reason all this has happened. And the key to getting me and

Terrance through this has somehow been laid at your feet. The preacher and you. So don't you go belittlin' the preacher."

I'd never heard Isabella raise her voice—not out of anger—but I'd managed to get her hackles up. Her words pierced me like a hot blade, and rightfully so. Samuel did seem to have the right heart, and though I despised him for saving me from the river then having the gall to make me bury a make-believe baby, I know he was trying to do right by me.

I placed Braden in a wrap and slipped him onto my back. Isabella filled a leather pouch with milk and I dropped it in my apron. She rolled my sleeves toward my elbows and patted my cheek. "I'm going with you today."

"Maybe. If I go."

"You'll go. And I need to go."

I snugged Braden against my back and headed onto the porch.

"Where you takin' my boy?" Isabella smiled as she patted the baby's back.

"To the garden. We're gonna hoe the tomatoes and cut some leaf lettuce. I got a hankering for lettuce and tomatoes for supper. Can you manage a loaf of sourdough?"

"Oh, that sounds good. Bread, milk, tomatoes, and salad greens. I'll handle the bread." Isabella kissed Braden. "His lips will never pinken. I know the good Lord has a plan for me and for Braden." She caressed his tiny head in her palm. "He's slipping away."

I couldn't believe Isabella was talking that way. She practically had the boy in the grave.

"It's important you let me walk with you to Angel's grave today," she said again. "You hear?"

"I hear." I squeezed her hand and headed to the garden.

I knew what Isabella was doing. She was preparing for the inevitable. She was readying herself for what she knew would come and, as much as I knew that, I wasn't ready to face another loss. Braden was nothing but skin stretched over bone. His sisters had more than doubled in size, while he had hardly grown an inch. I didn't want to admit it, but he was more than frail.

Isabella's only reason to follow me to the base of the mountain was to

prepare a spot to bury her son. That's what we do in the mountains—
prepare the ground. Pray over it. Ask God to make the ground warm to
cradle a baby. Not cold and hard. But I wasn't ready to let this baby go.
Not another one.

"Let's go, little man," I said. "I'm going to mash you some fresh 'maters,
strain the seed, and make you some creamy soup. And if I go to all that
trouble, you better hang 'round to eat it."

Never in my life had I seen a child stay so cold in the heat of a blanket
and the hot sun beaming down on him. Braden's skin was pasty, clammy,
and chilled. He'd already beat the odds by making it this long, but the
skin hung on his ribs, and regardless what I managed to poke into his
tummy, death hung over him.

Why would any God who calls hisself a God let a little one like this suffer?

Doc had come and gone more than once, and every trip he'd hold
the child and shake his head in disbelief. "He's a miracle. That's all I can
say. Can't nobody guess how long this baby will hold out." *Some doctor*, I
thought. He could at least have offered Terrance and Isabella hope.

I hoed the weeds from the row of tomatoes, and with each motion of
my arms I felt Braden's head wobble. He'd not opened his eyes in days,
and I'd gone to putting him against me when I slept. I was tired, but not
near as tired as Braden.

Samuel gently took the hoe from my hand and laid a bright yellow
tomato in my palm.

"The way you fade in and out without a sound, you scared the tarnation outta me."

The preacher laughed. "I'm not quiet. Birds scatter when I traipse
through the field. You're just off in a cloud somewhere." He flicked a fly
off Braden's head. "The boy isn't doing so good, is he?"

I nodded and changed the subject. "Well, I think you're of the devil,
possessing some ability to just pop up when you see fit."

Samuel walked the row, picking over yellow, orange, and red tomatoes,
pulling a few green ones.

"Those tomatoes are green," I said.

"I know. They can ripen on the porch . . . or they could be fried for
breakfast."

"Is that a hint?"

"Just a fact."

I twisted the cloth carry around to my chest and rubbed the baby's head. My fingers left a white trail in the blue color of his skin. Braden didn't move, and when I clasped my fingers around his tiny wrist the imprint of my fingers stayed as though I'd pressed them into clay. What tiny bit of warmth that held tight in his cheeks drained.

"Oh Lord," I said. "Baby boy, open your eyes. Braden." Tears filled my eyes. I dropped to my knees and cradled him. Samuel grasped at me.

"Don't you do this, child. No, don't you do this. You come back this minute." I pushed him tight against my breast. "Braden, please?" I felt him quiver in my clutch. His chest rose just a bit as he took in a half-hearted breath.

Samuel reached around my waist and untied the sling that held Braden. "What you doing?"

"I'm taking the boy to his mother. He needs to be cradled by his momma."

I slapped the preacher's hand away. "Leave Braden alone. He's fine. He's warm. He's mine." I couldn't believe the words slipped from my thoughts and onto my lips. Isabella stood on the porch and when she saw Samuel grab for Braden she slumped down the steps.

"Mercy, don't do this. You know this baby is dying. Let his mother cradle him."

"He's not dying. He's not." I stood and stumbled across the rows of green bean vines.

"Mercy. Please." Samuel came after me. "Stop."

I froze in my steps. The preacher wrapped his arms around me and twisted. He cradled me while I cuddled Braden. "Let him go, Mercy. Let me take him to his mother."

I glanced up as Terrance and Isabella come across the yard. Him with his one arm holding her, while she lugged both girls. Isabella sputtered coughs and tears.

Samuel turned me gently to face him, his deep eyes calm, and at peace. "Give me the baby," he whispered. "You've done all you can do. You loved him, fed him, warmed him. But he's not yours. He's Isabella's son."

A numbness crawled up my arms and they weakened, opening up and letting Braden gently slip into the preacher's arms. He kissed my forehead and turned.

Terrance loosened his grip on Isabella. He placed his hand on the preacher's shoulder. His eyes spoke what words couldn't say. Samuel loosened the sling wrapped around the baby and slipped Braden into the crook of Terrance's arm. Terrance's chin quivered as he tenderly kissed the baby's head. Braden's chest barely moved. Samuel took the girls from Isabella and held them close to his chest.

My heart was torn in two. Sobs seeped from the deepest part of me as I watched Isabella caress her baby. Her hair fell from her shoulders and blanketed Braden, while her mourns echoed across the pasture. And as I watched Braden take his last breath in the arms of his mother, my own scabs were scratched off and the blood of hurt poured out.

Edom used to say the deeper the love, the harder a body had to scratch the scabs in order to bleed out the pain. I mourned that day. A true mourn. I scratched the scab of Angel Grace, and now I dug at the wound with Braden. The blood that poured out of me covered me, and I remembered what Samuel had once said. "The blood of the Lamb covers you and His grace and mercy are ours."

Grace and mercy. Mercy. Mercy.

TWENTY-ONE

THE MOUNTAIN FOLK formed a black line of mourning that snaked across the field and past the newly finished barn.

Sawhorse tables lined the yard, and women filled it with bowls of cooked vegetables, ham, chicken, fresh baked breads, and jellies. It looked more like a church picnic than a funeral. Isabella carried Amelia on her back and Melody in her arms. A handkerchief dangled from her fingers. Her cheeks were sunken, and her eyes darkened from the agony of loss. Folks tried to comfort her with kind words and gestures. But I found myself making my way across the field to the base of the mountain. And there, alone and in the shade of the overhanging trees, I stood numb, staring at the two graves. One empty of a body, but filled with memory. The other stuffed to the gill with this child—the second one I'd loved.

"It's not fair." My voice cracked. "That little baby did nothing but fight to live."

"I know." A soft voice spoke. When I turned there was Isabella. She'd followed me back to the graves. In her grief, she tried to comfort me.

"I hate God for this. I hate Him," I mumbled. I didn't mean for Isabella to hear it, but she did. She turned me toward her and raised her finger to my face.

"Mercy, this ain't the cruelty of God, it's His mercy."

"Mercy? Taking an innocent child?"

"No. Saving an innocent child from a life of misery." Isabella leaned against me and sobbed. I grasped her elbows and tried to keep her knees from buckling.

There we stood. Two women. Both suffering loss. Both seeking peace. We must have stood by them graves the better part of an hour, sobbing relentlessly. Grieving, weeping, when Terrance come in search of us.

He scooped Isabella up in the one good arm he had, and pressed his forehead against hers. "Shhh. It'll be all right."

But to me, it wasn't going to be all right. It wasn't right at all. I'd done all I could to save that youngin. Isabella had too. We all had. I saw no favor in death. Little Angel entered my mind, and for a moment I thought of her loss. Her life snuffed out after her first breath. *Better dead than held captive by the devil*, I thought. It was then I began to understand Isabella's thinking. I didn't forgive the Lord for taking the life of this infant. But I could at least justify the means to the end.

A hand grasped my shoulder and I felt Samuel's breath against my ear. "They're playing together in heaven. Angel has a wonderful friend who can tell her all about her mother."

I tilted my shoulder and dropped Samuel's hand. "That supposed to make me feel better? That the best a man of the cloth can do?"

"Mercy, I understand your—"

"You understand what, Preacher? What? You tell me what good can come outta the death of two babies."

"We can't understand the will of God."

"Will of God," I shouted. "Will of God. I understand the will of God. He giveth and He taketh away. That's the will of God. He's an Indian giver. He tempts us with the goodness and purity of a baby, then snuffs it out." I fell to my knees across the graves and wailed.

In seconds Isabella was digging her fingers into the fresh dark dirt, overcome by the finality of it all. Clawing after her son. They comes a point where even when you can justify the loss, your heart has to thrash out the reality. At least she got to hold Braden. Nurse him. Touch his tender skin, kiss his tiny head. Isabella at least had fond memories.

I pressed my hands into the silty soil and knew the only thing there was the outline of my palms. Those handprints . . . they was a mirror of who murdered the Pastor.

Samuel did not leave my side. He said nothing, he knelt instead, clasped his hands together and prayed for my peace.

"Lord God, have mercy on this woman who hurts."

I buried my head in my arms. "Yes, Lord. Have mercy. 'Cause I ain't got none."

Twenty-Two

Fall 1897

Melody whined as I twisted the pouch that held her milk. Her mouth drew into a pucker at my touch. "You hungry?"

She clasped hold of the tip and commenced to draw on it. "That's my girl. You eat. The more you eat, the more the preacher has to wash diapers."

I laughed. It felt good to laugh. I don't think I'd cracked a smile in a month. It took me a day or two, but I shoveled my pain over my shoulder and straightened up. Isabella and the girls took precedence. The babies were standing with help and their sweet giggles filled the house with joy. I couldn't believe the April spring had bled into fall.

Terrance and Isabella had taken the preacher and me as family. I couldn't really grasp having a family. But when Terrance built that extra room onto the shack, I knew they had no intentions of letting either of us go, and I certainly had no intention of leaving them.

By the time I hit eighteen, I was beginning to put the pieces together. How the Pastor worked. Who he picked on and why. I just was slow to see it. Slower to admit it. But the muddy waters were becoming clearer.

I wanted a father to love, and like the Pastor used to preach, *love covers a multitude of sin*. Despite all his meanness, all his cruelty, I still wanted him to love me. I still wanted to love him, but truth was makin' that pertnear impossible.

The Pastor's personal demons pushed him to do despicable things. The

Widow, Stanley, my baby. They were all fallout from the Pastor trying to
hide his own evil. What he couldn't hurt, he snuffed out. Knowing that
. . . having lived that . . . I wasn't about to let Isabella's babies suffer at the
hand of another so-called man of God. My gut told me better. Samuel
had more than proved he was nothing like the Pastor. It was my own fear.
My own mistrust. It was all me.

It wasn't much . . . the shack. But I grew to call it home. It stood a few
feet from the house. And though the barn was rebuilt, it was too much
to ask Samuel to spend a cold winter there so Terrance added a room and
a fireplace. Terrance's house was a short distance from the base of the
mountain, a brisk walk across the field, but not bad. And you could stand
on the porch and see the babies' graves in the distance.

Samuel had since crossed back to his own home and turned his
church work there over to the men on that side of the mountain. After he
returned, I wasn't surprised when he told me he'd be working on a church
for Thunder Mountain. Not that I really cared. I could do without one,
but that seemed to be his passion.

Samuel, with the help of the mountain folk, built a small church just
across the field from the shack. It was simple, nothing fancy, but the
mountain folk were friendly and believed in helping one another. You
wouldn't find that kind of goodness just anywhere. People on the mountain understood it took everybody to survive, so every man, woman,
and child shared what they had. Folks bartered their talents and trades
because money was scarce.

The Simmons brothers built a small white picket fence around the two
graves, and Silas Martin carved a bench that sat at their foot. In turn
Isabella spun wool and knitted socks and gloves for them for the winter.
Isabella and I walked to the cemetery every week and sat. She pondered
Braden, and I silently grieved both Angel and Braden.

Sometimes healing comes in the simple silence.

"You doin' alright?" I slipped my arm around Isabella.

She nodded and swiped a tear with her apron tail. "I thought it would
get easier with time. But it ain't. The wound just gets bigger." She went to
her knees and brushed away bright red and gold leaves from Braden's bed.
"It's getting cooler and I think how cold he must be."

"We'll make grave covers. I'll go up the mountain. Maybe Samuel will help me, and we'll cut out some evergreen. I know Terrance has twine. We'll weave us some warm grave blankets."

I remembered Momma weaving a grave cover for the Widow after she died. Even though Momma and Mabel laid the Widow out in her best Sunday dress, all I could see was her naked body sprawled out on the bed and the blisters around her mouth after the Pastor poured that hot coffee down her throat. That picture never left me . . . even when we covered her grave with evergreen. I guessed some things were just meant to haunt us. And her screams and pleadin' haunted me.

Isabella clasped her fingers together across her face and sobbed. I understood her pain. I felt it too. Even wondered when the agony would leave. But, like Isabella said, it just grows worse. I swallowed my own tears, determined not to let Isabella see me in a moment of weakness. Besides, no one could know I was weak. No one. Ever.

"I feel so selfish," Isabella said.

"What? You're the most selfless person I know. Why would you feel selfish?"

"I still have two babies. Two sweet babies and . . ."

"I have none." She drew a second glance at me, stunned I'd said it for her.

"No, that's not what I meant."

"Sure it is. But I know you meant it in a good way. Or as good as it could be."

Isabella dropped her head. She reached to me and I took her hand. Then Isabella, being the kind soul she was, kissed my knuckles.

"Mercy, you are my gift from God. You saved me. You saved my babies. You loved Braden as I loved him. That was selfless. All I can do is mourn the loss of one, but you. You mourn the loss of two, and they ain't nothin' I can do to change that. Nothin' I can say to fill your void. I just pray for you."

I pulled her to her feet and brushed the dirt from her skirt. "Miss Isabella, don't waste your prayers on me. Spend them on someone who might believe they help." The words came out quiet, but they struck a mighty blow because Isabella broke into an all-out wail, crying tears of sadness for me. She wanted me to be happy. She wanted me to find peace, to reconcile with the good Lord. But I saw no need to make amends with a God who found His pleasure in the death of babies.

"Can you make your way back to the house on your own?" I asked.

Isabella shook her head. "You're not going back with me?"

"No, I'm going on up the mountain. Gonna follow the river a piece. See if I can find its beginning."

"Mercy, you climb that riverbed all the time. Why is it so important to you to find what can't be found?"

"It's what I have to do. It's my search for answers. My time to figure things out."

I'd walked the mountain over and over, hopping the boulders, searching for the spot where the river began. The farther I climbed the mountain, the bigger the boulders became until I couldn't shimmy up them anymore. I was so close to finding the source of the water, but every time the river swerved and I failed. Every time my search for who I was grew murkier than the trip before.

From high up on the ridge the Indian River sang its song to me. I'd sit on the edge of the rocks and watch the water race through the crevices. I'd stare into the water and wonder how on earth the rush of the river left the pebbles on the sandy bottom in place.

I tried to sleep at night, but memories like ghosts haunted me. Terrance built my door so I could bar it with two planks, assuring me no one could slip in during the night. Even though the Pastor was dead and gone, I still felt like his steel cold eyes hovered over me. So I walked the mountain, scaled the boulders, and found nothing but the continual wash of the water. I knew nothing more when I came down than I knew when I climbed up.

"God, I know You're there. I just can't figure out why in heaven's name You can't come outta that heavenly kingdom and answer me one question. *Why?*"

Samuel's church doors were propped open that fall Sunday. I lay in my bed and listened to the voices of the mountain folk as they sang "Onward

Christian Soldiers, marching as to war." Even the feather pillow couldn't drown out the bum, bum, bum rhythm of the song. I found myself lost in a wash of memories.

"Sing," Momma would say. "The Pastor wants us to set the example for the church people. Sing."

The Pastor entered the church from the rear, his heels clicking against the wood floor. He started preaching and shouting words from the Good Book before he got to the pulpit. Sweat beaded across his forehead as he pounded his Bible and spilled out his message. The Pastor pulled his handkerchief from his pocket and swiped his face, then leaned across the pew and kissed Momma. He grasped my arm. His touch appeared gentle to the churchgoers, but his nails dug deep into my flesh as he steered me to the front of the church.

"Mercy, stand before the congregation and sing. Show them how to sing. Sing."

I mouthed the words to "Amazing Grace."

"Louder. Louder so the people can hear you." He spun me around, my back now to the congregation. His fingers grasped my jaw and chin. I felt my knees shake.

"The devil has her tongue," he shouted.

"No sir, he doesn't. I can sing."

"No you can't. The devil has your throat sealed tight. Let's pray for this child to be healed." He grabbed my arms and pulled me close to his face.

"In the name of Jesus. Release this child's voice." My head bobbled as he shook me. Each time the shakes jarred my neck and pain shot down my legs. The Pastor shouted, "God heal this youngin." He went to praying and stomping around the front of the church like a chicken scratchin' for the last bite of corn. "Be healed. Come out of this child, demon." He wheeled around and smacked my forehead with his palm, sending me backward across the front pew.

My head smashed against the pew, making a gash the size of my little finger in my crown. I crawled to my feet, straightened my dress, and sang as loud as I could sing, "Praise God from whom all blessings flow . . ." I knew better than not to sing. My back ached from landing across the pew, and my head trickled blood from the whack it took.

As much as the Pastor said I needed healin' from demons, I didn't need nothin', and the Pastor knew that.

I glanced at Maddie and prayed she could read the fear in my eyes. I guess you could say the good Lord had mercy on Mercy that day because He opened Maddie's eyes. Maddie knew to be scared when she saw that look of terror in me. She took matters into her own hands and being the quick-witted little thing she was, she wasn't about to let the Pastor kill me in front of the congregation. After the Pastor preached, he called for Miss Mabel to play the organ for the invitation. Maddie stepped into the aisle and come forward. She glanced across the aisle at me and gave me a devilish grin.

"What has the Lord put on your heart, little Maddie?" The Pastor put both hands on his knees and bent into her face. She stepped back.

"I . . . uh . . . I . . ."

The Pastor straightened up and grasped her shoulder. "Does Satan have your tongue too?"

"No, Pastor. I'm just nervous. I wanna give my heart to Jesus."

I covered my eyes. *Please, Lord. Don't let the Pastor hurt Maddie.*

Maddie was always good at comin' up with ideas on the spur, and when the Pastor took to smiling at her decision, she wheeled around at me and winked. What happened next was nothing short of funny.

"Pastor, I feel the Lord movin' in my heart. I feeeel Him reachin' in and yankin' at the strings." Maddie pressed her hands against her chest, then fell to her knees. She commenced to flail at her chest. "Lord, come into my heart. Make me a child of Yours. Fill me, Lord." She stretched her hands toward the ceiling. I just prayed the Lord wouldn't strike her down for lyin'.

"Amen." The Pastor clapped his hands. "Amen. Make her a child of Yours."

Maddie jumped to her feet and commenced to hop around the front of the church squealing praises to God. "Praise the Lord, for I am a child of the King. Play me a song, Miss Mabel. I wanna sing this joy to the whole congregation. Play something lively."

Lively to Mabel Whaley was "Bringing in the Sheaves." She only knew a handful of songs and this was the toe tapper. She played an introduction and Maddie took hold of the Pastor's hand, leading him around the front and singing, "We shall come rejoicing, bringing in the sheaves."

Momma stood and began to clap. Pierce Thomas started to stomp his foot, and before you knew it, Maddie had the whole congregation belting out a melody. She jumped on the pew, waved her hands, praised God, and jumped down again. I couldn't help but giggle and join in the singing. I knew what Maddie was doing. But the Pastor . . . the Pastor was snowed. He thought he'd preached the sermon that moved the mountain. What with Maddie stirring the emotions of the people, there ended up being two baptisms and three rededications.

Maddie saved me that day. Who knows what the Pastor would have done because I couldn't open up and sing, but as it stood, the Pastor went home singing his own praises for doing the work of the Lord in a commendable way.

The dreaded trip home from church was not as bad as it could have been. Maddie's father lifted her into their wagon and tipped his hat to the Pastor. The girl lifted her hands into the air and hooted once more for good measure.

Slouch groaned as she pulled the wagon loose from a rut in the road. The Pastor took his hat and dropped it on my head.

"That was a good service, Pastor." I pushed his hat away from my face. "You preached a good sermon."

Momma smiled and nodded in agreement. "Mercy's right, Pastor. Look how the Lord worked in you today."

"You saved Maddie's soul, Pastor. Now I'll see her in heaven." I swallowed hard and crawled to my knees in the back of the wagon. I leaned forward and wrapped my arms around the Pastor's neck. "Thank you, Pastor. Thank you for saving Maddie."

The Pastor pulled back on the reins. "Whoa there, Slouch." The horse came to a halt. I wondered if I'd made a mistake hugging the Pastor. He crawled out of the wagon, wrapped his arms around my waist, and swung me around in a circle.

"It was a good day. And you sung a beautiful song." The Pastor squeezed me, then kissed my cheek. I was afraid 'cause the devil could turn on you like a mad cat. But even in my fear, for a brief moment I felt the loving arms of a father. I chose to claim his affection as real love, even when I knew better.

"Oh Pastor, you are a true servant," Momma added. The Pastor helped Momma down and the three of us walked a ways into the field. Grass stood knee high and the smell of lavender filled the air. The Pastor held my hand and Momma's too. Ever once in a while, he'd bring them to his lips and kiss 'em.

I reckon Maddie did me a real favor that day. She'd kept me out of harm's way and she'd softened the Pastor's heart just enough that I got to see a real man . . . not a monster.

———

The brisk mountain breeze carried the scent of the newly built cedar pews across the way. Along with it the sweet harmony of the congregation's voices. "Surely goodness and mercy shall follow me . . ."

I wondered if these melodious notes streaming across the mountain were God's way of pressing at me. I pulled the feather pillow over my head to muffle the convicting music. The tune and the words seared my mind, and they continued to burn clean through to my heart. Occasionally I'd catch a word or so from Samuel. He rarely raised his voice, but any good preacher who called himself a man of the cloth would shout every once in a while. Words like *forgiveness*, *sovereignty*, and *eternity* seeped through the pillow that covered my head. I don't doubt the Lord exists, but I question that He's good. As much as His words of forgiveness crept into my head, they were blocked from anywhere near my heart. *I blame You, God. Why would You let all the bad happen? That ain't love.*

"Surely goodness and mercy shall follow me, all the days, all the days of my life." I sat up on my bed and slung my pillow across the room. "Surely to goodness you can stop followin' me anytime now," I shouted. "Ain't it enough I have to live with Mercy as a name? Ain't it enough I have to hear it every day? Ain't it enough? Surely goodness . . . ain't it enough?"

I knew the Lord was gnawin' at my heart like a dog at a soup bone, but I was planning on starving if that was the only food offered.

TWENTY-THREE

IT SEEMED I SPENT every minute I was free of chores walking the riverbank. Listening. Searching. Some days I'd follow the river two or three miles up the mountain. Even as the season started to cool, the water never stopped bubblin', and the voice of the river never hushed. It just kept comin'. Just like Samuel.

"I thought I'd find you here." Samuel skipped a rock across a relatively still pool of water. He dropped a small flat stone in my lap. "Let's see what you got."

I rubbed the stone. "You challengin' me?"

Samuel winked. "Depends on what you call a challenge." His hand dug deep into his pocket and he dropped a fistful of stones on the ground. He raised his brow. "What do you consider a challenge?"

I stood up slowly and ran my finger around the thin edge of the stone. I set it perfect between my thumb and forefinger. Then I dropped my arm by my side and whipped my wrist toward the river, making the stone dance far across the water.

Samuel slapped his leg and laughed. "That was some toss. I reckon it skipped four times."

I pressed my hands against my hips, proud. "Doubt you can beat that. Took me forever to learn how much spin to put on a rock for four jumps."

Samuel knelt. He dug through the pile of stones searching for the perfect bullet. "I got an idea."

I burst out laughing. "Now you have an idea. Trying to save face?"

"Tryin' to help *you* save face." He grabbed a stone. "So here's the challenge. I hit five skips with this stone and you tell me a desire of your heart."

"Really, Samuel? You never let up." I sat on a rock and dangled my feet over the water.

"I thought it was a fair challenge."

"Ain't no challenge. It's blackmail."

"What I figured." He twisted the stone between his fingers.

"What you figured? What does that mean?" I crawled to my feet.

"You're so busy being tough, you ain't got the time or skill to take me up on the offer."

There was something about this man that drove me off the ledge. I've yet to figure if it was his straight, white teeth and strong smile, or his annoying way. But Samuel could raise a hair on me faster than a dog after a cat. "You ain't suckin' me into your game."

"It's not a game. It's a challenge."

"Pleeease." I turned my back.

Samuel's hand sneaked around my waist and waved the stone. I smacked him. "Stop it. I ain't no kid you can taunt."

He kicked a rock into the water. "Yep, guess you'll never know if I got five hops in me or not."

"You ain't," I snapped. "You're no real country boy."

"Oh, but I am a country boy. I ain't always been a preacher."

"Right. You ain't always been a preacher. Part of the time you were just a pain in the . . ."

Samuel bent his knees then drew back. He flicked the stone so hard I heard his fingers snap. The rock sailed over the bank, landed low on the edge of the water and skipped.

"There she goes. One, two, three, four, five . . . oh, yes. Six."

After I closed my mouth, I grabbed a stone from the pile and licked my fingers. I aimed downstream in hopes the current would catch it. One eye squinted and my tongue peeked out my mouth. I drew back and whipped the rock. "Now count, loser."

"Ohh! Good sling. One, two, three, four, five, six. Tie!" I felt rage rise to the surface. "Tie. Shucks. Couldn't meet the challenge." Samuel slapped his knee and laughed.

I walked straight to him, put out my hands and shoved. He went back on one foot, arms spinning trying to keep his balance. As he toppled over the edge of the rock, he did the unthinkable. He grabbed my arm. I went over top of him, headfirst into the river. When I opened my eyes I was staring at the bottom. A hand snugged around my shoulder and rolled me to my back. Samuel, laughing hard, pushed the wet strands of hair from my face. His hand tighted around my chin, and he pulled me into his lips.

The water was like ice and I was sure that was why I chilled. He'd caught me off guard. Pulled me straight into his trap and that made me mad. When I tried to pull away from him, his grip gently tightened. Samuel looked into my eyes and let go.

"I know what you want. Now, I know."

"You think you know everything. So you tell me what I want."

Samuel wrapped his arm around me and pressed my head into his shoulder. "You want to be loved, Mercy. Let me love you."

"Stop it."

"No. I won't stop. I won't quit. Because I knew the day I laid eyes on you that I—"

"You what?"

"That I wanted to . . . to . . ." He gently pressed his lips against mine again and for an instant I found comfort. Quiet. Peace.

Samuel helped steady me on my feet. He snagged his hat from an eddy circling a rock and started toward the bank.

A guy who can skip a stone six times can't be all bad.

Words stuck in my throat as he walked away. The water rushed past me and its voice seemed to guide me.

Speak. Say something.

"Gentleness." I took a step.

Samuel turned. "What?"

"I want gentleness. No pain, no torture. I want to close my eyes at night and know I can sleep in peace. I want to walk the river without looking over my shoulder and seeing the ghost of the Pastor. I want someone to be gentle to me."

"Easy enough."

Samuel slapped his hat against his leg. Water splattered. He nodded and walked away. I stood ankle deep in the icy waters of the Indian River watchin' him walk away . . . and I felt . . . warmed.

TWENTY-FOUR

EARLY NOVEMBER HAD taken the beauty of the colored leaves and changed them to brown.

Fall was taking a strong hold. The nip in the morning air became a bite and it hung on for the better part of the day. There was something comforting about the briskness of morning. The weight of the cool air pushed the smoke from Isabella's fireplace low to the ground, and the scent of fresh-burnt hickory made my stomach growl.

Isabella's trips to visit Braden dwindled to an occasional walk, and I found myself sitting by the river more than walking to the graves. If I didn't go there, I wouldn't be haunted by my loss. I didn't think as much of the Pastor either. I owe that purely to Samuel's continual prodding to tell him more of my past. There was one thing for sure. The nightmares might have lessened, but my hate for the Pastor and his unforgiving God remained kindled in my heart.

"Mercy." A whistle streamed across the field where I bundled the last remaining summer hay. "Hey, Mercy." The preacher flapped his arms as he ran across the hayfield.

"What? I'm busy."

"I can see that. I told you to wait and I'd help you finish baling this hay when it dried up in the afternoon."

"Well, Preacher, you know what they say. Idle hands is the devil's workshop."

The preacher took hold of the makeshift rake and pulled a pile of hay remnants into a stack. I snugged it tight then wound three strands of twine around the bundle.

"'And if one prevail against him, two shall withstand him; and a three-fold cord is not quickly broken.' That's from Ecclesiastes." Sweat dampened his face.

"I know. Ecclesiastes 4:12." I rolled my eyes and continued to work.

"I'm just saying, a cord of three strands is strong. That's how you wrapped the bundle. And why wouldn't you wait?" Samuel asked. "I'm a man of my word."

"I guess I wasn't in the mood to have you harp on my history . . . dig at my wounds. Sometimes you're like a youngin scratchin' off scabs making a sore bleed. Guess I ain't willin' to bleed today."

"Mercy, I'm only trying—"

"To help. I know, Samuel. But maybe what you don't get is I don't want help. I made this bed and I have to make my way out."

Samuel swiped his forehead with his handkerchief. "You'd be a wonderful mother."

"What?" I stopped bailing the hay and stared into his deep green eyes.

"I was just thinkin' how good you are with Isabella's girls and with Braden."

"I guess I appreciate the thought. But lovin' youngins and being a mother are two different things, Preacher. They ain't no room in my life for a youngin." I went back to working on the hay. "Or a man for that fact."

"Can't you let me just once offer you a compliment? Just once?"

He dropped the rake and turned to stand toe-to-toe with me. The cool fall breeze turned into a constant wind that whipped my hair in circles. Samuel lifted my chin and looked me in the eye.

"You would be a beautiful bride. A wonderful wife." He pressed his palm against my cheek. "You would. Maybe someday you'll open your eyes to that."

Samuel dropped his hand and walked away.

I stood there for some time and watched him make his way across the field, kicking at weeds. I wondered just how foolish I was. That was the closest thing to a proposal I'd had since Thomas. But when your life is consumed with hate and vengeance, there's no room for forgiveness and love. So I watched as Samuel walked away from me. I'd made a choice, and the choice was not him.

Maybe someday, I thought. Right now, though, I had to live with the guilt.

Isabella stood carving a pumpkin into slices while the girls watched. She laid bits of mashed pumpkin on a plate for them to finger. I pushed open the door and carried a newly dressed hen toward the fire pit next to the house.

"Baked chicken," I said.

"Oh good. Terrance told me this morning he was toting home a guest today."

"I hope it's not one of them Ramey boys. Those varmints are good workers, but they have yet to learn basic table manners."

Isabella laughed. "I don't think you have to worry about that. He told me to make a bed for a guest in the loft. Said it was a surprise."

"I can't imagine what kind of surprise Terrance would find on this mountain. We know everybody they is to know."

I scraped some salt from the block over the hen, then covered the pot.

"The preacher is holding a fall prayer meeting in the church tonight too. Can I twist your arm to come along?"

"You can twist, but I probably won't come."

"Mercy Roller, you've been mad at God long enough. When are you going to make peace?"

I hung the cast iron pot close to the fire. "This ought to be ready about the time you get home. Providin', that is, the preacher don't go off on a tangent."

"I pray for you every day." Isabella squeezed my arm. "I pray the good Lord will drop them scales off your eyes, just like He did Paul, and let you see there's a man here who loves you, who wants you. I pray for your peace, and I hope you'll give up the bitterness."

I kissed Isabella's cheek. "You, Terrance, and these babies is all I need. It's all I want. I'm happy."

I was happy. I guess I was . . . as happy as I could be considering the circumstances. It wasn't easy learning to love a family, or to let them love me back. And it was just as hard getting used to the fact they weren't going to wake me up from a dead sleep to torture me. Isabella was right. I needed to let the scales fall off my eyes, but what I was afraid of was worse than being blinded.

"The green beans are cooking and the corn is laying shuck side up by the fire. That hen will be ready in a couple of hours. Now get those girls bundled up and in the wagon." I headed into the house to get an extra blanket to cover them on the trip across the field.

The sound of a team of horses pulled to a halt in front of the house. I grabbed the blanket and opened the door. "Wait, Isabella. Them girls need an extra blanket."

I thought I'd experienced all the hurt, surprise, and sin a person could. But nothing prepared me for what I saw when I opened that door. Nothing readied me for the wrath of the good Lord.

Isabella stood at the porch steps, both girls in tow, and Terrance in all his innocence, stood there smiling like a cat who'd brought his master a catch. I heard it loud and clear—the voice of the Lord: *Mercy, it's time.*

I didn't know whether to be joyous or filled with despair. Terrance stepped forward.

"I reckon I've brung home a stray. Found this woman down in Chattanooga. She was headin' back across the gap. Thought she could use a little rest, seein' her condition and all."

The moment was odd. Awkward. When I finally managed to find my words, I stepped toward the stairs.

"Momma?"

TWENTY-FIVE

"MOMMA?" I STOOD in shock.

"Mercy, Mercy. My baby girl."

Her face was drawn and wrinkled, her eyes sunken and her stomach stretched well into the eighth month of pregnancy. Skin sagged from her arms and around her neck. Despite the size of her stomach, she was thin and frail. She giggled as she touched a strand of my hair.

"Cat got your tongue?"

I grabbed at my mouth, remembering this was the Pastor's cue to cast out a demon.

"You're pregnant? When did you get married? Better yet, what are you doing here?" It had only been a few months since the Pastor died.

Momma rubbed her hands up and down her arms and shivered. "Mr. Johnson here helped fix my cabin after a rain storm broke down one side of the roof. When he run into me in Chattanooga, we got to talking and, seein' I was a widow and all, he offered to bring me here till this youngin comes."

"Widow?" I'd thought of Momma as a lot of things, but widowed was never one.

"When he was workin' on my house, I told him I put my only daughter out on her own and I'd prayed the good Lord would forgive my sin. Bring her back to me."

"You're pregnant. Why would you want me?" I asked.

Terrance pushed his hat back on his head. "You mean to tell me *Mercy* is your *daughter*?"

Momma ignored him and kept talkin'.

"I've been sick. Real sick. That's why I was in Chattanooga, huntin' for Doc Mosley. And now that I'm with child, I need to know you forgive me. I need to know you'll be here to help me raise this baby."

"Hold up here a minute." Terrance stepped between me and Momma. "You're the Pastor's wife?" His head swung toward me. "Mercy, this your momma?"

"Raise your baby?" I burst into laughter. "Why ain't the daddy stepping out like a man and taking hold of his child?"

"He can't, Mercy."

"Can't or won't?"

"Now just hold it a cotton pickin' minute." Terrance rubbed his chin. "I want an answer."

I went toe-to-toe with Terrance. "You want answers. I'll give you answers. Yes! Terrance, meet my momma. Of all the strays you coulda dragged in, you found my momma. Reckon that's fate?"

Momma shoved her way around Terrance. "Mercy, wait."

I stepped inside the cabin and tried to push the door closed but Momma's hand slipped inside. I couldn't believe Momma had the gall to hunt me down like an animal then hit me up to nurse her and help her raise a child. Lord knows she needed help. She sure as the devil didn't raise me like she shoulda.

"Any real man would take his rightful place and help you raise your baby. This ain't my concern."

"Oh, but it is your concern."

I looked to the sky and laughed. "This is some joke, God. You're just a regular jester."

There was nothing, as far as I could see, that was my concern. She'd gone and got herself in a family way. That wasn't my doin'.

"Wait, Mercy." Momma's voice trembled and cracked. "I'm pregnant with the Pastor's last seed."

"Well, if that ain't a face slapper." I started counting days in my head. "So," I said at last, "you was carryin' this baby when I whacked that horse and set you free. Right?"

It made sense. The months would be about right for her to give birth to a dead man's child. A man I'd killed. That made it my concern.

"I reckon you're right. It's my fault that baby ain't got no daddy." I looked at Samuel then glanced toward Isabella and shrugged. "Life has a way of coming back to bite you, don't it, Preacher?"

"I suspected I was new with a child, but I wasn't sure. It was early on."

"No, Momma, you knew. You knew and you never said a word. Afraid the Pastor would call your baby a demon and kill it too?"

Isabella slipped her arm around Momma's fat waist and helped her inside. "Mercy."

"Don't say it, Isabella. Don't utter the words. I'll do what is right."

I brushed past Samuel and walked outside. I picked up a basket and shoved in a few pieces of wood.

"Mercy," Samuel said.

"I need to build a fire in the shack. It's getting cold and she looks ready to pop. Babies don't need no chill."

"Mercy?"

"You'll have to give up your side of the shack. Momma will need some space till after this baby comes. I know you won't mind. You're good like that."

"Mercy!" Samuel's voice was stern.

"What, Samuel? What?" The evening wind was brisk and the steam from my breath begin to show.

"Gentleness comes when gentleness is given."

I dropped the bucket and walked right up to Samuel. "So this is how you twist my words?"

"No. It's that usually our greatest needs are our greatest weaknesses. Me, I want more than anything to have the same thing Isabella and Terrance have. A family, a home, someone to talk to. But my greatest desire is my biggest weakness. Sometimes you have to give that desire before you can have it. That's all I'm saying."

I put my hand against his chest and shoved him back a step. "Bring an extra log or two when you come. Give me some time to make space for Momma."

The Pastor's last seed. That just figures. He was like a weed. Pull him from one garden and he sprouts again in the next.

The wind howled around the edge of the shack and as the sun set, the

sky turned a deep orange. The glow across the river should have brought
me peace. Instead, it brought me rage. It looked like hell had opened up
over the ridge.

I lifted my hand toward the blazing sky and shouted, "This your way
of getting even?"

I know it ain't possible, but I could have sworn I heard the river talk.
It was as clear as a bell:

Blessed are the poor in spirit for theirs is the kingdom of heaven. Blessed
are they that mourn: for they shall be comforted. Blessed are the meek: for
they shall inherit the earth. Blessed are they which do hunger and thirst after
righteousness: for they shall be filled. Blessed are the merciful: for they shall
obtain mercy.

There it was. My name and Samuel's wisdom, put together. "I get it.
You have to give mercy to get it."

I headed into the shack to make room for Momma.

I was stubborn. Even hateful at times. But stupid was never one of my
gifts. Fate had brought hate and guilt to me, just like a cat dropping its
mouse at my feet. Now I had to accept the gift and open it. It was time
to give some mercy.

TWENTY-SIX

"MERCY, GET ME OUT of this bed."

Momma's voice screeched like a tattered bow on a beat-up fiddle. Her sweet nature had soured. I reckon that was my fault too. Here she was. Pregnant and bossin' me around. Where was the mercy in that? I got her to her feet and walked her to the porch.

It wasn't right of me, but I leaned against the door frame and hollered and laughed. There was nothing left for me to do but laugh. In the months I'd been with the Johnsons and the preacher, I'd about cried all the tears I could cry. I'd managed to tell Isabella and the preacher about all I could tell them . . . all I could remember about the Pastor, Thomas, and my baby, Angel.

"I know forgiveness is hard, Mercy," the preacher said. "But they won't never be peace until you come to grips with it, face it, and let it go."

"Let it go," I shouted. "Let it go. Easy for you to say. It wasn't you the Pastor beat to an inch of your life. It wasn't you he raped and tortured. It wasn't you he forced to have a hand in his killins."

"Mercy, listen to me. The good Lord used you to save Isabella and those babies. He used you to love little Braden with the kind of love few understand. Let Him help you this time. Let me . . ."

It wasn't that I didn't appreciate what the preacher was trying to do. He'd managed to peel away one layer of my pain. I know he was trying to look out for my best interest. His heart was good and intentions right. But I was a stubborn cuss and the taste of bitterness don't go away easy. I wondered at times how I could hold those sweet babies of Isabella's and love them like I did, what with the bitterness that welled up inside me.

I was considering looking up to the Lord, pondering drawing a truce, and then this. Bringing Momma back into my life, and bringing her in pregnant. What kind of God would do that? Fact was, here she stood in front of me, ripe with a youngin and somewhat proud this child was the Pastor's last seed. All I could think was *lordy, lordy*.

Crazy as it was, I found myself echoing my own name the way the mountain folk did. *Lord have mercy.* It stung enough to hear others say it, but it burned when I said it myself.

Isabella stared at me. "Mercy, I want you to know, you don't have to do this. But if you do, we'll be right here ready to help." She climbed the step to the porch and leaned into my cheek, her arms filled with babies. "I know you'll do the right thing." She kissed my cheek and I wrapped the wool Indian blanket around the girls—the same blanket Momma was wrapped in when Terrance delivered her to the door.

"Isabella, stop worrying." I leaned to whisper. "I'll take care of Momma. I promise not to kill her." I chuckled at my joke, but Isabella found no laughter in it.

I wanted to smack Terrance. How could he do this to me? But the truth was, he didn't know Reba was my momma. Momma couldn't have known I was the one who delivered babies. It all boiled back around to God Almighty. Him and His so called "plan," as the preacher reminded me.

Terrance pulled the wagon around to the shack and helped Isabella in, then bedded the girls into a warm nest of hay just behind the wagon seat.

"We're goin' down to the Whaley's for a spell. You be alright here with your momma?"

I gritted my teeth. My eyes squeezed into a squint. I reckon that was Terrance's way of letting me know he expected me to behave without actually sayin' it.

"Yeah." I glanced at Momma. "We'll be fine. I guess we got a lot of catchin' up to do. You know, things like her bein' pregnant and all. Guess it would be nice to find out if there's anything else I need to know."

Terrance pressed his fingers to his lips, and pointed them toward me. I could have sworn I felt the kiss land on my forehead.

"Hup, there, horse. Hup."

Slouch had made her place on the farm. Terrance had promoted her to lead on the yoke. Funny that the horse was happy and I still struggled.

The wagon pulled loose from the grass. Isabella turned and waved. Then there I stood. Eyeball to eyeball with the woman who'd given birth to me. I stood looking her in the face, and wondered how she could have allowed the Pastor to do the horrible things he'd done to me.

"How could you, Momma?" The November wind was piercing but my heart already felt cold.

"How could I what, Mercy?" She clasped her hands beneath her belly to support the weight of the child. "How could I what?"

All them years of hate boiled to the surface. I drew back my hand to slap her. She closed her eyes and flinched, waiting for the blow. I dropped my hand to my side.

"No, I ain't my daddy. I ain't him."

It wasn't that I hated Momma. I did, but I didn't. It was bittersweet. More like I loved the woman but hated her ways. I couldn't understand why she did what she did. Why she condoned the Pastor's actions, hid away his nasty secrets. Fear and force do terrible things to a body. But when I set us both free, she sent me packin'. Said I wasn't her child. I wonder now, if she knew she was carrying that baby. It was her own little secret.

"You knew," I said. "You knew about them horrible acts. All of them."

She bent her head toward the floor.

"You knew the Widow was one of the Pastor's monthly visits. You knew he mauled her when his sick passions flooded."

"I knew."

"You knew and you let him." She said nothing. "You let him do the same thing to Mabel, to Elsi all in the name of cleansing. All in the name of God. And you knew Bet was the Pastor's seed, not Stanley's."

"I knew." Her voice cracked when she spoke and her chin commenced to quiver.

"And Stanley. Poor Stanley."

That day by the river flooded back to me. It rushed over me like a wild rapids over the rocks. A sharp wind sent a chill over me, and Momma waivered as she stood. She pressed her hand against the side of the house to hold herself upright. I had no intentions of offering to help. *Let her fall,* I thought. *Serves her right.* And she did just that. Momma's knees buckled and she went to all fours on the porch.

"I did what I did to save your life. To save my life."

"Save my life? You let him nearly beat me to death to save my life? You defended that evil son of the devil, and let him kill Stanley, a repentant man. You knew about the Widow, and when she got drunk she got loose-lipped. You let him kill her to keep his nasty secret."

I suddenly understood the power behind the river. The power of the rush of the water and how such a crystal blue beauty could become the devil itself. I suddenly understood how in one swift swoosh, the river could wash the land clean, and every bit of the power bubbled inside of me. I went to my hands and knees and stared in her eyes.

"You let him kill my baby. You let him kill Thomas. You, you . . . are as much Satan as he was."

Momma lifted her hand and sobbed. "Forgive me, baby. Mercy, forgive me."

I glared into her face and all the hate of almost twenty years rose up in me like a monster.

"God have mercy on me and my child." Momma crawled to the porch rail and pulled herself up. She wept like none I'd ever heard. Her cries echoed across the valley. I could have killed her at that second. I could have grabbed her by the neck and snapped it like a chicken neck. All the horrible things the Pastor had done twisted through my head. My hands balled into fists, I thought of wailing her to death.

Momma slumped there like a lump of unmolded clay. She was beat down, broken, and begging *me* for mercy.

The wind whistled and brought back to mind the words of the congregants singing in the church the night before. *Surely goodness and mercy shall follow me. All the days, all the days of my life.* I touched Momma's face, deep with wrinkles. My fingers followed along her jaw and around her chin.

The years of torment from the Pastor had taken their toll on her. The skin that was so tight and soft when I was a child had hardened into crevices. The eyes I remembered were no longer sky blue, but were beads of black. She'd paid a price. One certainly as big, if not bigger than mine.

They say when a man finds forgiveness he feels it deep inside. Samuel told me over and over how it felt to be a changed man, but I could never get ahold of the idea. Now, here I sat with the perfect chance to end my hate. To snuff out the last ember of a life that haunted me. I could have my revenge. Make her pay. Make the Pastor pay. But all I did was wrap my arms around Momma while she sobbed. I gave her mercy. Grace.

Every bit of the anger I'd harbored blew away like leaves in the breeze. A burden was lifted from my shoulders. I stood Momma to her feet and guided her back inside the shack. I stoked the fire, covered her with two blankets, and sat in the pinewood rocker to hold vigil.

Gentleness comes when gentleness is given.

I hated it when Samuel was right. But he was and it was time I learned how to give instead of how to survive.

I brushed my hand across Momma's cheek and uttered the second hardest thing I'd ever said. "I hate you've been through this, Momma. I hate it for both of us." I wanted to tell her I forgave her, but my heart wasn't ready. It was takin' on a soft spot, feeling compassion, but I wasn't in no place yet to say I'd forgive her, so I leaned to her ear and whispered, "I love you, Momma. Despite it all. I love you."

Her face twisted and her eyes took on a glassy look. I saw her change. Something about her changed. She said nothing.

After a long silence, I poured a cup of hot coffee and set it by her. "How long until this baby comes?" I asked.

"Days, hours. It's close."

The latch on the door clicked and Isabella popped her head around the door.

"You're back. I thought you'd gone to the Whaley's with Terrance."

"I did, but I couldn't leave you alone, so I trekked back across the fields. Their place ain't that far. Samuel went with Terrance, and the girls are with them. Seems Terrance wants to show off his youngins." She leaned over Momma and checked her. "She's weak."

"I know."

"I can stay tonight and you stay with the girls at the house."

"No. Your place is with your babies."

"Mercy."

"I know, Isabella." And I did know. I knew exactly what she wanted to say, but there was no point. My heart was changing. Momma had dozed off to sleep so I pulled Isabella to the far side of the cabin. "I know you love me. I've never been loved like you and Terrance love me. Even from this woman that gave me birth, I've never felt the love of a family except what has come from you."

"Like Samuel loves you?"

I'd seen the look in Samuel's eyes. I knew his thoughts. But at the same time, he didn't deserve a wretch like me. "Samuel deserves better."

I remembered the time Momma rocked me and sang *Amazing Grace, how sweet the sound that saved a wretch like me.* It was a bit of a comfort, but Samuel . . . he was a good man. He didn't need my hand of cards dealt to him too. I'd never be able to offer him the comfort and love he deserved. "I'm broke. Used. Worthless. A man like Samuel is owed someone who's complete."

Isabella sat at my feet and laid her head in my lap. She wrapped her arms around my legs and squeezed. "We're gonna have us a baby." A smile came across her face. "Another sweet baby. Come get me if you need me." She climbed to her feet and headed out the door.

That was the night I found an ounce of love, or it found me . . . and I let it. It was the start. And like a vine, once its seeds are planted, you can't stop them from sprouting. Good vines produce good fruit, and I knew through the years they was good planted in me. Edom and Pactol always seemed to be the Johnny Appleseed of my life, poking words of encouragement, hope, and forgiveness in the tilled dirt of my soul. I wondered for a time, how I could have forgotten them. I suppose a body gets so tied up in their own pain, they tend to lose sight of the tidbits that make them decent folk.

Momma wallowed back and forth on the bed, half in sleep and half out. "Lord, Lord have mercy," she muttered.

My heart was pierced by the words. And for the first time, I felt like the Lord really did have mercy.

This time . . . it was on me.

Twenty-Seven

The door to the shack creaked open and Samuel peered around the edge. The soft golden glow of the oil lamp caught a glint of his clear green eyes. His hat in his hand, he nudged the heavy door. The wind had simmered down, but the night air sneaked in behind him, blowing up the edge of the blankets that covered Momma.

"Everything quiet here?" he whispered. "May I?" He pointed to Momma. I nodded and he gently eased the corner of the blanket around her neck. "She nodded off a while ago. I ain't rightly sure she's slept much in days."

"When's the baby coming?"

"Don't know. Anytime I guess. She ain't real sure, but she's ripe."

Samuel knelt in front of me and brushed my face. There were those eyes again. They'd called to my heart more than once, and that night they wormed their way in. Goosebumps rose on my arms at the touch of his knuckles against my cheek. I wanted to let him in. Wanted to say yes to his kindness, but fear just wouldn't let me.

"It's been several months since you last saw her. Did you know she was pregnant when you left?" He reached and pulled a stool close. Its feet scrubbed across the rugged plank floor, sending a screech through the room.

"She sent me away. And no, I didn't know she was pregnant."

"It was good of you to take her in."

"Maybe," I said.

"She don't look well."

"She ain't. She's half starved, half crazy, and pregnant. The odds is stacked against her."

Samuel tossed a log on top of the fire. It caught and blazed. The flames grew blue, and the hickory popped and cracked as the fire whittled into its flesh. There was little as soothing as the smell of hickory. Its woodsy scent carried the beauty of the fall inside. It made things feel like, well . . . home.

"Wanna tell me what happened?" Samuel asked.

"Not really. But you're just like an old hound. Once you got a bone, can't nobody take it from you."

He smiled and rested his arm on the back of my chair. "That be the case, then just tell me."

I stood and moved to the small stove that heated the brass coffeepot. Samuel followed.

"Coffee?" I whispered.

"Yep. And you will tell me, won't you?"

"Preacher, I ain't figured you out yet. Either you're just nosey, or the good Lord give you the gift of persistence."

"I like to think it's a gift," he said. I was sure he did. Who wouldn't prefer to think their bad habit is a gift of God, rather than a true annoyance? "But I reckon it's divided. One half nosey and one half caring for you."

"She admitted everything," I said.

"Everything?"

"Yes. Everything. She didn't deny one thing I threw at her from the Widow up the holler to Stanley, to the horrible things she let happen to me. All of it."

"And how did that make you feel?"

I stood and wrapped my blanket tight around my shoulders. My patience were slim, but I tried to contain the frustration. "I'll tell you how it made me feel. I wanted to wail her to death. Actually considered it. I wanted to beat her like the Pastor beat me. And every hit would be for someone else's indiscretion. I wanted to kill her, Samuel. Kill her."

Samuel stood quiet.

"Ain't you got no words from the Good Book for that?"

"Keep your voice down. Let's not wake her," he said.

I threw my arms into the air. "Not wake her?"

Like I needed to care. And I did . . . need to care. I felt the words come from my mouth, but the sting didn't seem as harsh, and that sorta made me mad.

"Mercy is right. I take the blame," Momma whispered. Samuel pulled his chair next to the bed and took Momma's hand.

"Mrs. Roller, I'm Samuel Stone. I'm the preacher on this side of the mountain." Momma strained a smile. "Mercy, would you get her some soup? Look in my bag. Isabella sent hot soup."

I was a little surprised Samuel had given me an order. Well at least something close to one. He did at least ask. I opened his bag and pulled out the leather stitched bowl, damp with hot soup. I gathered a wood bowl from the shelf, and a cup, then poured Momma a sip. Samuel lifted her by the shoulders and tipped the cup gently against Momma's lips.

"You're a preacher?"

"Yes'm. I'm a preacher."

"I remember when the Pastor was young and handsome like you." She lifted her hand to Samuel's cheek.

"Momma. Stop." I pushed her hand away from Samuel. He looked at me as though I'd slapped him. "She's got no business touching you."

"Mercy. You have to give gentleness to get it."

I caught myself. For an instant, I'd taken on protector of the preacher. Maybe it was jealousy. I just knew Momma had no right touching this kind man. It was like I thought her touch would ruin him. Ruin his heart. Ruin his attention toward me. He was a good man and I couldn't bear Momma's hands on his skin. I shoved Samuel to one side and took the cup.

"Momma, sit up. Let's get some warm soup down you." Samuel helped me lift her and I supported her with a pillow, just like I did Braden when I needed him to sit straight.

"Preacher, I need to talk. I need to tell you some things." Momma groaned.

Fear wrapped around me like a dark, cold night. What could she possibly want to tell Samuel?

"Momma, I ain't sure you're talking in your right mind just now. You're tired and starved. You ain't got your wits about you. Wait and talk to Samuel in a couple of days."

"No, Mercy. Let her talk. When the good Lord lays something on someone's heart, it ain't ours to stifle."

Momma proceeded to tell Samuel a list of her indiscretions. She admitted to telling the Pastor about me and Thomas running off to get married. And how she told the Pastor where to look for me. Then she babbled on about Elsi, Stanley, the Widow, others.

I knew these things. I remembered them. I just never wanted to believe Momma had a hand in them.

"A woman does things she'd not ordinarily do when she's afraid," Momma told Samuel. "I was afraid of the Pastor. Afraid if I didn't tell him, he'd not just beat me or Mercy, but he'd kill us."

She went on for the better part of an hour and with each story she told, Samuel's green eyes filled with tears. His chin trembled and he bit his lip to stop himself from sobbing. Once he pulled out his Bible and started to read from the Psalms. "The Lord is my shepherd; I shall not want." He knew those Scripture by heart, so I knew he didn't need to be opening his Bible to read them. His hands shook and I couldn't tell if it was from anger or from sickness.

Momma finally fell off to sleep. I let her lay to her side, so the weight of that baby was off her body.

Samuel stood and walked outside the door. I heard him pace the porch, and when his heels stopped clicking against the planks, I walked out to see where he was. There he stood, in the middle of the hayfield, hands stretched up toward heaven, bellowing like an angry bull. He slung his head from side to side. Wrapped his arms around himself and sobbed.

I wasn't sure what the right thing to do was. Did I dare talk to him?

Before I knew it, I'd walked across the field and stood behind him as he cried. This man who'd been the rock of strength for me, was now a mound of mush thanks to Momma.

"Preacher?" I whispered.

"I understand now, Mercy."

Those weren't words I expected to hear.

"I know you kept saying they wasn't no way I could understand. But I do. My eyes are opened."

"Are you saying you didn't believe me?"

"I didn't know, Mercy. I didn't know how much was truth and how much was just anger."

"You thought I made this up?"

"No. I didn't think that. I just didn't know how . . . how . . ."

"How true the stories were. Let me say it for you."

I felt my temper boil. Just when I thought there might be a chance for me to find peace, I learned that the one person I shared my secrets with didn't believe me, or that's how it seemed. "Well, that's just peachy."

I turned and headed toward the barn. My feet stomped so hard my knees hurt.

"Mercy, wait," Samuel called. "Wait. What about your mother?"

"What about her, Preacher? What about her?"

I pulled the latch on the barn door and walked inside. Terrance had left a lamp lit for the preacher so he could bed down. It hung several inches from the wall and well above the reach of any animal. The light cast my shadow across the barn floor and up the wall. I wanted to cry. I wanted to hit something. But instead, I dropped to my knees in the hay and cried out to the cruel God who'd brought this wrath on me.

"O Lord. My heart is broke. My life is shattered. My soul is lost. Mercy, Lord. Mercy."

Twenty-Eight

The preacher and me got to making it a habit to walk the river.

We'd managed to forge a way up the better part of the mountain until the path became nothing but boulders. I think Samuel understood my need to find the river's beginning, and though he tried to help me see that finding it would not change my life, I appreciated his efforts.

"You ain't such a bad old cuss." I pushed a tree limb from the path.

"I reckon that's a compliment. Hey, let me up ahead of you."

I smiled as Samuel slipped past me. "Can't stand being in back, Preacher?"

"Oh, no. Bein' behind you is a mighty fine view."

"Reckon God will hold you accountable for that." I tossed my walking stick to the side.

Where the path turned into boulders, Samuel extended his hand to help me. We halted at the top of the ridge. The view of the mountains went on and on. The day was crisp and cold but the sun warmed my heart.

"This is what I call the door to heaven."

"Yes, I know. You've told me before," I teased.

"You sayin' I say the same thing over and over?"

"If the shoe fits." I walked to the edge of the summit. Nothing but air on my left and a rushing river on my right. I knelt and leaned over the edge. "Makes a body want to fly like the eagle."

"Indeed." Samuel took hold of the back of my dress. "If you don't mind, I'd like to hold on to keep you from making the effort to soar."

I stood. "Samuel, can I ask you a question?"

"Sure."

"Why haven't you gone back across the mountain anymore? You made that one trip to hand over your church, but no more. You must have family. You've been here for months. Terrance and Isabella are fine. Why ain't you gone back home?"

Samuel was silent. He tinkered with his jacket. "I like it here. We've started the church on the back of Terrance's property. The neighbor folks are coming."

I knew that already. I knew those reasons. What I was hoping he'd say was he stayed because of me. I hated to admit it, but Samuel had begun to make his way into my heart and though I wasn't, what a body would say, ready to have a man in my life, I did find myself . . . comfortable around him. I guess I was looking for some sort of confirmation.

Why would a man like Samuel want to stay on Thunder Mountain because of someone like me? There was the thought and there, one more time, was a wall that protected me.

"Besides, there's work to be done. The good Lord calls and I answer. Here's where He's called me."

I felt my anger rise. "Of course. Why else would you stay?" I turned in a snit and headed down the mountain. I looked over my shoulder and saw Samuel throw up his arms.

"You never give me a minute," he shouted.

"You're a man of God. You're supposed to be up-to-snuff on things. Don't you have a divine connection with the Almighty?"

"That's stupid. You think because I'm a preacher I can read your mind?"

"No. I think you're a man of God who should be smarter than what you are."

I stormed toward the path down the mountain. Half mad, half hurt. I knew I was wrong, but just like the day I slapped that horse, I couldn't stop myself.

My reason for coming to this mountain was to save a woman and her baby from the wicked hands of a preacher. I didn't expect the hands to be kind and generous. What Samuel didn't understand was, I didn't know how to act. I didn't know how to show love. I'd never received it . . . how could I show it?

I made my way down the path, fuming and ranting under my breath.

After a spell I got the feeling I was alone, which just fueled my anger more. I'd wasted a good grumblin' comin' down the mountain.

"Samuel," I yelled. "Samuel?"

The only noise I heard was the running water of the river. I put two fingers inside my mouth and blew. A loud whistle rang up the path. Still nothing. It was like someone hit me in the stomach. What if something had happened to Samuel and I was too busy growlin' to hear? I started back up the path, first in a fast walk and then breaking into a run.

"Samuel. Where are you?"

"Down here." His voiced sounded far away.

"Down where? Where are you?" I grabbed hold of a small beech tree and leaned over the edge of the ridge. There, several feet below me, sat Samuel, cradling a woman.

"What in tarnation?"

"Run get Terrance. Get him to bring the horse and some rope. Hurry."

I strained to see the face of the wounded woman. "She conscious?"

"She is. She's weak. Go. Now!"

I know it was selfish, but even seein' this was an innocent thing, I found myself a little jealous. "Who is that, Samuel? That woman got a name?"

Samuel bent his head close to the woman's face. I saw him nod. "Sounds like she said her name's Maddie."

Twenty-Nine

I WAS NUMB. Surely Samuel didn't say Maddie. Not my Maddie. Not the Maddie from my childhood. Not the Maddie who walked away from me while the Pastor swung from the tree. Surely not.

"Mercy, go! Now!" Samuel's voice echoed up the side of the ridge. "She looks to have broke her back and she may be sufferin' some frostbite."

I couldn't believe we'd walked past her going up the mountain and didn't hear her moans. If this was my Maddie, it would be another thing to hate myself for. I pulled my skirt to my knees and run like greased lightnin' down the mountain. Overhanging branches slapped my face and briars grabbed at my ankles as I come within sight of the farm. The mountain air, fresh as it was, stung the lungs that pleaded for it.

Terrance stood splitting logs with his one good arm. I could see the sweat slinging off him when he'd swing that axe. "Terrance!" I screamed. "Come quick. Get the horse and rope. Hurry."

It took a minute for my words to register, but when they did, Terrance dropped the axe and tore across the field to the barn. I whistled and Slouch raised her head. One more whistle and she kicked into a gallop. I reckon she figured there was a carrot for her. It was only minutes, but it felt like hours.

"What's goin' on?" He threw the harness over Slouch, then tossed the ropes in the back of the wagon.

"A woman. Samuel found her down over the bluff. He ain't sure, but he thinks her back is broke."

"Land's sake. We best make haste."

Terrance slapped Slouch and took off like a raccoon after a fish. The wagon bounced hard over the lumps in the field. So hard, I grabbed around Terrance's waist and held on for dear life.

"Terrance?"

"Sorry for the bumpy ride."

"No. It ain't about the bumpy ride. I think I know that woman."

"I didn't think you was from around this part of the mountain." The wagon slammed against a rock and jumped into the air. My feet flew up and I tumbled into the flat of the wagon.

"You hurt?" Terrance peered over his shoulder.

"No worries about me. We just need to get to the end of the path." If that was Maddie, I wasn't sure what I'd do. It would be uneasy at best . . . facin' her after what I did.

The path narrowed and the hillside grew steep. Terrance pulled Slouch to a walk. She snorted and huffed as she struggled to pull the wagon.

"Ho there, girl. This is as far as the old girl can pull the weight of the wagon. How much farther?" He unharnessed Slouch and threw the ropes over his shoulder.

"Just around the bend. Quarter mile or so." I hopped over the bed of the wagon and pulled the brake against the wheels.

"You carry the ropes. I'll pull the backboard off the end of the wagon. We can lay her on that and pull her if need be."

Terrance loosened the straps that held the backboard then yanked it off the wagon. "Let's go."

I took Slouch by the harness and tugged. "Hup, girl. Come on, now."

We made our way around the bend, and when we come around the edge of the bluff I commenced to holler for Samuel.

"Samuel. You hear me?"

"Down here. We're down here. Me and Miss Maddie are down here."

Terrance peered over the edge of the bluff. "I tell you, Preacher. You got yourself in a real pickle. Ain't ya?"

Samuel chuckled. "Looks so. Toss me the rope."

"No. I'll be down there in a few. Keep your britches on."

Terrance tied one rope through the hole on the backboard and the other rope around his waist. He dropped both ropes over a strong tree limb and handed me one.

I'd not felt a rope in my hands since . . . Especially one draped over a tree limb. My palm began to burn. Sweat dripped down my cheek. It wasn't but a minute, still it was like I was holding the rope that tightened around the Pastor's neck. My stomach rolled and I tasted vomit.

"Mercy, you got the backboard. Dig one foot in the dirt and rest your other knee agin that tree. Lower that rascal down slow. You understand?"

I stared into his eyes, motionless.

"Mercy! You understand?"

"Yeah, I understand."

I did what Terrance told me, slowly slipping the backboard toward Samuel. Terrance wrapped his rope once again around the tree and then eased hisself over the bluff.

"Preacher. Help is on the way."

I couldn't see over the bluff and hold the backboard of the wagon at the same time, but I could hear Samuel and the faint voice of a woman. My mind wandered back to the day the Pastor dangled from that tree. Maddie stood eyeing me with a cold, dark stare. Too angry to see real clear that day, I later recalled seeing a tear trickle down her face. I don't think Maddie was angry at me. I think she was brokenhearted. Me and her had been through a lot as youngins, and when nobody else on earth cared an iota about me, Maddie did. When I slapped that horse and took the Pastor's life, I believe Maddie knew I'd took my own too. And she was right. That was the day I lost my innocence.

Living with Terrance and Isabella, taking care of her and the babies, getting to know Samuel, had softened me. I didn't want it to, but it seems goodness has a way of doin' just that. It put me in the mind of an old dog . . . lovin' me with no strings attached.

I thought the good Lord would leave me alone for a spell. Let me heal. But it seemed what He required of me was remorse. Samuel called it "repentance." I knew what repentance was. After all I'd been through with the Pastor, I didn't reckon it was me that needed to repent.

Here I stood, never expectin' ever to care for another human as long as I lived. Yet I did. I'd grown to love Terrance and Isabella. God knows I loved them little babies, and Samuel . . . well . . . he was wormin' his way into my heart too. Through it all, even through Momma showin' back up on our doorstep, the biggest surprise was the nudge from within. Those little hints that life wasn't always so bad.

The rope jiggled in my hands and tightened against the limb. "Brace your foot on that tree trunk and pull," Terrance shouted. "Can you do that, Mercy?"

I wrapped the rope around my wrist and snugged my foot against the poplar tree. I leaned back and felt the weight of the backboard, twice its weight. "Pull, Mercy. Come on. Put your back in it."

"I got my back in it," I hollered. A groan slipped from my mouth. My arms shook from the weight of the woman. "Hold up. Let me hook up Slouch."

I anchored the rope around the tree and whistled for Slouch. She raised her head from a stand of grass she was gnawing on. "Come here, horse." Slouch stretched her snout toward me and I grabbed the harness. I slipped the rope through the leather collar around the animal's shoulders.

"Ready," I hollered. "Push, boys."

"It's gotta be all you, Mercy. We'll push, but you gotta be the one to do the brunt."

"Aaaaaarrrrgggh," I shouted. "Aaaarrrggghh. Come on, horse. Easy, hup. Hup." Slouch leaned against the weight of rope and slowly took a few steps. Bit by bit, I held the reins and guided the rope. With each pull, Samuel and Terrance lifted the woman lying on the backboard.

"Come on, Mercy. Pull."

I slapped the reins against Slouch and she jumped. "Easy, girl. I don't need to be hung between you and a tree." The horse huffed and continued to pull.

I wanted to scream at Terrance. But the burden was worth more than a smart remark. My body ached as I tugged against the rope and the horse. It felt like I was being pulled in two.

"Push, Mercy." That was all Momma could say when I was having that baby. "Come on, push. You can do this." I wanted to slap her too, but it wouldn't have done me no good. All I could do was just what she told me. Ever time a pain would come, I'd grit my teeth and push. At least until the Pastor showed up.

I shook my head to clear the horrible memory. *Keep your mind on what you're doin'. Keep your head on.*

I pulled hard against the rope, guiding it toward a smooth place in the bluff. The tip of the backboard popped above the ledge. "Come on, Slouch, one more tug," Samuel shouted. "You can do this. I have great faith in you, Mercy Roller."

Great faith. Faith in me? I nearly let go of the rope. I don't recollect anybody ever saying they had faith in me, much less, great faith. But I could tell Samuel meant it. It wasn't just some sentence he threw at me in the heat of the moment. His head topped the bluff and he wrapped his hand around the tree, heaving himself up.

"I knew you could do it." Samuel grabbed Terrance by the waist of his trousers and dragged him up and over the ledge. My knees were weak. I couldn't tell if it was from his words, or from all the pulling I'd done. Either way, it was a minute I would never forget.

Terrance pulled the woman, board and all, the rest of the way over the rocks. Samuel and me grabbed the sides of the backboard and lifted. "Not bad for a man short a limb," Terrance said. He swiped his only hand across his forehead leaving a streak of mud.

Samuel leaned against the wagon and roared. "Terrance, this ain't funny, but then, it is."

For the next few minutes the two men slung jokes about Terrance's nub like Momma used to sling slop for the pigs. I believe the two tried to hide their worry for the woman under their sour jokes. She was in a serious shape.

Once we had her safe on the hill, I knelt to look. Leaves matted her dark hair and her face was covered in mud, but when she rolled her head toward me and smiled, I knew.

"Dear God. Maddie."

"Mercy. I found you."

THIRTY

I WALKED THE riverbank like I'd done so many times, trying to follow the river. Taking my quest. Searching.

The night was dark yet the moon, even cut in half, brightened the river. Silver streaks of moonlight bent and blurred with the eddies. I'd never heard the river cry my name like it did that night. At first I wondered if it wanted me to sink beneath its icy shield and die, then I realized the call I heard was restful.

"What you are sayin' to me?" I asked the river.

If Samuel hadda walked up on me he'd have sworn on his Bible I was lock, stock, and barrel crazy . . . talking to the river. But even when I tried for the water to snuff out my life, it spit me out. Not once, but twice. I climbed the moss-covered rocks and leaned against an overhanging tree limb. I pulled the wool coat Isabella had bartered for me tight around my neck. What I heard was a lullaby, a soothing melody as the water cascaded over boulders and made its way to who knows where.

I didn't know how much was truth and how much was just anger.

Samuel's words seared my heart. I didn't volunteer the truths of my life. They—Samuel and Isabella—forced them out of me. I was content to suffer in my own right. Be left alone. My job, I'd convinced myself, was to make sure Isabella and her girls never fell prey to a man of God and his self-righteous permissions.

Still my heart throbbed like someone stomped on it. Relentless. Harsh. The bushes behind me rustled. I jumped, startled, and my heart sank.

"Who's there?" I snapped. "Can't a person even come to the river to find peace without being hunted like a wild animal?"

Terrance stepped onto the boulder and threw one leg over the tree limb where I sat. He crawled over and tugged at the scarf tied around my head.

"What in tarnation are you doin' out here? You ought to be home with Isabella," I said.

He scooted close to me and patted my knee.

"I ought to be a lot of places but I ain't. Oughta be down by Chattanooga sawing a stand of trees for old man Hurley. He offered me enough money to last us the winter. But I ain't. Oughta be down by the house finishin' up that second bedroom for the girls. Ain't doin' that neither. But here I am. Searchin' to find you. Reckon I'm meant to be right here."

"Alright. I get it, Terrance. You oughta be a lot of places but you choose to be here, on a rock by the river with me in the middle of the night, freezing your back-of-behind off."

"Not really. Isabella got to worrying about you, so I told her I'd check on you. They wasn't no lamp lit in the window and when I pecked on the door, Samuel said he'd come to sit with Reba a spell so you could go out for a bit. I figured you'd be here somewhere. Gatherin' your thoughts."

"Well, well. Aren't you just Mr. Know-it-all?"

"That's my girl. Now you're getting it." He leaned against the tree limb. Taking ahold of his empty coat sleeve, he began to slap it against his stomach.

"What's on your mind, Terrance?" I pulled a wool saddle blanket I'd gotten from the barn, around my shoulders. The smell of hay made me sneeze.

"That was some work you did pullin' that girl up the bluff. Usin' old Slouch. It was hard to guide that rope and the horse. You did good."

"We do what we have to do. That ain't why you're here. What brings you out in the cold? Something wearin' on your mind?"

"I told you, Isabella was worried. But it's more what's on *your* mind."

"Oh great. Now I get it from you."

"Naw. Now listen. I knowed from the first day you laid eyes on me you had something you wanted to ask me and you wouldn't. So let's have it. Go ahead. Spit it out."

A smile tipped the corner of my lips. "You're kidding, right?"

"Oh no siree. I ain't a kiddin' man. It's bothered me from that first day here. So I'm here to get your peace of mind."

I wasn't sure if Terrance was messing with me or if he was serious. I had to admit through all the hardships, through all my suffering, he never once opened his mouth. Never once asked me to tell him what was wrong. Never once.

"I'll play this game of cat and mouse. I want to know what happened to make you cut off your arm. There. You happy?" I growled.

"Now that wasn't so hard, was it?" A grin widened and I looked into the hole where two teeth once lived. "I can answer that question."

"Good. See that you do. It's bugged the devil outta me since I met you."

Terrance rared back and let out a laugh. He dropped his arm around my shoulder and pulled me close. "I'll tell you what happened, if you'll tell me why you ain't been up to the house to see that girl."

"I figured as much." I turned my back to Terrance. "Wondered when you or the preacher would get around to houndin' me about Maddie."

"Ah. So you do know the girl?"

I rolled my eyes. I'd been at ease with Terrance until now. That "never asking" just turned the corner. "You'll tell me about the arm? What happened?"

Terrance pulled his hat from his head and scooped his fingers through his hair. "I reckon. It's a fair trade. But you go first. I've knowed you for a short time, Mercy Roller, but it didn't take me long to figure you was slippery as a carp. So you go first."

I couldn't help but smile. It seemed Terrance had a way of making the worst situation . . . light.

"Maddie Holmes. Her name is Maddie. We was kids on the mountain together. The girl got me in more trouble than a weasel in a mole hole. Trouble I couldn't always afford to have. But she was always my friend. Even in the worst of times."

The breeze sent a chill across the river that blistered through my coat and made me shake. Terrance nodded. He kicked the heel of his boots against the ground. I could see why Isabella loved him so much. He didn't have to say a word to let you know things would be fine. Edom would have called Terrance an encourager. Strong. Safe. A rock to lean on. He wasn't much older than Samuel, but Terrance had a wisdom about him. One that made me respect him.

"Go on," he said. "I'm listenin'."

"Me and Maddie was hitched at the hip. She always was quick on her feet. Her wit saved my hide more than once. And I'm grateful. The day I left home though, I think I broke Maddie's heart with my actions. I ain't seen her since she turned and walked away."

Terrance bumped his shoulder against mine. "Mercy, you is one of the hardest women I've ever met. You always figure folks is disappointed in you. Did it ever occur to you, they might just be surprised you took a stand?"

That was a novel idea. I was so used to people cursing the things I did . . . I just never thought the day Maddie walked away from me, that she might not have knowed what to say.

"So Mercy, why ain't you been up to talk to that girl?"

I wasn't real sure why. "I don't know, Terrance. I reckon I was afraid of what might happen. What if she hates me?"

"Ain't no sign of hate when a body searches you out. That appears to me to be love. Just like the love you showed me and Isabella. I know your reason for comin' here. I ain't no idiot. You don't have to tell me where your hate lies, or what your fear is. It screams out of you in your actions, and in the way you try to block out Samuel."

I was stunned. Terrance could read me that good?

"So here's what I'm sayin' you need to do. And I ain't really givin' you no option here, Mercy. This here family loves you and, to tell the truth, I'm dern tired of you shuttin' the barn door on us. So you're gonna get that pretty little bustle of yours up to the house, and you are goin' welcome that girl here. Thank God, she was just banged up and not broke up like we thought."

I sat straight. *How dare he tell me, Mercy Roller, what to do!*

"My family don't shun visitors. Nobody shunned you and your junk, and I expect nothin' less from you. You clear?"

I sat staring at Terrance. So this was what it was like to have a friend show you the error of your ways without beatin' the fool out of you. I wasn't scared, wasn't bleeding. But I understood Terrance not only cared for me, but he meant business.

"Yes sir. I understand."

"Good we see eye to eye here."

And we did see eye to eye. They was no shame in my rebuke, just love and direction. "So it's your turn, big boy. Tell me about the arm."

Terrance broke into a laugh. "Well, here's what happened. See, I was cutting a stand of trees out by the south field. It was the early part of the year. And ole Bull . . . you know ole Bull, right?"

I nodded. "The bull behind the barn."

"Yeah, that's the one. Well, ole Bull followed me out to the stand of trees. He's been testy with me since I slapped him on the end of the nose with a plank. That taught him to stop shoving my fence down in the back field."

"Terrance, I appreciate what you're doing here . . . tryin' to make me feel better and all, but—"

"Then you'll oblige me to finish my story." He looked me square in the eye. "Ole Bull kept eyein' me every time I'd bend over that sawmill belt. I'd push a log through and stand, push a log through and stand. But I noticed he kept watchin'. And when I finally picked up one last log, he dug them front hooves into the ground, threw some dirt, and charged me. The ole cuss did a head butt straight into the sawmill, tipping it over and knocking me under. When I tried to shove the sawmill off me, the stack of sawed logs dropped over my arm. They was so blamed heavy I couldn't pull my arm out."

I sat straight and covered my mouth with my hand. "Oh, Terrance. How did you get out?"

"Well, that's the miracle. See, Isabella had taken the team to the village at the foot of the mountain. She was aimin' to help serve up some vittles for some miners passing through town. So I was here by myself. I laid there for some time before it commenced to rain. And not just any rain. It come a gully washer. I thought I'd drown buried under those logs and that's when one of them mountain wolves come outta the woods. They smell a weak prey. I knew they wasn't nothing left to do, but coax that varmint over. So I did."

The night was bright with fireflies. The last of the warmth faded into the chill of the air. I couldn't believe my ears. Poor Terrance.

"What did you do?" I asked.

"I coaxed that critter over and it commenced to gnaw at my arm until it chewed clean through the bone."

I jumped to my feet and kicked Terrance in the hip. "You're such a liar." He'd tried hard to sucker me into his story.

He leaned back and roared in laughter, grabbing that empty sleeve and flapping it at me. Before I knew it, I was laughing too. Tears dripped off my cheeks. *What a moment*, I thought. *What a time for this kind man to get up, hunt me down in the night, and make jokes.* I couldn't stop laughing. In fact, I couldn't really remember the last time I'd laughed.

Terrance pulled me down next to him and swiped the tears off my cheek. "Now see. Them is happy tears. Them is the kind I like to see you have." He took my hand and gently lifted it to his lips. "Mercy, we call you family."

My laughter eased. "I know."

"I owe you the life of my girls and the only woman I've ever loved."

"No, you don't."

"Yes, I do. Now it ain't none of my business. And I can't say I hear the good Lord speak to me often. But when I saw that woman pregnant and sick down in the town, I knew where to bring her. I knew I needed to bring her to *our* angel of mercy. I had no idea she was your momma. None." I'd never heard my name used with such compassion. *Angel of mercy.* My heart was pricked.

He dropped his head and whispered, "I'd never hurt you . . . not intentionally." He clasped my hand tighter. "I swear I didn't know. And I didn't know Maddie was a friend. But it looks to me like you have business to take care of. It's come huntin' you. So you need to oblige it."

"Terrance. You did right. And I believe you. This has been what I've run from since the early part of the year. It's time to face the ghosts. First Momma and now Maddie. One bad and one good. But ghosts . . . memories from the past, nonetheless."

"Miss Mercy. I ain't goin' ask you to tell me all that happened. All I can say is a man can have a lot of slop throwed in his trough, but he can still pick out the bacon. And I know they is bacon here, Mercy. I know it." Terrance stood. "Baby girl. Don't stay here all night. It's droppin' to freezin', and I need both your arms."

He nudged his boot against me and I smiled.

"You sayin' I need to pick out the good things about Momma?"

"Could be. Even the bad milk makes buttermilk. And while you're at it, you might give the preacher a little slack. He's had his share of hardships too. He cares about you just like we do. I'd be willing to step out on a log and say the man loves you. Maybe you oughta best consider letting him do just that."

He took a few steps and turned back. "Oh, and ole Bull did turn the mill over on me. Broke my arm so bad, Doc couldn't fix it. So he took it off above the elbow. See," he said. "Sour milk turned to buttermilk." I watched as he disappeared into the darkness.

Terrance Johnson had the soul of a saint. A man who listened more than he spoke, who spit more than he chewed. But what an oak. Mighty. Strong. And he was right. Between the preacher and Isabella harping at me, the death of Braden, and now Momma and Maddie showin' up. Maybe, just maybe it was time to answer the restful call of the water.

I put my hands on my hips and pointed my nose toward the sky. Some last leaves clung stubbornly to the trees. I took in a deep breath of icy, damp air. The water whispered its song over the rocks.

"Will I ever know where you begin? Will I?" I reckon Terrance was right. All the ghosts had hunted me down. Guess they was no place left to run.

An owl landed in the treetop above me. Its eyes glowed like two moons. Whoo-it-whooo. Whoo-it-whooo.

"Who?" I asked. "Mercy Roller. Mercy Roller, is who."

THIRTY-ONE

I PUSHED OPEN THE wire door to the chicken coop. Terrance had sawed lumber for Milsap Whaley who owned the general store down in Chattanooga. A few years back, he'd traded his lumbering for some octagon shaped chicken wire, a precious commodity in the mountains. A body was lucky to have it. Most folks kept quiet about owning chicken wire lest they'd find it missing the next day.

I shoved the slate lid off the corn bin and buried my hand wrist-deep into the dried kernels. The hens started their morning chatter, hustling from their nests onto the dirt floor.

"Here ya go. Mornin', ladies," I said, strewing corn across the ground. "How many eggs you leave me today? From the smell of this pen, egg layin' wasn't your priority." I lifted my feet over the plump, feathered bodies and stepped alongside the row of nests made in a wooden trough. "You gals got it easy. Ain't many men I know who'd lay such a nice bed for their ladies."

"True enough." Samuel's fingers poked through the wire and waved. "You still mad at me?"

"I'm not mad."

"You're not a good liar either."

"Law help. Samuel, can't you just stop reading into my head for one day?"

"I like your head." He stepped up on the framed edge of the coop. "You have a very . . . um, very uniquely shaped head."

I pulled three eggs from the bantys' nests. "Now you're just making no sense. Or you're just some schoolboy trying to bully the younger kids."

Samuel laughed. He leaned his head against the cage. The shape of the wire pressed into his forehead.

"Naw, I was always a good kid. It was me who kept the bullies away. But I did flirt with Becky Ottman. She was a peach in my second year. Long black hair, plaited down her back. Big ole' blue eyes. Round cheeks."

"And I guess you suckered all the girls with your charm. Mr. Big Man, savin' them from the bad boys."

"Well, now that would have been a nice prize, but best I recall, most it got me was a slice of homemade pie from a happy momma the next day."

The weatherworn basket slipped into the bend of my arm. I rummaged around the nests. "Hum. Only about a dozen today. Looks like we might just boil eggs for breakfast this mornin'. Not enough to scramble." I toed my way past the feeding hens. Samuel opened the coop door.

"You didn't answer my question."

"I did. But you chose not to accept it. So once more"—I brushed past him—"I'm not mad."

The morning sun slipped behind a grey cloud. Thunder rumbled across the mountain.

"Looks like rain, Samuel. Is there wood under the shack?"

He stepped in front of me and took me by the shoulders. His face boasted a bright red color. "Mercy, I like you a lot."

I stared into his eyes. "Well, that's nice to know, Preacher. You hungry for breakfast?"

Samuel leaned in and kissed my cheek. Then he did an about-face and headed toward the barn.

"That's it?" I shouted. "A peck on the cheek. They don't mean nothing but trouble."

Samuel turned and came back. "I'm not good at such things."

"What things? You tell me you like me and then give me a peck on the cheek. Good for you. I like you too . . . for a preacher. But that's about as far as it goes."

Samuel's face lost the crimson hue and the sweet expression in his eyes dimmed. "I was trying to be serious, Mercy." He walked away kicking at the ground.

My stomach twitched and my hands shook. I liked him too, but there was no way I'd let him into my heart. There was no room to like a man. No space for my past.

The river's roar spoke over the breeze. *Not like thisss. Not like thisss.* I turned toward the river then back again. I'd looked for a long time, set and listened longer for the river to show me something . . . anything. Looks like on the breath of the wind, it finally spoke, or at least in my mind it did . . . warning me. *Not like this. Don't push him away like this.*

I swallowed. "Samuel," I called out. "Wait. Samuel, wait." He stopped, but did not turn around. "Wait up a minute. I was . . . I was . . . awe heck. I like you too. I'm rough around the edges." I sat the basket of eggs on the ground and grasped hold of his arm. Samuel stared at the grass. "I ain't polished at letting anyone into my heart. Especially a man of the cloth. My experience with your type wasn't exactly like eating strawberries." Samuel wouldn't look at me. Instead he turned his back.

I yanked on his arm. "Heck, I'm tryin' to tell you I was wrong, all right?"

Samuel twisted to one side and cupped his hand around my cheek. He pressed against me and faintly touched his lips to mine. I felt the warmth of his breath against my face. Goose bumps raced up my arms. "You're forgiven."

Well, that took me back a few steps. Can't recollect a time someone told me I was forgiven, but there was one thing for sure. There was a kind of peace about them words.

Samuel immediately dropped his hand from my cheek. His face grew the color of cherries in the spring. "I'm sorry, Mercy."

"Oh hells bells. Are we gonna start goin' back an forth with the I'm sorrys?"

A grin broke. Samuel patted my arm. "No. We can call it even."

"Samuel," I said. "Can I ask you a question?"

"Shoot. I'm ready."

"What exactly do you see in me? I'm like a busted bowl that leaks."

"I reckon, Miss Mercy"—he turned to walk away—"that's for me to know and you to find out."

Momma sat wrapped in a blanket on Isabella's porch. Maddie, sore and bent from her fall, sat on a stool at Momma's feet. Isabella had bundled Momma up and stuffed her into one of the rockers. One hand peeked through the covers. A cup balanced on her fingers. Steam circled around Momma's face. I watched as she took in the bittersweet smell of Isabella's coffee. She caught a glimpse of me and a smile split her lips. Her free hand slipped out of the blanket and patted Maddie's shoulder. It was like Momma's touch was saying, "Look, Maddie, there she is." I hesitated and took in a deep breath. Terrance had gently but sternly told me the way things was gonna be. But I needed a minute. Looking at both them women stirred me so that all I wanted to do was run away.

Momma had changed. Outside of being pregnant, her eyes were sunken and dark circles filled the drooping skin beneath them. Deep wrinkles etched her forehead and the corners of her eyes. Her hands were shriveled and drawn. I could tell she'd not taken care of herself, coming to us half starved like she did. Had I not done the smack that sent the Pastor to his grave, I'd have sworn by the looks of her that he was still living with Momma.

She looked worse than the time he set her out in the snow after a Sunday service. We were leaving the church and Nate Carson gave Momma a set of winter mums.

"These is for you, Ms. Roller. My girls told me you like winter mums to warm up your cabin in the winter. And you was good to them when Emma passed. God rest my good wife's soul."

Momma took the basket of sets and kissed Nate's cheek. I thought the Pastor would explode. Momma was just thanking Nate. That was all. The Pastor come up behind her and wrapped one monster hand around her arm. His knuckles turned white as he squeezed into her flesh.

"Nice of you to bring my wife flowers. I'll see to it she takes good care of them." The Pastor elbowed past Nate, his two young girls huddled at his side. The Pastor hesitated and looked at the girls. Nellie's long blond hair hung in ringlets around her face, and Rose's beautiful smile beamed. The Pastor snarled. He sounded like a mad coyote.

He shoved Momma into the wagon and tipped his hat toward Nate. He spent the bigger part of the ride home preaching to Momma about fornication and adultery. The Pastor quoted Scripture, and every time he wanted to make a point, he smacked Momma with the horse whip.

I huddled down in the back of the wagon and prayed the good Lord would strike him dead. But like always, the good Lord ignored my prayers.

The snow was knee deep. When the horses came to a halt at the cabin, the Pastor took both hands and hit Momma square in the chest, sending her sailing backward into the snow. He stomped around the horses, yanked Momma up, then took one of the leather straps off the wagon hitch and lashed it around her wrists.

"Pastor, please. Don't punish Momma. Please don't punish Momma. She was just sayin' thank you." I grabbed at his hands and tried to untie Momma, but he put his knee into my stomach. The Pastor dragged Momma out to the big oak tree in the back and nailed that leather strap high above Momma's head. He pulled off her coat and boots and left her hanging by the wrists on that oak tree.

"Scripture says those who lust must be punished."

I pleaded for hours. "Please, Pastor. Momma will freeze. Please let me get her down. She's punished now. Let me get her down."

"Shut up the pleading. It ain't lady-like," he shouted. Every time I asked, he'd smack me in the mouth. But I kept asking and he finally gave up on me. My mouth bled. Both lips swelled twice their size. I felt a tooth dangle, but I kept pleading.

When the Pastor finally tossed me a bar to pry the nail loose, Momma had already turned blue. Her hands were black where blood pooled around her wrists. The leather strap had cut off the blood from her hands, and her feet looked as though they were on fire. I couldn't reach the nail and I could hear the Pastor laughing from the porch. I ran to the barn and mounted Slouch. She stood tall enough for me to pry loose the nail. Momma dropped to the ground. I tied one end of a rope around Slouch's neck and the other end around Momma's waist, then dragged her through the snow to the barn.

Me and Momma stayed two days in the barn. I built a fire and kept water warming to soak her hands and feet. It was so cold, ice grew on my eyebrows. Momma came in and out of consciousness. When she finally got where she could hold her eyes open, I fed her dried corn kernels just to get food in her.

"Get in the house. You'll freeze out here. Just let me die." But I didn't. I couldn't leave Momma for fear she would die. That would leave me alone with the Pastor. Even with the fire, the slats on the barn wall was wide cracks and the winter cold poured through like water through a sieve. Once or twice I heard the Pastor ranting about Momma lusting over Nate and I wondered when he'd bust in and finish us both off.

It was late on the third day when the Pastor opened the barn door and come in. He stood with his hands behind his back, staring at me and Momma shivering by the tiny fire. I'd buried Momma chin deep in hay to try and keep her warm.

The Pastor nodded. "I didn't know you was so smart, Mercy. I reckon you kept the adulteress alive. He pulled the winter mums from behind his back. The pot cracked when he slammed it on a wooden shelf. "I'm going across the mountain. Won't be home for a few days. Enjoy your flowers."

He turned and stormed out of the barn. Tears trickled down Momma's face. The Pastor had cut every bloom and leaf off the plant. All that stood in the bowl was a bunch of shaved stems.

Though it was only a couple winters back, it felt longer.

I glanced toward the house. Momma eased her cup onto the porch rail and motioned for me to come to her. It took me a while—them memories flashed in my head like a never-ending nightmare. Some made me feel bad for her whilst others made me hate her. My head played this hard game of tug-o-war.

Go to her or not, I thought. *Go to her or walk away.*

Walking away seemed to be the logical thing to do, but in the midst of my anger and hate, a sense of compassion rose from deep within me. Pity, I think. Sadness.

Isabella stepped onto the porch and forced my hand. "Mercy, them eggs in that basket?"

I could hear the girls squawking in the house. "These kids are hungry and, well, so am I."

I held the basket into the air and headed toward the porch. With each step my feet grew heavier. Isabella met me at the foot of the stairs. "Good mornin', glory. Your momma is looking a little better this morning and that Maddie, she's a charm. She's not well. Still spittin' blood from her fall, but she's managin' for now."

I looked at Momma. "I guess it depends on what you consider *better*."

"Mercy, sit. Talk to your momma. You can do this. I got great faith in you."

She stuffed a hot mug in my hand and pointed to another rocker. I handed her the basket and she vanished into the house. That was the second time somebody said they had great faith in me. I think, though I wasn't sure, that I was touched by it. Hearing it gave me a certain amount of strength. The chains my mind had locked around my ankles, clicked, and fell away.

"Good morning, sweet pea," Momma said. Her voice was weak and strained.

I nodded.

She picked up her cup and blew the steam across the brim, then sipped the coffee. The blanket around her shoulders dropped to her elbows and I found myself grabbing at it—pulling it back tight around her neck. I didn't want to care about her, but I did.

Maddie came to her feet. She took me by the shoulders. Tears dripped from her swollen eyes. "Ain't you a sight? I never thought I'd see you again."

That was Maddie. I knew better than to think she'd not love me, but it was easier to accuse her—to assume—than it was to face her. That day I hung the Pastor I still remember her begging me not to do anything foolish. But the rage inside me boiled out and her voice was nothing more than an echo in the crowd. Maddie wrapped her arms around me and squeezed so tight the air hissed from my lips. She turned me toward Momma.

"Your momma is having another youngin. Ain't that wonderful?"

Maddie lifted my arms and placed them around Momma's neck. "There. A reunion."

It was just like Maddie. The peacemaker. Always tryin' to make things right, even when she had no power to *right* with.

Momma smiled and kissed my cheek. "I know you're fightin' a battle inside you," she said. "Love and hate at the same time."

"You know that? How could you know that, Momma?"

"'Cause I fight the same battle. I love you and I hate you."

"You love me and hate me?" I twisted to face Momma eye to eye. "What did I ever do to you, but try to save your cowardly neck?"

Samuel turned the corner from the house and headed onto the porch. "Mercy, I'd like to—"

"Not now, Samuel. Momma here says she fights a battle with love and hate for me. Imagine that. She hates me."

Momma's eyes looked like dark caves, empty and cold. "You fight the same war. You know you do."

I stood speechless.

How could she hate me? After all I'd done? I did everything to save her sorry hide. I took beatings to keep her safe. I took on the Pastor at night to draw his vengeance off her. Hell, I'd killed the Pastor to save Momma from more misery. How could she dare hate me?

"I think what your Momma means is she hates the deed, Mercy. Not you. Just like you hate the deeds she did at times."

I glared at Samuel. "And this is your business because?"

"In fact, it is my business. As someone who cares about you, it's my business." He towered over me. "Today, it's my business. Sit down."

I guess I was stunned Samuel took charge. It wasn't his nature to be harsh. But he pretty much put me and Momma on the fence. He wasn't about to let either of us move until there was some sort of resolve. Samuel just didn't know Momma's manipulative ways, and it was only a minute before she tossed her words at him.

Momma smiled. "You sweet on my daughter, Preacher?"

Samuel glanced at Momma. His stare brought silence. I could tell he didn't know what to say. Especially since he'd just bared his feelings to me in the field and I'd made such an idiot of myself.

"This ain't about my feelings for Mercy. This is about you makin' peace with the only daughter you have. It's high time the both of you met on solid ground."

Maddie stepped between me and Momma. "The preacher is right. I come all this way to try and tell you I was wrong walkin' away that day. Mercy, I was wrong and I'm sorry. You did what most wished to do in their hearts. I was wrong to let you take on this burden by yourself. I knew the torture you endured. And to this day, I ain't never met no stronger woman than Mercy Roller." Her voice quivered.

I couldn't ignore Maddie's boldness. And though I couldn't tell you why, I understood her guilt. My heart began to thaw. I reached around Momma and took Maddie's hand.

For a brief moment, Momma softened. She patted my hand. "I do love you," she said. I could tell Momma's mind was comin' and goin'. It was hard to tell if it was from being so frail or if the Pastor's deeds had just drove her mad.

Momma snapped. What little kindness she'd had, left. They wasn't nothing a body could do but watch as her mind commenced to slip from weak and gentle to downright mean. The momma I'd known was gone and the devil in her reared his head.

"Well ain't that just peachy?" Momma sneered. "Two peas in a pod. Bad and badder. Stupid and stupider."

"Mrs. Roller, that'll be enough." Samuel pulled me behind him. "The good Lord tells us to love those who wrong us, even when it hurts."

"Pitiful and pitifuler." Momma spit on Samuel's boot and smirked. "They're both trash."

"Momma, that's enough. You might come after me, but you don't sink your claws into Maddie, you hear me?" For all the times Maddie stepped up for me, this time instinct took me to make a stand . . . a stand for Maddie.

I could tell by the look in her eyes she wasn't the same woman she was the day before, even minutes before. There was an emptiness in her face. It was like her soul left her body and all that remained was the banshee waiting to open her mouth and scream a horrible blood curtlin' screech.

"Ain't got no daughter," Momma said. "My daughter is dead. Died after she killed her father."

"No," Samuel said sternly. "Here's your daughter. The one who has loved you despite your ways. Who suffers because of your ways." He grabbed my wrist and pulled me close to Momma. She looked right through me. Just like she did that day at the river when the Pastor drowned Stanley— the day I took the Pastor's life.

A soft misty rain began to fall. The patter of the drops brought a restful release to the tension. It would not be long before the cold would take hold and the mist would become snow, bringing a winter hush over the mountain. We sat there eyeing one another, waiting for who'd break the silence.

I turned my hand, palm up, and studied the lines in the skin. "Momma," I said holding my hand up, "look at my palm."

Her eyes turned toward my hand. "This is the palm that slapped the horse the Pastor sat on that day. This is the hand that caused that horse to bolt, and the Pastor to hang. This, Momma, is the hand that killed the Pastor. And just so you know . . . it still burns."

THIRTY-TWO

"BREAKFAST IS READY. They ain't room in that kitchen for all of us, so I figured me and the preacher could eat out here on the porch. Do some talkin' about the weather and winter planning." The screen door squeaked as it closed behind Terrance.

Momma's stare was as cold as the fall rain. Every time I came close to her, her eyes fixed on my hands. Her glare burned a hole in my palm. She said nothing.

Terrance blew across his hot plate of food. A waft of fried potatoes and onions circled my head. My mouth watered. Isabella had fixed breakfast without me. It was the first time since I'd come to Thunder Mountain that I didn't have a hand in a meal. I rubbed my arms, but the damp morning air left a sticky dew on my skin—the same coating that turned warmth to frigid.

The three of us stood motionless. Wordless. Terrance pulled a cane bottomed chair close to the porch rail with his foot. He propped his plate on the rail. "Come on now, folks. Breakfast won't stay hot long." He scooped a fork of potatoes into his jaw.

Neither the preacher, Momma, Maddie, or me moved. It reminded me of the time Eli Morris, a friend of Terrance's, went head to head with a bear. He swore he froze in his tracks and the bear stopped, one foot reared in the air. "Whoever moved first gave the other an unspoken permission to attack," he said. Eli moved and the bear charged. He says to this day, that's how he lost the hair on the back of his head. "That there bear swatted me while I was hightailing it down the mountain. Scalped me bald."

Terrance took three bites of food before he slid his chair back from the rail and stood. His muddy boots popped against the weather-worn planks. He pulled his handkerchief from his back pocket and swiped his mouth.

"I see we have ourself a standoff. And since this here is my house, I can call a truce. Isabella has whipped up a fine breakfast. So Mercy, you and Maddie help your momma into the house. Fix her a plate. Preacher, you grab the door and hold it for the women. Get yourself some breakfast and join me back here on the porch." He covered his mouth and belched. "Everybody clear?"

Samuel stepped to the door and pulled it wide open. His hands trembled. I'd never seen a hint of anger in him. Least not till then. The color was drained from his face and his eyes were so wide, they could've shot flames. This was a side of Samuel he rarely let loose. And I was beginning to see a bit deeper into his soul. What I saw was a man who seemed to care for me, and to his side, Maddie, a long lost friendship now restored.

I glanced at Terrance. He motioned for me to move. I slid my arms around Momma and lifted her to her feet. Though she felt better that morning, her legs were weak and the weight of that baby pulled hard against her. She slipped her arm around my waist and leaned into me.

"Thank you." She patted my cheek. Her meanness suddenly turned to a childlike kindness. It made me sad because the woman I'd called my Momma had not always been right and fair to me, but I knew her heart, and I wanted to believe she knew mine . . . despite.

It took a few minutes, but I managed to finagle her into the house and to the table. Isabella had fixed Momma a plate. It sat steaming on the table.

"Here you go, Mrs. Roller." Isabella placed a fork next to the plate and warmed Momma's coffee. "I hope you don't mind boiled eggs. Seems the hens skimped today."

"Boiled eggs is fine." Momma fingered her knife, then slowly pressed it through the egg.

"I didn't give you too much this morning. I know your stomach was a mess last night. So I figured I'd ease you into breakfast. There's always more where that came from if you want it."

"It'll do," I said. "It looks wonderful, Isabella. Thank you."

Maddie scooped a spoon of potatoes onto her plate. "This smells so good, Isabella. I'll be happy to help you with the meals. I'm a right good cook."

Isabella nodded. That was the Maddie I knew. The fixer, the helper, the peacemaker. She'd proved that once again by huntin' me down. Lost memories of the joys Maddie and I shared flooded back. Her smile had not changed over the years and her laughter still lightened the room. I suppose, were it not for Maddie, I'd have died when I was a kid. She'd saved my hide and my sanity more than once.

Maddie coughed. Then coughed again. She lifted a cloth to her mouth and spit. Red seeped through the white material. She was hurt worse from the fall than she let on. But like any mountain woman, they was work to be done and she moved past the pain.

Samuel took hold of Isabella's hand and reached out to me. "Let's say grace." He jabbed his open hand toward me and I took hold. His hands felt as tender as his heart and his intentions. I knew Samuel meant well. He had my best interest at heart, but shoving Momma down my throat wasn't the way to do it.

Isabella took hold of Momma's hand and she took Maddie's. With that, Samuel prayed.

"Well, Sir, You're almighty. You've created this world and not without a plan. You have brought together those of us You need to complete Your work. Bless this food. We're much obliged. I pray for Your hand of mercy on us."

Samuel squeezed my fingers, then let go. Isabella filled a plate and offered it to him. "There you go. Now you can just go sit down." He nudged past me and pushed open the screen door to leave.

Terrance went to tellin' some silly yarn, and before we could finish filling our plates, the men were laughing.

"Let me help you, Mrs. Roller." Maddie laid a cloth across Momma's belly and set her plate on the table. She scooped a small bite of potatoes onto a fork and gently prompted Momma to eat. I wondered how Maddie could do it. How she could help Momma after the terrible things she'd said. But lookin' back, I see Maddie was showing me what I needed to do.

She glanced toward Momma and handed me the fork. "Here, you help.

I'll help Isabella." So I did what I was told and helped Momma eat. In the beginning it was hard, feeding the mouth that could eat me up and spit me out, but after a minute, I begin to sense the overwhelming weakness in Momma. I could see how her mind had faded. Years of the Pastor had finally taken its toll on her. Just like the Pastor . . . to give Momma his last seed but take her mind in return.

"You need me, Momma." I scraped the end of the potatoes from her plate.

Momma opened her mouth for the last bite. "I know," she said. "I know."

Melody and Amelia cooed their own language back and forth. Each fingered at the tiny white slivers of egg in front of them. I couldn't help but laugh as the girls giggled. "There's nothing sweeter than a baby's laugh."

"I know, ain't they the best?" Isabella chuckled. "You should have heard them girls last night. I was trying to bed them down and Terrance was dancing around like a rooster. Had them babies in stitches. It was a sight."

"They'll be walking before you know it," Momma said, wiping her mouth. "Then they'll be courtin'."

"Momma," I said. "This ain't the time. Let Isabella enjoy the babies while they are still babies."

"I'm just saying, they grow up fast. Too fast."

"These babies were small when they were born. Took them a couple of months to catch up to a regular newborn. But now they are sproutin' up like new shoots." Isabella poked a bite of egg in Melody's mouth.

I scooted eggs around on my plate, slowly picking at them. Things weren't going to hold much longer. All my frustration and hurt bubbled. I couldn't separate the feelings of sorrow for Momma and the anger. There was so much I wanted to say to Momma. So much I needed to say, but couldn't. I glanced across the table and once again, was taken back by her sad state. Never once had Momma made over this youngin on the way. I mean, she acknowledged it once, but other than that, it was like she'd forgotten she was pregnant. I couldn't understand that.

When I met Isabella in early spring, she was excited about her baby. It seemed every other sentence had something in it about babies. But not

Momma. She was numb to this child, just going through the motions. She was here. She was pregnant, yet she seemed calloused. Why was she really here? Unless this really was another trick of the good Lord. A way to make me pay.

Amelia choked on a sliver of egg. Me and Isabella both jumped toward her, one holding her tiny arm above her head while the other firmly patted her back. Momma didn't flinch.

"You know. I remember a time when Mercy was just toddling. She choked on a piece of cut apple John gave her."

"John?" I asked. "Who's John?" I'd never heard the Pastor or Momma ever talk about anyone named John, except for the one in the Bible.

"Why, Mercy. Don't you know your own daddy?" She gazed at me hard.

"What? Pastor Roller was my father." It hurt to utter those words.

"I know." Momma stared toward the ceiling. "John was his name."

I dropped to my seat. The Pastor had a name. Something besides Devil, Satan, or baby killer. Something besides Pastor.

"You remember your daddy. John Roller. Pastor of Rudman's Gap Baptist Church." I dabbed drool from her chin. She took my hand. "John loved you so much, Mercy. He was thrilled when you were born. I remember him taking you in his arms and spinning you around. Holding you high above his head and praising God for a daughter."

"We need to get you to bed. Come on." I tried to lift her from the chair, but she held tight to the table.

"Remember when you called the Pastor daddy?" Momma began to sob. "Tell me you remember when John was your papa."

Suddenly, I remembered the disconnect . . . the moment I stopped calling him *daddy* stood out loud and clear. I called him daddy when I was tiny. Maybe even until I was about seven. It came to me why I started calling him Pastor. It was hard to believe I was so innocent. So naive that I'd overlook what I knew in my heart was wrong. All for the love of a father.

"What I remember was asking the Pastor to go to school with me for show and tell."

"I remember that too. He was so excited."

"I remember introducing him as my father and in front of the entire class he smacked me across the mouth. Then he commenced to preach to the class about sparing the rod and spoiling the child. I was his example."

Momma gasped. "But he—"

"But he what, Momma? He said he loved me? No. No, that's not what happened. He whipped me in front of the class for being disrespectful and calling him *daddy*. In public, he was to be called *the Pastor*."

Maddie grabbed my arm. "Mercy, I remember that. I never did nothing. I'm sorry. I was—"

"Scared? Of course you wouldn't do nothing. That's how the Pastor liked it. He liked his congregation scared. I hate to say it, but Momma needs to hear some of these things."

"No, Mercy, she doesn't. Can't you see? She's this way because she does know. She knew. She don't need remindin'." Maddie led Momma around the edge of the table. That's when Momma started to wail. Her legs buckled and neither me nor Maddie could hold her.

Isabella dropped to her knees and wrapped her arms around Momma. "There, there. You cry. It's just fine. Go ahead and cry."

I watched as Isabella comforted Momma. Once again, I realized I was being taught how to care.

Maddie kept the girls busy, while we managed to get Momma out the back door and down to the shack. She wouldn't walk. Isabella and I draped her arms around our necks and tried to support her. All Momma would do was drag her feet then wail about John and how he loved her. How he loved me.

"Now that we got her bedded down, I'll run back to the house and send Maddie down with some more of that chicken soup. Mrs. Roller needs to eat a little more to keep up her strength," Isabella said. She covered her head with her shawl and slipped out the door.

There we were. Momma sobbing and me numb with shock. How could I have never known the Pastor's name? Momma never called him by his name. Neither did Granny when she came to visit. She just called him her boy.

For the first time in my life the man who'd never showed me any love had a name. John. Best I remember, John was the one Jesus loved most.

I sat next to Momma and watched as the baby inside her stomach kicked around. She was pitiful. I couldn't believe I was thinking this. But she was.

I thought I'd have my opportunity to shove the Pastor back in Momma's face, but what I got instead was an urge. A tingling. Signs of grace. Forgiveness. Mercy.

THIRTY-THREE

I SET THE BIGGEST PART of the day spoon-feeding Momma soup while Maddie kept the fire stoked. Maddie said little, but just her presence reminded me of her faithfulness as a child. Always close by . . . even in the rough patches.

Momma's face twisted with pain as she tried to find a comfortable position. She took a fever so I unbuttoned her dress and pulled her arms out of the sleeves. I was stunned at the sight.

She was scarred from front to back. Skin pulled over old holes looked like spider webs grasping to hold on to something to heal. Deep gashes, black spots left from burns. Two ribs jutted against the skin in her back. Probably broken and healed over years earlier. I lifted her arms and the scars continued. Long ugly stripes wrapped around her arms. Each bore the appearance of rope and when I rubbed my hands over hers, I realized she had no fingernails.

"Lord, have mercy," I said. Only this time I meant it. "Lord, please have mercy. I didn't know."

Tears flooded. "Maddie, I didn't know. I never saw these things on Momma."

"How could you, Mercy? You was too busy stayin' alive yourself. They ain't to be no guilt here. None. You hear me?"

I thought after Braden died, I'd cried all my tears. But from nowhere they flooded over me like the river running over its banks. I poured a pan of warm water and picked up a square of soap. Wetting her hands, I soaped them up and gently rubbed finger after finger on Momma's hand. Twisting and weaving my fingers through Momma's then rinsing. I pulled her dress away from her body. It was so worn and tattered that a puff of dust flew into the air when the material ripped.

There she lay, naked in front of me. And there before me, I saw every sin of every person who ever crossed the Pastor. I saw where she bore the payment to protect others. I soaped my hands and tenderly rubbed circles across the tight skin on her belly. Chill bumps popped up on her.

Maddie kept the water warmed and as I washed Momma, she rinsed. I slowly worked the soap up her stomach and across her chest. *Have you ever really had a bath, Momma? Or at least one when you could have it in peace?* Isabella pecked on the door and stuck her head in.

"Mercy?"

"Come on in. You can add some more water to the pot."

"I brought some clean clothes. Thought your momma would like a change."

"Couldn't be better timing," Maddie said. "Her dress is rotted to strings."

Isabella gasped at the sight of Momma's naked body. "Oh Lord."

She carried fresh water and together the three of us bathed Momma and washed her hair. Her hair was like straw when I unpinned it. After we washed it, it lay like fine silk. We dried her disfigured body and Isabella pulled on the dress from the basket she'd carried down.

I knew what scars my body held, but they was nothing like Momma's. One reason I had refused love was because I wondered how a husband could ever want a scarred mess, could ever love a damaged body and a broken spirit like I had. This though . . . the sight of Momma ripped my heart in half.

"Isabella, I can't get over this."

"I know. It's a lot to take in. Who'd have thought one person could have withstood that kind of torture?" She wrapped her arm around me. "I know it was hard for you. I can't imagine what the Pastor put you through."

When Isabella said that, I dropped my own dress and let her and Maddie see the wounds I'd taken in the name of God. She reached to the floor and pulled my dress over by body. "There ain't nothing I can say. Nothing. Nothing but they is more to you than scars."

"Who could ever love this?" I asked.

Isabella buttoned the front of my dress. "Someone who sees only the beauty in you. I believe the good Lord hides our imperfections from the eyes of those who love us. Otherwise, we'd be fixed on all that was wrong. People who love us don't see our flaws. They see us for who we are. I see you for who you are. My babies see you for the gentle woman who cuddles them close. Samuel sees you for the strong and beautiful woman you are."

"I ain't never showed no one those scars."

"I know." Isabella pulled a chair close to the fire and sat me down. Maddie finished getting Momma dressed and propped up in the bed.

"I'm lost here, Isabella. I'm torn just like Momma said. Caught between love and hate. And I don't know how to get away."

The fire popped and Maddie tossed on a log. Isabella checked on Momma then kissed my head. "I need to check on Terrance and the girls. It's hard to say what he's got them into. I'll be back later. Until then, I'm sending Samuel down."

"You don't need to do that. Me and Maddie are here."

She pushed her shoulder against the door. "Yes, I do. It's time you two talked. Maddie, last of the strawberries for the season makes an extra sweet pie. Comin'?"

"There's not a strawberry pie around I've ever refused." Maddie giggled and leaned against me. She blotted her mouth and I could again see tinges of red. She clasped my cheek and patted. "You remember strawberry pickin', don't you?"

The rain slowed and when Isabella opened the door I could hear the runoff passing under the plank porch. In the background the river roared and swelled its banks. It had been a good rain. I walked onto the porch and gazed at the river. Its song rang through the pass, splashes dancing off rocks and trees that lined its banks.

I glanced back and saw that Momma slept, so I stepped off the porch and walked the few feet to the river. I squatted and dropped my fingers into the cloudy water. The icy cold quickly numbed them.

"Where do you begin?" I whispered to the river. "Why don't you answer?" Tears dripped down my cheeks and dropped into the wash.

I looked up and there was Samuel, Bible in hand. "Mercy, can't you see that the one soul you think has deserted you, has brought you into a place where you can find peace?"

I set quiet, gazing into the water. A hundred thoughts whirled like eddies. "I reckon the mud is startin' to clear."

"'Lo, I am with you always, even unto the end of the world. Amen.' That's from—"

"The book of Matthew. I know."

"Do you believe that, Mercy?"

I tinkered with the string of my boot. "The Pastor was a sick man."

"I know." Samuel rested his hand on my shoulder.

"He did horrible things in the name of Jesus. But he also taught me the things the Good Book said."

"He did."

"I reckon I've seen about all the nastiness of the world they is to see. But you are right. Being here . . . with you, Isabella, and Terrance ain't no coincidence. And it sure ain't a coincidence that Momma and Maddie showed up. I figure the good Lord is grinding that in. I just know I can't live like this no more. I can't live stuck between love and hate."

"So choose. Which one do you want to live with? Love or hate?"

I set there. Pondering. Thinking. I can't remember what come over me, but I took Samuel's hand and walked into that river. This was the first step. He lifted his arm into the mountain's mist and said, "I baptize you in the name of God Almighty."

They was never any middle ground for me. I either trusted a body or I didn't. I either liked one, or not. I kept that line drawn betwixt the two. But at that moment, the moment I rested my neck and head in Samuel's palm, I remembered a Scripture Edom Strong would say. *Behold, I have graven thee upon the palms of my hands; thy walls are continually before me.* With that I leaned back. Samuel pressed his hand over my nose, then laid me gently beneath the rushing water.

For an instant a lack of trust brushed through my thoughts. Was he holding me under the water to drown me like the Pastor drowned Stanley, or was he holding on to keep me safe? The water rushed across my face and I waited for Samuel to turn loose of my nose and for the water to fill my nostrils then seep into my lungs. Three of his fingers cupped my cheek and his other hand gently cradled my neck.

I opened my eyes under the water of the Indian River—that same water I'd gazed into the day I tried to end my own life. I saw the ripples that distorted the shape of Samuel's body and dampness that took hold of his shirt and floated the material upward. My head rested firmly in the palm of Samuel's grasp, and my arm wrapped around his waist. As he lifted me through the clear ceiling of the river wash, my hair pulled tight around his arm. I felt the warmth of his skin through the cold autumn waters and suddenly I understood what it was to trust.

Without hesitation, I stepped across the line between yes and no and stood on the side of trust. I relaxed my body into the hands of a preacher. Not a man who called hisself a man of God, but a real man who loved God. I opened my heart to him. I opened my heart to the Almighty and I trusted. I wasn't sure what lay ahead. Didn't know if my life would really be any different, but I thought something must have to change. Something had to ease this pain. And I was ready to concede. I was ready to give it up. It was time to let the good Lord prove my worth.

When I come up, Samuel wrapped his arms around me. He pulled my face close to his cheek and I felt the tight grip of a man who cared. My teeth chattered and I felt Samuel's body shiver, but we stood in the water, entwined and warmed on the inside. He pressed his lips against mine and when he broke his kiss, he clasped both hands tight around my face. He didn't have to say nothing. I knew what his heart was saying. I saw the gentleness of a man who'd prayed over me, dodged my insults, and took my punches.

Samuel scooped me into his arms and carried me onto the bank of the river. Each step he took, the words of his song sank into my mind. "Showers of blessing, showers of blessing we need: Mercy-drops round us are falling, but for the showers we plead." Samuel sang quietly in my ear. "This ain't the fix-all, Mercy, but it's a start. I can't promise how you'll take hold of this newfound forgiveness . . . or me. But I can tell you, this is a start. And I will be here for you. I'll wait until you're ready."

And that's what happened.

Samuel began to wait.

THIRTY-FOUR

I RECKON I GAVE IN that day. I wasn't sure where I was going or what I'd do, but I supposed Samuel was right. This was a start and maybe, just maybe, I was ready for something new. I'd taken the first step toward finding peace. It started with trust.

Trust was a foreign thing and I wasn't sure what it meant, except that the fear seemed to be gone. I wasn't sure I could love, but I was willing to find out.

Maddie came from Isabella's house. She caught a glimpse of me and Samuel at the river. It only took minutes before she figured out what had happened. She broke into a run toward the river, one hand clutched the blanket around her shoulders. When Samuel got me to the bank she threw that blanket over me.

"Preacher, this is a real miracle. A blessing."

My teeth chattered like a squirrel titterin' with his mate, but I knew something was different. I couldn't have told you what, but I knew.

"Samuel," I asked, "how'd you know what I was thinkin'? How'd you know what my heart was seekin'?"

"Sometimes the Lord just pushes us into the spot He wants us to be. I reckon, today, He pushed. But it was right. I knew in my heart it was the right thing to do. The Lord called you as His child, Mercy."

"I know."

"And you didn't fight Him on it. He will be the Father you have longed for. This don't mean life'll be easy, though."

"I can't argue that fact." My chin shook and my teeth beat together like a woodpecker banging the side of an oak. "I'm pretty cold right now and it sure as whiz ain't easy to keep standin' here freezin'."

Maddie laughed and rubbed my arms. "Let's get you dried off."

Samuel kissed my forehead. "God bless you, Mercy Roller. God bless." Then he took his jacket from a tree limb and slipped his arms inside. "How about stoking the fire in the shack?" he said. Maddie smiled and nodded.

"I'll be happy to do just that. You be all right?" Maddie glanced at me.

"She'll be fine. I'll get her up to the shack in a minute. Now, go stoke that fire." Maddie trailed off toward the shack, stopping at the woodpile and grabbing a log.

I set on a rock next to the river, water dripping from strands of soaked hair. I felt different, I think. But I didn't feel like I thought I would.

"Just ponder on things," Samuel said. "Just ponder." He squeezed my shoulder.

I wondered what more I needed to ponder. I'd done nothing but that. Ponder my life, ponder my naivety, and stupidity. Trying to understand—worse, searching to blame someone. I'd just given in to the pain and hurt. Where was this life-changing thing that was supposed to happen?

God, I said, *I give in. Did what the preacher said I needed to do. Ain't You gonna talk to me now? Ain't You got something to say?*

I didn't hear a voice and I waited for a while. Samuel watched me waiting, and then he stepped in.

"It don't work like that, Mercy," he said. "God don't just open up the heavens and thunder in your ears. Just think on the fact you've surrendered. Let God speak on His terms and not yours."

Maybe the preacher was right. Maybe I just needed to mull over things and then the good Lord would give me some fancy revelation. I didn't want to think I was disappointed, but I was. I'd stepped out on faith, walked into the icy Indian River water, trusted God enough . . . and trusted Samuel enough, to let him press me under the water. I'd let the waters wash away the old, and I'd let the preacher into my heart right along with God Almighty.

Now all I felt was wet and froze solid.

"How long does this take?" I asked Samuel, but he didn't answer. When I turned all I saw was his back as he trekked toward the shack.

"Where you goin'?" I shouted.

Samuel poked his hands deep into his coat pocket. "To the shack. I'm nearly froze. Don't take long, but think on things a minute and then come on up."

"Just like that, you're leavin' me here on this rock?"

"Oh Mercy, for a smart woman you ain't always real swift. You're on the rock now. Ain't nobody ever leavin' you again. Like I said, don't be long. You'll catch your death of a cold."

But there I was, alone again. Filled with questions and nobody to answer them. I wondered for a time if this was all there was to God Almighty. A big hoopla and then disappointment. After all, that's how it'd been most of my life.

I turned back toward the river. Crumpled brown leaves circled and spun in tiny whirlpools, then snagged against fallen limbs along its edge. The sun seemed to move further above the mountains, allowing the season to grab and chill me.

"Mercy." A faint voice from behind me caught on a breeze. There was a twinge of excitement in my stomach.

"Yes, Lord. Are You finally talking to me?"

"Mercy Roller."

"Yes, Sir," I said. And then I felt a hand on my shoulder.

As fast as the excitement came, it left. God had failed me again. It wasn't Him who called my name.

"Momma, what you doing out here? You should be in bed. And where's your shoes?"

"You're one to ask questions. Why are you soakin' wet?"

I stood and took her by the arm. "How'd you get past Maddie? Let's get you and this baby-to-be back to the shack."

Samuel had his coat and shirt off before he got to the shack. He draped them across the clothesline and yanked a dry shirt loose from the clothespins as he stepped onto the porch. Momma rubbed her eyes with her fists. "That boy is soakin' wet too."

"Momma, why did you venture out? You're too weak."

She straightened her shoulders and pressed her palm against her hip. "My Lord. The preacher baptized you, didn't he?"

My stomach turned and I thought, for an instant, I'd vomit. The tone in Momma's voice was snide and condemning. She had that same hateful questioning that the Pastor had. She made it sound like I had done something wrong.

"You let that preacher baptize you, didn't you?" She braced her back with her hands and stretched. "I never thought I'd see that happen. Whatever in heaven's name possessed you to give it up to the Lord?"

I slipped my arm under hers and ignored the question. "Come on, Momma. Let's get you back to bed."

Isabella pulled a braided rug from the line behind the house. I saw her glance up and see me, soaking wet, leading Momma back to the shack. She dropped her broom and grabbed both babies, one under her arm and the other on her hip. I had to chuckle that she'd managed to run so fast with both girls.

"Mercy, what are you doing?" Her voice raspy from running. "Mrs. Roller, why are you out here and Mercy, you're soaking wet? You both owe me a passel of explainin'." A bead of sweat rolled down her temple. Maddie took Amelia and rested her on her hip.

Isabella shifted Melody to the other hip then slipped her free hand under Momma's arm. Together Isabella and me waddled Momma to the shack. Just as we reached the porch Samuel opened the door.

"Good land, Mrs. Roller."

He reached around her and took her from me and Isabella. Samuel's hair was brushed back from his face and the hint of a beard edged his jaw. His shirt half buttoned, and the suspenders on his trousers hung to his knees. I caught myself smiling in between my teeth clicking together. He was a handsome man and I wasn't sure why or how he'd managed, but he'd broken through the barrier around my heart. I suppose, like he'd said . . . that was a start.

Maddie took Amelia and Melody and sat with them on the floor while we bedded Momma down. Amelia crawled across the pine planks and grasped hold of Samuel's pant leg then pulled herself to her feet. He squatted to her level and lifted her into him. "Hello, sweet baby." He tipped her nose with his finger.

Momma groaned as she tried to work herself into a comfortable position. "You baptized my girl." She pointed her bony finger toward Samuel.

Isabella's eyes met mine and she mouthed, "You what?"

"I performed the act, but the Lord did the baptizing."

"You know Mercy's daddy was a pastor? How dare you do his job?"

"I've heard about the Pastor. In fact, I was headed across the mountain to visit him when I met Mercy on the trail."

"You met Mercy on a trail? Don't seem to surprise me." Momma grunted.

I stepped between her bed and the preacher. "Samuel don't want to hear your tales about the Pastor."

"Ha." Momma laughed but it was a hard sound. "I was gonna tell him about the daughter I had that killed her father."

"That's enough, Momma."

"Enough? You're telling me what enough is? You should have seen her, Preacher."

"Momma, stop."

"She stood there on that hill whilst them men strung up the only family I had left, and she never did a thing to stop them. In fact, she drew that arm back and slapped the horse on the rear. She killed her own daddy."

Momma grabbed my arm and twisted my hand palm up.

I felt the anger in me rise. Pulling my hand away, I took the Pastor's Bible off the small table in the corner and threw it across the room. It slammed against the wall and fell face down on the floor. Melody whimpered and started to cry.

"Isabella, let me have them girls. It's gettin' ready to be hotter than blue blazes in this shack." Maddie scooped up the babies. She groaned and coughed. "You okay, Maddie?" Isabella grabbed at Maddie's elbow.

"We do what we must despite the hurts. You don't fret over me. Come on, girls. Let's head up and see your daddy."

It was too late for me, for my fury rose hard and fast. Momma dropped her feet over the edge of the bed. Samuel stood fast.

"Don't you dare accuse me of stopping justice." I shoved my palm into her face. "I done told you this palm still burns from the slap. But you know, Momma, whether I'd have spoke up or walked away and never touched that horse, them men was gonna hang the Pastor. I've come to understand that."

"Understand what? That you killed your daddy?" Momma cried. Her voice caught between the sobs.

"I killed the Pastor. He was never a daddy. He was never a husband, Momma. We've been through this and I'm tired of it. I'm tired of explainin'. That man was Satan hiding behind the black coat and white shirt of a Pastor. He was a killer. A cold-blooded killer and had I not done what I'd done, he'd have killed you next." Momma covered her ears with her hands.

"Your daddy was a good man. Oh . . . he was a good man."

"The Pastor killed people, Momma. He beat you and me. For heaven's sake, he took me and then killed the child he planted inside me. The Pastor was everything the Bible speaks out against."

"No. No. Noooo," she screamed.

Samuel took me by the shoulders. "Mercy, stop."

"No, I won't stop. I've been made to feel like an animal most of my life. I've been forced to do things that'd even make God's skin crawl. And what I did the day the Pastor was set on that horse, that's what set us all free."

"Mercy!" Samuel shouted. "That is enough. Go put on some dry clothes. We'll manage Mrs. Roller."

Isabella walked toward me and lifted her hand. Once again she placed that tender hand of hers against my cheek. It was like a fresh drink of cool water.

"Darlin', you ain't no animal. You are the product of a man and woman who aren't right. Now shhhh." Her fingers slipped onto my lips and pressed. "Shhhhh. Quiet now, sweetie."

I never figured what it was about Isabella that always eased my anger, but she could. Maybe it was her soft voice or maybe her gentle touch. Perhaps it was her eyes that burrowed into my soul. A kindred spirit . . . I don't know. But she calmed me in a heartbeat. Isabella nudged me into the other room and handed me some dry clothes.

"Turn loose of the demons, child," Isabella said. "Turn loose." But turnin' loose wasn't something I could do all of a sudden. That was like askin' me to let loose of the rope that kept me from falling off the mountain. Who, in their right mind, could loosen their grip and let go?

The rays of the day streamed a pinkish purple through the window. Momma sat crying into her hands and Samuel tried to reassure her she'd be fine when she let out a squall that scared us all. She doubled over and grabbed her stomach, letting out a loud groan.

Isabella wrapped her arm around Momma. "It's time for that baby."

Samuel came to his feet like he'd been shot. "What can I do?"

"You can get Maddie from the house. Ring the bell and bring Terrance up from the barn." Isabella barked orders like a wild dog. "Then, Preacher, you can do what you do best. Pray."

"Samuel," I said, ashamed of my disagreement with Momma, "when you get back from gettin' Maddie, will you build up the fire and haul us some water in?" He pulled my hair behind my shoulder.

"Done." He started to the door and stopped. "Mercy, ponder. Think on things."

"Ain't no time for ponderin' now, Preacher." How he expected me to think on things was beyond me. Still I got what he was asking.

We laid Momma on the bed and rolled her to her side. She let out a scream that made your hair curl. "Lord, help me."

I'd watched Momma help birth over a dozen babies on the mountain. She was always a tower of strength. Her hand firm and steady. Her instructions clear and perfect. Her voice soft yet commanding. To see her weak left me confused. I thought my head was in a quandary when I left home. My heart was broken and the one woman I'd always looked toward was now like a bowl of mush. We'd always had each other's back. I thought Momma loved me in a twisted sort of way. But the way she attacked me. The way her eyes shouted hate. What little hope of family love was shattered.

I'd let Samuel baptize me. I waited for this whoosh of cleansing power to wash over me, but it didn't. Instead, I now stood looking at the hand dealt me by God Almighty, and I wondered if He was laughing out loud.

Momma retched and the soup I'd given her earlier spewed from her mouth. "Look out," Isabella said as she dropped a blanket over the puddle. "Get me a bucket off one of them maples outside. They ain't no syrup running now."

Maddie had hardly gotten in the door before she turned and headed toward the stand of maples behind the shack. Terrance had tapped them in early spring to catch the sweet liquid that flowed through the trunk. Maddie unhooked a bucket. I sopped up the vomit and carried the blanket outside.

Surely to goodness things will change. Is they anything else that could crumble?

I hesitated and cocked my head. I'd have sworn my heart stopped beating so I could hear the whisper. Nothing but the rustle of tree tops swaying in the breeze. All my life I wanted to hear my named called with love. Just once. I dunked the blanket in a bucket and rinsed it then threw it over the clothesline. From out by the trees I heard Momma cry again. "Lordy, lordy. Help me."

What I heard must have been the distant echo of her cry.

I stepped over some logs Terrance had cut and laid to ready for sawin'. I pulled my dress to the knees and dropped in a few small pieces of wood for the fire. There it was again. *Have mercy.*

Isabella stepped onto the porch and hollered, "Hurry!" I wanted to oblige, but my feet grew weighted and my heart grew cold. Why should I hurry to help this woman? She hated me.

I remembered not long after Braden passed, Samuel made a trip to visit some folks and preach in town. He was gone the better part of three days. When he returned, I found him out by those babies' graves.

"What are you doin'?" I asked. Samuel held up a small set of tin chimes. The top was a cross and hanging from the crossties were tiny tin angels.

"Listen." He jiggled the chimes and they tinged. "I thought this would be nice to put over the babies' graves. Every time you hear them clang, you know the souls of these sweet infants are safe in the good Lord's arms." It was a sweet gesture on his part. I had to give him credit. I stopped and tipped my head. It was faint, but I heard the tingling of the chimes.

Isabella waited for me on the porch. Her hand waved wildly for me to hurry. *Ting-a-ling. Mercy. Have mercy.*

I had to be crazier than Momma to hear a voice. Clang, clang. The wind whipped across the pasture and up and over the mountain. Ting. The chimes played an eerie melody. I looked up into the sky. A few soft wispy clouds floated in a sea of blue behind what was left of the dull grey rain clouds. Clang. Tingle, clang. As I stared into the clouds one seemed to shape into a tiny angel. Chills run across my arms. I looked toward the river and the song of the waters rolling around the rocks seemed to form words.

And I wondered . . . was this the Lord speaking?

The anger in my heart melted as I listened to the melding of music from the water, the wind, and the chimes. I wanted to be mad at Momma. I thought I was, but what I found was pity. Pity and the love a child has for her mother, despite hard times. My feet lightened and I broke into a run toward the shack. Maybe this was the breaking free of the ties that bound me. "Bless be the tie that binds." I began to sing as I ran toward the shack. "If you're gonna speak, Lord, now might be a good time."

All I heard was the ringing of the chimes. I guess God was with me. I wasn't sure, but the chimes reminded me He had our babies in His arms. Now they was about to be another baby. Another life. One I might have a chance to change.

My feet hit the porch and I slipped and fell to my knees, the wood rolled to Maddie's feet. "You alright?" Maddie stretched out her hand to help me up. "Guess the Lord was takin' you to your knees when you least expected."

Her humor, as untimely as it seemed, still eased the hardness of the moment. "Let's have us a baby."

I smiled. "Yes, let's do. Let's have us a baby." And for a moment, even in the harshness of Momma's cries, the thought of a new baby brought joy to my heart.

"What took you so long?" Isabella stuffed a sweater in my arms, then smacked my rear as I passed. "I'm proud of you, Mercy. Giving your heart to the Lord. Now, put that on to knock the chill. Your hair is still drippin' wet."

I stepped behind a curtain I'd hung on the far side of the room to hide what few possessions I had from sight. My wet clothes lay on the floor, a puddle of water trailed down the wood floor. I brushed out my hair and twisted it into a bun. Isabella had been sewing the bigger part of late summer and I now wore a dress she'd made from wool. *Your needs have been met*. I shook my head thinkin' I must be goin' crazier than Momma, but in my heart I knew the Lord was reminding me.

I stood speechless. I could never remember a time when Momma or the Pastor ever said they was proud of me. I felt joy rise from my toes to my head. A grin popped across my face and Isabella motioned me to hand her the wet clothes.

Momma rolled from side to side trying to pull her knees up to her chest, but that baby was so big, hanging so low and clawing to get out, that they was no way in hades she'd get her arms around her knees.

I swiped a wet cloth across her face. "Momma. Hold on. We'll get this baby out." She gritted her teeth and turned her face away from me.

Maddie draped her arm around me and twisted me toward her. She whispered, "Mercy, this ain't Reba. You know it ain't. Forgive her trespasses and care for the shell of a woman that is left. I'll be right here."

For years I'd been angry, scared . . . hurt. But now, I simply felt compassion. Momma's mind was gone. I knew that in my heart. Oddly enough, I realized even *my* broken heart could still feel.

"Lord, give us strength. Lord, I forgive Momma. I ain't mad at her no more." Then I said it. "Lord, have mercy." Little did I know, the mercy would be for me.

"Momma," I said. "I only tried to save you. To save me. I never meant to tear apart your idea of family. I never meant to destroy the man you loved. Can you forgive me?" She turned her head toward me and spit in my face.

Spit slivered down my cheek as Momma drew back to hit me. I flinched and closed my eyes waiting for the hit. Her saliva smelled like rotten eggs. My gut told me to hightail it to the bucket of water on the porch and wash my face.

The closest thing to forgiveness I'd got from Momma was the day before. I know under the madness, she loved me. I'd have to hold on to that 'cause Momma, the woman I knew as my mother, was gone.

THIRTY-FIVE

HOURS PASSED AND they was nothing we could do to move that baby into the world.

"Try to relax, Momma." I leaned down and kissed her. She grunted in response.

"Set her up so we can rub her back," Maddie said. "Maybe we can ease her pain."

Isabella took old of Momma's wrists.

Samuel paced on the porch. Momma was fightin' so hard, we needed help.

"Get in here, Samuel," I shouted.

Maddie covered Momma as he burst through the door. "Step on the bed and squat behind her. Push her forward with your knees," I commanded.

Maddie soaked us some rags in warm water as Momma commenced to yell. I can't ever remember her being this way, but then I never saw her pregnant and in labor either. Not to mention out of her mind. She fought Isabella and Samuel. At times all I did was stand and watch, too numb to move—too shocked at her behavior to know what to do next. Samuel would snap me out of it, and I'd go back to trying to help Momma rid her body of that baby. Nothing worked. And when I tried to get a look, Momma would shove me away. That baby wasn't gonna come on its own.

I wanted to run. Wanted to get away, but something held me there. I couldn't explain it.

"You can do this, Mercy." Maddie continued to whisper in my ear, words that helped me hang on. "Do what Reba taught you. Bring that baby out."

"There's too much blood. This ain't right." I rubbed my apron over my face. "I can't stop this bleedin'."

"Reba, let us see if we can get a look at this baby." Isabella tried to pull Momma's dress up to check the baby's progress. Momma kicked her, sending her backward over a chair. She elbowed Samuel in the stomach.

"They ain't no baby!" Momma screamed. "This is Satan ripping out my soul."

Momma focused on me. She gained a strength none of us could explain and pulled herself out of the bed.

"God Almighty will send your soul straight to the bowels of hell." She grabbed my dress and pulled me to her face.

I did nothing.

"Only God can save your wretched soul."

Samuel pulled Momma's arms behind her and dragged her up into the bed.

"You'll be sorry you were born," she shouted. "Oh Lord. Stop stabbin' me. You're stabbin' me."

Momma didn't know how right she was. She had no idea how many times I'd wished I was never born.

Like the time the Pastor come to me in the night. I heard him slip next to my bed and when his hand crawled across the covers toward me, I jumped and started to scream.

"You little wench," he whispered. "I come to you in the name of the Lord Jesus. You get down on your knees and give yourself to the Lord."

"No, Pastor. I won't."

He grabbed me by the hair and yanked so hard my feet left the ground. "You're a disobedient child. Kneel and let me take you. The Lord requires it of you. Kneel."

"Ain't falling to you. Ain't no God who requires you to maul me. Stay away."

Before I knew what hit me I was tumbling down the steps into the root cellar. My feet caught on the wood shelf that sat at the edge of the stairs. I hadn't had a chance to right myself and climb up before the Pastor slammed the doors and slid a wood plank through the handle.

"Pastor, let me out," I cried. "Let me out!" I beat the door with my fists until I felt the warmth of blood trickle down my arms.

"You'll be sorry you was ever born." His voice rang through the wood door. I don't know how many days he left me in that underground pit, but I remember kickin' at the rats that tried to gnaw at my dress. The Pastor was right. I wished I'd never been born.

"Mrs. Roller, Mercy ain't hurtin' you. It's the baby. The baby is comin'. You're in labor." Isabella grabbed her feet and together she and Samuel straightened Momma in the bed. Maddie tore strips of material and they tied Momma's hands to the bed to keep her from scratching at us.

"Baby? You're crazy. They ain't no baby." Momma's voice raised a pitch. "Lord. Lord! Stop stabbin' me. Ain't it enough you killed the Pastor. Now you're killin' me."

Tears filled my eyes. I could see there was no forgiveness coming from Momma. The only act of forgiveness would be what I chose to give. The Pastor's last act to Momma, ended up drivin' her mad.

Momma kicked at Isabella again, catching her just below the belly. Isabella doubled over. That was all I could take. I drew up a bowl of water from the bucket Samuel carried in and threw it in Momma's face.

"Simmer down."

Maddie jumped up and commenced to dry Momma off. "Oh, Mercy. That ain't necessary."

"It calmed her didn't it?"

"Come on, Reba. Let me help you," Maddie said.

I moved toward Momma and leaned into her face. "I don't care if you hate me. Lord knows I deserve it. But the past is past. You need to know . . ." And that's when the words slipped out and the weight I'd carried fell away. "You need to know I forgive you. Momma, I forgive John, the Pastor . . . Daddy." For an instant she quieted and I thought I saw a remnant of the woman I once knew. "Now, lay back so we can deliver this baby."

Momma hushed. A calm came over her and her eyes rolled back in her head. Her body went limp. Samuel and Isabella were finally able to straighten her in the bed.

I don't know how much time passed before I'd noticed the preacher lit the oil lamps. The soft yellow glow of the light cast shadows across the room. "Dark comes earlier these days," Samuel said. He patted my shoulder. "Be strong."

Samuel stoked the fire. Isabella opened the door. "I'll bring some vittles back shortly." She headed up to the house.

Momma hardly opened her eyes. She'd flinch and her face would twist when the pain of the labor would grab. Her body would rest a spell then start to shake so hard it would take me and Samuel both to hold her down. Still the baby wasn't coming.

That baby fought like the devil to free itself from the womb, but it was like Satan himself was hanging on to its feet. No amount of rubbing on Momma's back or stretching her legs apart opened her enough for that baby to slide out. I'd tried all I knew and when Samuel asked about layin' Momma over the rail like we did Isabella, I shook my head no. "You can't push out what ain't showin'. And this baby ain't give us one peek at its head."

I was tired and I know Momma was worn to a frazzle. Her pains come hard, one right after the other, and there seemed to be no relief for her. Still nothing.

Isabella came back a bit later. "Here's supper. I made stew. At least it's warm on a cold night." She sat a bowl on the table. The aroma of cooked beef and vegetables made my stomach growl. "It's heading into the wee hours. This ain't much but it'll keep your strength up. How is Miss Reba?"

"She's not good. That baby just ain't makin' its way out," Maddie said. "It ain't lookin' good for either of them."

Samuel poured a cup of coffee. "She lays quiet for a while then she starts to convulse like a mad dog. I ain't never seen nothing like it." He blew across the cup and steam twirled around his face.

I dabbed a cool cloth over her neck, but I couldn't seem to comfort her. "Momma can you hear me?" She cracked her eyelids open and hissed at me like a cat.

I cried.

I sent Isabella back to her house to rest. Maddie inched closer to Momma. "I'll stay with her. Go out and rest a few minutes."

Samuel took me by the arm and led me onto the porch. My knees shook from fatigue. The sky was dark, but over the south side of the mountain the night clouds cleared. The moon burst from behind the trees and it lit the pasture. I gasped.

"It's full and it's orange."

"Beautiful, ain't it?" Samuel shoved his hands into his pockets.

"You know that means death, right?" I asked.

"Don't be silly. Only the Lord knows the hour a man's life ends."

"I'm tellin' you. Here on the mountain, we ain't stupid. An orange moon means a death."

I readied myself for Momma or the baby to die. Even both.

"I was raised on the mountain too, Mercy. I know the wives' tales."

"Wives' tales? That's what you call this?"

"Well, yes. My momma and daddy taught me the good things about life. Like the beauty of a full moon. They didn't spend time waitin' for the bad. Even when I wasn't perfect, they looked at the good in me."

I wasn't sure how to respond. I guess in a strange sort of way, Samuel was trying to teach me something new. Something good.

"Can't none of us know if someone will die. And it ain't our place to make that judgment. What we can do is look at what's real, and the fact is, your Momma ain't herself. I know beneath the pain and sadness, she loves you."

I appreciated what Samuel was trying to do, but I knew what I knew. This night was not going to end well.

"She's outta her mind." Samuel tried to comfort me.

"She *lost* her mind. They's a difference. Between the life she suffered with the Pastor, and me taking the Pastor's life, Momma's gone crazy. And all that hoopla about being baptized. It ain't done nothing. I thought the Lord would change things. But ain't nothing changed."

I could hear Maddie in the shack trying to comfort Momma. Nothing stopped her from screaming my name. "Mercy, help me," Momma shouted. I turned to head inside and Samuel gently grasped my arm.

"She's in good hands. Maddie can manage her for a few more minutes."

"I guess," I said. "It's just hearing my name screamed. You'd think a body who lived with this name all her life could do something. I ain't sure I know what mercy is, much less how to give it."

"Well, now that's the wonder of the good Lord. He offers you mercy and forgiveness. They ain't no guessing. You're the only one who refuses to forgive yourself. The good Lord has done forgot your wrongs. It's history. Or as my momma used to say, his-story." Samuel flipped my braid over my shoulder.

"My name haunts me."

"Maybe it haunts you because you ain't learned its meaning. It's all about forgiveness. There is mercy in the forgiveness."

I looked at Samuel. "I reckon I'm sortin' through tryin' to understand."

"It'll come," Samuel said. Momma shouted again. One minute she had her wits about her, the next she was somebody different—violent and ugly. Samuel loosened his grip.

"Go."

I turned toward the shack.

"Mercy," Samuel said.

"Yes."

"A body can't give mercy until they've accepted it."

I nodded then drew up to him again, searching his face. I kissed his cheek.

"How is it you're this way, Samuel?"

"Way?"

"How do you understand pain and comfort when you ain't never suffered no pain or hurt?"

"Never said I ain't had no hurt. I told you way back I was raised by a good man and woman. Folks that loved the Lord. I never once said I ain't had no pain."

"Then what have you had?" I leaned into him, his chest firm from the hours of work on the homestead.

"I fought God. Guess I fought Him worse than you. I knew my callin' but it was more interesting being something different. I found out about pain and loss."

I shoved him gently. "Just what have you ever lost? Your hands didn't have a callus until you come here to help Terrance."

He hung his head and his eyes proved he'd suffered something. "I lost my wife."

I stood straight. "You was married?"

"Yep. Married purt near three years before . . ."

"Before what?"

"Well, it ain't important, Mercy. What counts is you know your momma loves you deep beneath her shroud of misery."

"Oh, no. You don't get off that easy. Not after all the razzin' I've taken from you about my past. Who was she?"

Samuel sighed and kicked a stone off the porch. "Meredith. Her name was Meredith. She was weak from the gitgo. Sickly since we was kids. But she saw things in me nobody else saw. She saw good when I was no good."

I stepped back. The preacher had a past and it wasn't all fried sweet apples. "Go on."

"I took a corner of dad's homestead and built us a cabin," Samuel said. "It was about a half mile to a natural crossover. A body couldn't get from one summit to the next lest they passed through my place. I took men's money to cross the summit. Took their food or pelts. Anything for pay. If they couldn't pay, they couldn't cross."

Samuel's voice had softened. He turned to move away.

"Wait. That's makin' a livin'."

"It went beyond that. When men couldn't pay, I sent them away."

"That ain't that bad," I said.

Samuel dragged his toe in a circle on the porch. "Meredith told me to be forgiving of those who couldn't pay. She kept telling me money was the root of all kinds of evil. Sad thing was, she was right and I wouldn't listen."

"A man has a right to make a livin'."

"That's true, Mercy. But an honest livin', not one like me. And I paid the price for my greed."

"They ain't a greedy bone in your body," I said. Samuel smiled and shrugged.

"No man really knows another man's heart or his true intentions."

I was shocked at what Samuel shared. He hung his head in shame and it nearly broke my heart.

"One day, Dallas Ensor come ridin' up with his six-year-old girl." Samuel paced the porch. "She was sick. In his rush to get her to Doc, he didn't have no money. He didn't have nothing. And me being who I was then, said . . . no payment, no crossing."

"Samuel, his child was sick." I crossed my arms to block the chill of the wind.

"I know, and I wouldn't let him cross the summit."

"It was a mistake. We all make mistakes," I said.

"It was a mistake. It was a serious mistake 'cause that little girl died while I argued with Dallas. I won't never forget it. He swore I'd pay. And I did. When the day come I needed to get help to Meredith, the only person within ridin' distance was Dallas. My folks had traveled down the mountain the day before. I was alone with my wife."

I knew what was coming. The end of the story spoke before Samuel got the words out. "Dallas wouldn't help you get her to the doctor," I said.

Tears welled in Samuel's eyes. "No. He walked away. An eye for an eye, was what he said. Guess that's why I understood what you meant when you talked about spoutin' that Scripture to the Pastor. An eye for an eye really struck home. I understood what it meant to take revenge that day because Dallas took his revenge on me. The result of my greed came back to bite me. Before I could get Meredith loaded on my horse and down the mountain, she passed over."

"What did you do?"

"Buried my wife. Learned just what greed can do to a man's life. Stopped fighting God and let the past go. Became a preacher . . . one determined to serve, not take."

I felt bad for Samuel. Maybe it was the good Lord working in me, but I felt. That was an odd feeling . . . to feel for someone else. My feelings had been numbed for so many years, all I knew how to feel was bitterness. But now that I knew his weakness, maybe I could be the one to help him.

"So you think the good Lord has forgive you?" I asked.

"I have to trust He has. He promises to."

"But you don't know for sure?"

"I know what I believe, Mercy. And I believe what I was taught. Every man is full of bad things. We all do and act on greed, selfishness, and bitterness. But when we take the leap of faith to trust—trust in something higher, something besides ourself, then we can make a difference. It's just a shame we have to do something plum outright stupid to figure out what goodness and love really are."

"I'm sorry," I said.

Samuel looked at me and smiled. "Did you hear yourself?"

"What?"

"Did you hear yourself? A few months ago, you'd have never uttered the words, I'm sorry. Guess that dunkin' in the river made a dent in your heart after all."

I wasn't sure it was the baptizing that made a difference. I was still waiting on that big moment when God opened up and talked. But I was softening.

I laid my head on his shoulder. "Momma hasn't forgave me, and it ain't lookin' good she will. She ain't even acknowledged that baby more than once or twice. It just ain't right."

"The Lord will make things right. You'll see. She knows your aim was to save her. A person knows deep in their heart. She forgives you. You have to trust in that. Make it right as best you can." Samuel tightened his arms around me. His hug was tender, gentle.

"Merccccyyyy." Momma let out a wail that echoed across the night. The wind took a chill to me; her scream was like ice.

Maddie pushed open the shack door and hollered, "Get in here, now!"

Isabella tried to hold Momma, but the pain of that baby was too great. Blood gushed from Momma's mouth. The tears that streamed down her cheeks dripped red. I rushed to her side and scooped her into my arms.

"Momma," I cried. "Momma, I love you. Please don't do this. Momma, don't die."

She lifted her bloodstained hand and grasped my dress. With her last breath she cursed my name.

They wasn't no forgiveness from Momma. Nothing for me to receive.

Terrance heard Momma scream and he made his way to the shack. His face grew pale when he entered.

"Is she . . ."

"Dead?" I said. "She's gone."

I shouldn't have. I didn't want to, but I burst into tears. I ain't sure why.

Maybe it was because Momma refused to forgive me out loud, or maybe it was relief and sadness. Either way, it didn't seem right.

I rested my hand on Momma's belly and that baby kicked. "Oh Lord, that youngin has survived."

Isabella come to her feet and the preacher went to his knees. I looked at Terrance then at Maddie. We all knew what needed to be done.

Time fought against us and my courage grew weaker by the moment. I gazed toward the ceiling, then prayed out loud. "Lord, I haven't prayed in years but today I tried to set things right. You didn't see fit to let Momma forgive me, but I'm asking You now. If You forgive me like the preacher said, help me save this baby."

I reached toward my boot and yanked my knife from the shank. In one swift stroke, I drew the razor-sharp blade across Momma's belly letting that baby spill out into my arms. My fingers grew weak and the knife dropped to the floor. Isabella grabbed it and sliced the life cord to that baby. She turned the infant over and held it into the air.

I snatched the child from her and flipped it upside down, and shook it. Liquid poured from its nose and the baby sucked in a breath. Its mouth opened and its weakened cry turned powerful. I wiped its face with the tail of my skirt.

Maddie held a blanket next to the fire and warmed it so I could wrap the little varmint up. The baby's skin turned a perfect pink and the blue that had encircled its mouth faded. Clear blue eyes blinked and its lips wrapped around my finger as it began to suckle. Isabella wet a cloth and washed the baby's face clean of the milky white coating. Sandy hair loosened from the skin and curled.

Samuel lifted his hands toward heaven. "Dear Lord, You have saved this infant. Let this little one be a blessing to You." I wasn't sure I needed to be thankful to God for the life that was given or to plead for the one that was lost.

"I'll tend to her body." Isabella covered Momma with a quilt. It wasn't long before Terrance and the preacher lifted the bed and all and carried it to the barn.

She was gone. At rest, or at least as much at rest as a troubled soul could be.

What was I to do? Where was I to go? I was alone. No more family. Then it occurred to me the infant I held in my arms was family.

I gazed into the child's eyes and my heart melted. I'd not even taken time to see if I held a boy or a girl, so I peeled away the blanket that held the baby. What I held in my arms was the opportunity to right a host of wrongs.

It was a boy.

Thirty-Six

Three days passed and a hard winter freeze come to the mountain.

Weeks of the black-and-brown wooly worms held true to the Almanac's prediction of snow. The cold snap hardened the ground and made it too brittle for Samuel and Terrance to dig a grave. Terrance even rode down the mountain a mile or so and called on Ben Stetson to help. Between the icy mountainside and the frozen ground, they decided to stack wood from the fallen trees on the hillside and set blaze to Momma's remains.

Isabella dressed Momma in one of her few dresses. The material was a brown tea-stained cotton she'd sewn into a skirt and collared blouse. Buttons were scarce in the hills of the Appalachians, and I made her cut them off the blouse and stitch the opening closed. Momma wouldn't care if her blouse was buttoned or sewn. The flames that waited for her cared even less.

I'd cried years worth of pain and loss over Momma. Now they was no more tears to shed. I brushed a comb through her hair and braded it into a strand that draped over her shoulder. That was when I saw a glint of rest on Momma's face.

I only remembered seeing that look once before. The Pastor had taken off for a few weeks to tend his congregations by the coal mines in the spring of 1887. I was just a girl. Momma had worked hard the day the Pastor left.

"Mercy," she said. "I've got a surprise for you."

"I love surprises, Momma."

"The Pastor has left for his fall preachin' along the coal mines, so I thought you and me would take the wagon up to the meadow."

The meadow was a few miles up the mountain. It lay between Wadalow Mountain and Reeves Bluff. The fields reached so far it seemed like the fingers of the clouds could pick blades of grass. I'd only been there a couple of times. Once, when I was allowed to go to school, the teacher took our class to learn about the birds that flocked there to feed. The other time I sneaked off with Maddie. We hiked the better part of a day to hide in the knee-deep grass and giggle at the butterflies.

Momma was excited to go. She packed us some sourdough bread and jelly, and filled a leather poke with icy water from the river. She'd baked some cookies from some oats she'd snatched from Slouch's feed. Off we went singing and laughing up the trail. When we got to the pass, Momma spread a quilt. We lay down and watched the clouds pass above us. The sun warmed our cheeks and after a time, I noticed Momma had fallen asleep.

A soft smile edged the corners of her lips upward. The wrinkles across her forehead seemed to ease and fade. I rolled to my stomach and gazed at her. Momma's hair was a shiny yellow. She'd pulled the braid loose and her locks spread around her head like an angel's halo. Her lips were the color of strawberries, and her eyelashes were long enough to bat away butterflies that tickled at her lids. Momma, as best I remember, was once a beautiful woman. And as she lay there on the quilt, her arm resting across her forehead, sun kissing her cheeks, I wanted to look like her.

"Momma," I said. "Can I eat a cookie?" She cracked open one eye and smiled.

"Only if you share a bite with me."

I dug my hand into the basket of goodies and retrieved two cookies. Momma bit into hers and rolled her eyes toward the sky. "Savor them oats. Oh my word. They's sinfully good."

And they were good. But what was better was the rest, the peace, the freedom I saw on Momma's face. With the Pastor gone, Momma was almost giddy.

The memory quickly faded as I laid her braid over her shoulder and across her chest. Her hair, now dull and thin, bore a yellow hint of its past color. Momma never had a wedding ring. The Pastor said jewelry was nothing but trinkets that led women to covet the wealth of Satan.

She deserved better so I twisted together some blades of grass and slipped it over her finger. The brownish green grass added a tinge of color to the pasty grey of death.

I leaned over and kissed her. "Momma," I whispered. "I forgive you even if you never forgave me."

Samuel took hold of my elbow and eased me away. "It's time."

"Time?"

"The men from the church are here. It's time to take Mrs. Roller to meet her maker."

I walked beside Samuel down the path toward the back pasture. Maddie wrapped her arm through mine, offering me some balance even though she stumbled a bit herself. The trail was lined with men and women from the mountain. I eased down the trail, amazed by the folks who cared enough to come stand by me. My chin quivered and my nose began to drip. Samuel reached out his arms to me and all I could do was fall into them and cry. He pulled me close and I felt his lips gently kiss my head. His hand cupped my face and he wiped the tears with his thumb.

"I'm so sorry. May she finally rest in peace."

I nodded. "Isabella"—my voice shook from sadness—"I'm so sorry too. Sorry for everything that happened to the people I loved. Those folks the Pastor took out his wrath on."

"The good Lord makes good come from the hard times. And thanks to you, my girls are alive and happy. Able to enjoy the sun. Play with their daddy. All thanks to you. They ain't a day that passes that I don't lift my hands to the heavens and pray the Lord watches over you, and gives you peace."

There was a sweet gentleness in Isabella. And it spilled over onto me. I felt my sin, and the Pastor's, get covered with love.

I needed peace. I needed to be able to go to bed just one night, and not have my palm burn. Not be plagued with nightmares of the Pastor and his sick ways. I wanted to make things right for everyone. That's why I took it on myself to slap the horse. I wanted to right the Pastor's wrongs. Momma called it revenge. I called it salvation.

Samuel tugged at my elbow again and nudged me on. As we passed, the mountain folk fell in behind us. I heard a baritone voice start to sing,

> *Going forth with weeping, sowing for the Master,*
> *Though the loss sustained our spirit often grieves;*
> *When our weeping's over, He will bid us welcome,*
> *We shall come rejoicing, bringing in the sheaves.*

The voices of the people joined, and their harmony floated across the valley. These people cared so much about me. They loved me. Folks from all around our side of the mountain came to pay their respects. I reckon they figured out their faith and trust needn't be in man, but in the Almighty, 'cause the man just might turn out to be warped like the Pastor.

The men lifted Momma on her bed of hay and rested it atop the huge pile of dead trees. Samuel preached a tender funeral for her. He found words that were soothing. Words that softened the loss. Words that did Momma justice.

Maddie pulled me close.

"I'm sorry this happened, Mercy. I wish you could have worked things out with your Momma. I'm so sorry." She squeezed my shoulder with her arm.

"Lord, take this woman into Your presence. For I know You have written her name on Your palm." And after he prayed over her, Terrance lit the woodpile soaked in oil.

Flames quickly rose and the crack and pop of the wood sounded like gunfire. It was hard to watch. Momma always feared the fire of hell and here she was, being eaten by the flames that hell was best known for. Isabella carried the baby strapped to her back. She held Amelia on one hip and Maddie snuggled Melody tight against her chest.

"Samuel, you think Momma is in heaven?"

"I think the Lord has mercy on the souls who are hard-pressed to know the difference between truth and lies."

This . . . today . . . ended my anger toward Momma. She was dead and gone. A flake of snow floated from the sky and landed on my face. Then another. And another. Momma's ashes would soon be blanketed in a quilt of white. *Bittersweet*, I thought. *Bittersweet.*

I raised my face toward the falling snow. "Autumn has become winter. An old life is gone and a new one has come." I glanced at the baby tied tight against Isabella. "A new season of life."

Thirty-Seven

THE MOUNTAIN'S WEATHER was like a cranky old man, turning on you without a moment's notice. A few scattered snowflakes soon turned to a blinding curtain.

Still, mountain women were known for their generosity to others, especially upon the loss of a family member. The weather didn't pose problem one. They'd cook regardless. And they'd cook a feast. Today was no different, despite the snow.

After Terrance lit the wood to take Momma back to the ash of the earth, several of the women made their way to Isabella's house to prepare for us. They'd celebrate Momma's life with a feast, and her death with memories.

Horses groaned as they jarred their wagon wheels loose from the frozen ground. The men opened up the barn so folks could get out of the cold, setting up sawhorses and laying planks across them for tables, while the women laid out a spread.

I saw Maddie hug Isabella, then take the baby from her. She looked weak but I figured it was just the turn in the season. Samuel tightened my cloak around me.

"Did you see Maddie take hold of Momma's baby?"

Samuel looked at me with those deep green eyes and nodded. "He's a sweet baby. Who wouldn't want to love on him?"

I don't think Samuel realized the depth of his question. But I did.

Who would want to love on this child? The Pastor's blood runs through him, and like they say, "The apple don't fall far from the tree." I pitied that child. Almost wished the infant had died so his life following behind the tread of the Pastor wouldn't be hell on earth.

"Women folk keep passing that child around, one after the other." I
groaned.

"He's a baby, Mercy. An infant. Helpless. Vulnerable. "

Samuel sounded as though I didn't understand helpless. Oh, I understood helpless and vulnerable all too well. He'd never know how much.
The mountain winds whipped through the holler and screamed past like
a banshee. I was chilled to the bone.

Samuel rested his hand on my shoulder. "You named that boy yet?"

I shot him a look that oughta have sent him sailing. "Lordy, Samuel.
Momma's hardly gone yet and you're already pushing this baby on me."
My words were harsh and colder than the mountain wind.

"I'm just sayin', this life ain't the boy's choice. But since the Lord has
sent him for a reason, the child deserves his life. And a name."

Samuel scratched his fingers across my back. His touch was tender. I'd
grown less fidgety when Samuel touched me. At times his touch was comforting. Still if he caught me off guard, I'd catch myself swinging a punch.

"I'm not sure what to do, Samuel. Isabella has taken to the child. It's
almost like she has Braden back. She seems to love him."

"But this child isn't Isabella's. This baby is your sibling."

"I know what he is, Samuel."

"Then you understand he's your blood. Your family."

"Dang it, Samuel. Yes, I understand all that. The baby is my brother.
Is that what you're aimin' to hear? This baby is my brother. I'll thank you
not to remind me of what lies ahead."

Silas Martin pulled his wagon next to me and the preacher. Samuel
helped me up. "Thanks for the ride, Silas," he said. "It's a long walk on a
cold day."

"Silas," I said. "Can you turn the wagon back toward Momma?"

"Miss Mercy, I really don't think you wanna see that fire." He pulled
his glove tight around his fingers.

Maddie tugged at my arm as I sat in the wagon. "Mercy, let's just go to
the house. You don't need to go back."

I yanked my arm away.

"But I do want to see. I need to see. So you can take me, or I can walk."

Samuel nodded and Silas pulled the team around. When we rounded the bend, the flames were as tall as the trees. The smell of burning flesh took my breath, and I covered my mouth with my hand. Embers shot toward the sky and mixed with the falling snow raining down over us. Some touched my skin with a hot burn, others icy.

There was a time when Momma refused to go to the church with the Pastor. I was sick with the fever. "You'll get in the wagon and go." The Pastor grabbed Momma by the back of her dress and shoved her toward the door.

"Mercy has the fever and I won't leave her. She's a child. She can't care for herself."

The Pastor stormed out the door and within minutes he'd built a fire close to the old elm tree. He took Momma out to the elm. When she took to runnin' from him, he roped her like a calf then tied her inches from the flame.

"Pastor, I'll catch fire," Momma screamed.

"I told you . . . you were needed in the Lord's house. You're to stand by me regardless. Now we'll see if your flesh runs as hot as that child's."

The Pastor stoked the fire. He walked away from Momma screaming for help then blocked the cabin door so I couldn't get out. I could hear Momma shouting. I knew she must be burning and there was nothing I could do.

The Pastor left. I laid on the cabin floor imagining Momma burning alive. Tate Colby was passing by and heard Momma screaming. He was her savior that day, releasing her from her binding and rushing her to the river to cool her skin.

"I'll get the sheriff," Tate told Momma.

"No. Don't you dare. The Pastor will kill you when you least expect it. I can't have that on my conscience. I can cover for myself, but I can't cover for you. Go. Don't never speak of this."

I reckon Tate took Momma's advice. Least we thought he did. We never saw him on our side of the mountain again.

I buried my head into Samuel's shoulder. "Momma was so afraid of flames. She was afraid of burning in hell. Wasn't there any other way we could have done this?"

"Let's go. Silas, I think she's seen enough," Samuel said. "There's no other way with the ground so hard, Mercy."

"Lord, I'm so sorry. Momma, I'm so sorry." I couldn't control the emotion any longer. The tears that I thought had run out, came back. Sobs bubbled from the depths of my soul. I felt as though I'd killed Momma too. I knew her fear of fire. I knew her fear. My shoulders shook as I cried. I found myself trying to climb out of the wagon, but Samuel held me in.

Silas took me by the arm and jerked me toward him. "Mercy, listen. Death happens and according to the preacher here, you, Maddie, and Isabella did all you could for your momma. Now stop this."

I was shocked. Silas, a soft and gentle man, stunned me to my senses. "We do what we must on the mountain. We mourn the way that suits us best. Then we move on. Now let's go. Let's head back."

———✦———

They say time heals and the good Lord comforts. It seemed to me both were a little slow. I cried the tears of a broken woman. One who'd lost her childhood, her own baby, and now her mother. It was time to move on.

Time to walk the river again.

THIRTY-EIGHT

Winter 1897–1898

HAD IT NOT BEEN FOR Isabella, Maddie and I wouldn't have had anything to keep us warm through the winter. She'd gone into the foothills and traded some of the goods she'd canned for boots with no holes and heavy coats. Her spinning gave us fabric for shirts and dresses.

"These'll fit the two of you perfect. It gets bitter cold, bein' hung in the lap of the mountain," Isabella said. She held her thumb into the air and closed one eye to measure me up.

"You've been far too good to me. I don't know what I'd done without you, and you allowing my Maddie to stay with us a while . . ."

They was a tender silence between us, then, "You know, Mercy. You ain't named the boy yet. It's been a week. The youngin needs a name."

Maddie tilted the baby forward and rubbed his back. "Come on, littlun. Burp."

I wasn't prepared for a baby. Especially not Momma's son. Not the Pastor's son . . . if that's really who he was. Momma was so crazy by the time we got her here, that only the Lord knows the real truth. I guess they was no real reason to doubt her.

"Funny you'd say that Isabella. It was me sayin' the same thing to Terrance when you was so sick. Took him several days to agree to name them babies."

Isabella had taken to the boy. I'd done little with him. This baby, I'm sure, seemed like the likely replacement for Braden. Truth was, sooner or later I was gonna have to face the fact this infant was my blood, and I was going to have to raise him.

"The good Lord never saw fit to provide me a son." That's what the Pastor said every time I didn't please him. "A son could be raised up to follow in his daddy's ways."

Memories flooded back. If anything, I'd never let this baby grow up in the Pastor's ways. I needed to talk to Isabella. Needed to talk to Samuel. I needed answers.

I'd not had a chance to be a momma. Not with the Pastor stealing it away from me. Lovin' on little Braden was easy. He wasn't mine, even though they was times I'd wished he was.

What kind of a momma would I be?

"Look at this." Isabella held up a shirt she'd crocheted for the baby. "Ain't this the cutest?" She held it up to the child's chest and measured. "Now you'll stay warm too, little boy."

The baby burped a loud one. "Atta boy. Good strong burp means you'll be a big boy." Maddie giggled just like she did when we were kids. "You wanna go to your momma?"

I stopped dead in my tracks. "I ain't his momma."

Maddie stared at me. The color drained from her face. "I didn't mean nothin' by that Mercy. But you are his only kin."

"I'm his only kin? That ain't sayin' much, now is it?"

"Looks like we need to find two names." Isabella pointed her boney finger at me. "A name for the child and a name for you."

A hush fell over the room. Isabella made it clear the next thing for me was to decide the role I'd play in this little feller's life. Momma, sister? Whatever it seemed to be, I could see nothing but bad coming from it. The child would be warped just from trying to explain who I was.

"I can see this comin'. Momma and sister both. Won't that be a real hoot to hear him explain. 'My momma is my sister.' Just the sound of that is terrible."

Isabella came to her feet. She took the baby from Maddie and wrapped him in a blanket. "Take this baby." She stuck him tight against my chest.

I could tell I'd made her mad. Just listening to her heels click across the floor pretty much told a tale.

"Ponder on this." She kissed his head and walked out.

Maddie coughed and a trickle of blood dripped from the corner of her mouth. "You ain't well. Did this start after the fall?" I pressed the baby against my shoulder and leaned to look Maddie eye to eye.

She wiggled around and tried to ignore me. After all, it was odd Maddie showed up out of the blue. They had to be a reason.

"Did I tell you I lost Momma and Daddy to a sickness? Not long after you left the holler. That's when I best thought I needed to find the one person that I always called my sister."

"Maddie. Stop sidesteppin'. Answer me. Was you sick like your folks or is this blood still comin' from your fall? Why come lookin' for me?" It was strange Maddie needed me. It was always me who needed her and always her who come to the rescue.

She stared at the floor. "I reckon after the fall. They's days it's bad and days it ain't. But lately it's gettin' to be more." She dabbed the corner of her mouth. "I needed to tell you I wasn't angry with you. I needed you. I figured of all the times I'd been there for you, the one you really needed, I snuffed out."

I understood what Maddie was aiming at and I reckoned this was another time the good Lord was rakin' at my soul. *Forgiveness.*

"There ain't nothin' for you to feel bad about. I did what I did on my own accord. It was me that walked away." I squeezed her hand. "I'll get Samuel to fetch the doc. He can help."

"Mercy, I'm fine. Or as fine as I'll ever be. Besides, we all have our days numbered."

I felt a cold chill. "Are you tellin' me you think you're gonna die?"

"I ain't tellin' you nothin' except I'm grateful I found you again."

I didn't like the feeling I was getting from Maddie. It was like she had some idea of what was to come. Almost like she came here for a purpose, and well, I guess she did. Right now, I had no intentions of lettin' go of her.

The harshness of winter dug its heels deep into the mountain. In the midst of the bitterness, all we had to look forward to . . . was the hope of a new year.

The winter didn't ease. Its winds grew stronger and colder as they filled the pass. The days grew longer but the sun seemed to struggle to drag itself up in the mornings. Winter on the mountain was hard.

Weeks slugged by and I still couldn't find my way clear to name the boy. We'd all taken to calling him *Bub*, the sound Amelia mimicked when we'd say *baby*. The child was the better part of a month old and Isabella nagged at me every day to offer the boy his own calling.

I don't know what made me do it. Guess maybe it was the good Lord, but I woke up from a dead sleep. Maddie had been sharing my bed. She'd started to cough, a hard cough that wouldn't let go. I'd gotten used to her barking through the night, but that night . . . the night the wind howled its deepest, Maddie's cough stopped.

I slapped my hand against the bed behind me. Nothing. Maddie was gone.

"Maddie." I whispered so as not to wake Samuel on his side of the shack. It had grown too cold for him to bunk in the barn any longer.

"Maddie." I struck the flint and lit the lamp. The baby slept sound, bundled tight in his blankets. The shack was filled with small cracks that welcomed the cold winds of winter.

"Maddie?" I slipped my boots on and wrapped the wool blanket tight around me. I eased out the door. A dark figure stood at the end of the porch.

"Maddie?"

"Shhhh." She motioned me toward her. "Look at that moon."

"Maddie, what you doing? It's cold enough inside. Why are you outside?"

"I . . ." Her cough made it hard to speak. "Darned old cough. It's gonna be the death of me." She'd lit an oil lamp on the porch. "I reckon I need to show you this."

Maddie inched close to the light and pulled up her shirt. A dark red bruise the size of a plate covered her lower back.

"What in tarnation?" I gently rubbed the spot. The skin was mushy, filled with liquid. "You're bleeding under the skin. Why didn't you say somethin'? Let's get inside." I took her arm and pulled her toward the door.

"No, Mercy. You don't get it. You've always been a little shy of smarts."
Maddie smiled.

"What? Now you're sounding like Momma. You got your wits about
you?"

Maddie pulled the cane-bottom chair to the edge of the porch. "Really,
Mercy. This cough is gonna be the death of me. This bruise has just kept
growin' over the weeks."

My stomach turned. "Maddie, this cough will pass. You'll see."

"No, I'll pass. *You'll* see."

Anger raised its head. "Maddie, is everything a joke to you?"

"Mercy, is everything so dire straits to you? It's death. I'm a child of
God or have you forgot the day I saved your hide at the church while God
saved me? 'Member that? You was afraid to sing. I hopped up and claimed
the Spirit had got aholt of me. Jumped around. Cried repentance so the
Pastor would baptize me. You remember?"

Her cough was hard and she gagged as she struggled to breathe.

Maddie had always had a flare for the unexpected. I smiled and took
her hand. "I remember."

"I've made my peace. Set out on the mountain to find you. Made
things right with you. I didn't expect to fall off the bluff and bang myself
up like this. But I can see, now it's my time. Good Lord brought me into
the arms of the friend I love the most. He let me find you. He restored us."

"Stop it. Don't be silly. You'll be fine. Besides, Isabella has really taken
to you. And Samuel loves to tease with you."

She gagged again as she pulled in the cold air. "Let's talk Samuel. You
know if it wasn't for you, I'd marry that man myself. So here's my advice.
You best be hooking your claws into that fish and reelin' him in. Lest
some little one snatches him from underneath you."

I couldn't help but laugh. "You are my dearest friend. The closest thing
I have to a sister. And besides, I can't marry anybody or raise a baby without you. Somebody has to teach them how life really is. Somebody who
understands the good in life. Now let's go inside, Maddie."

She pulled her arm from me. "I want to see the moon. The beautiful
moon. Besides, I'm not sure I can get up. My rear is froze to the chair." I
burst into laughter.

"Mercy, I come here as a reminder that they was always some good in your life. Me and you . . . we was good. They was fun memories. Things to be happy about."

"Please, Maddie, let's go inside." Her hands were stiff from the cold.

"You need to know that life is good. Even in the bad, life is good. The Lord granted me a short time to remind you of that. So take it to heart. Take to heart the wonders that you have right here at your fingertips." She held her hand in front of my face. I'd not realized how thin she'd grown.

"Maddie, you're my sister. Thank you for coming to find me. Thank you for standing with me through this mess with Momma. Thank you, sweet friend, for being my friend when the Pastor said no."

She patted my hand. "Maybe you should wake Samuel. I'm not sure I can stand." Maddie took my hand and pressed it against her cheek. She closed her eyes and commenced to hum. "What a friend we have in Jesus . . ."

I could tell things weren't right. I rushed to the door. "Samuel. Hurry. Help me! It's Maddie."

Samuel came out of his bed in a rush. It was so cold we all slept in our clothes. He threw on his shoes and tore out the door. His eyes were as big as saucers. I knew I'd scared him to death.

"Help me get Maddie inside. She's been coughin' so bad she come out here. She keeps talkin' crazy. She says it's her time to go."

Samuel touched Maddie. She toppled to one side.

"Maddie. Maddddiiieee!" Grief swept over me and every bone in my body ached. My chest grabbed and my heart broke open. "Nooo. Maddie."

Samuel scooped Maddie in his arms and carried her inside. I stood howling sobs into the wind like a wolf. The baby started to scream and together we wailed. A light came on inside Isabella's house and it wasn't long before Terrance stood beside Samuel, praying over the shell Maddie had left behind.

That was it. There was no more ties for me. No more reasons for me to move ahead. I'd killed my father, cut open my dead mother to save a baby that was the seed of Satan himself, and now, I'd lost the last person that tied me to my past.

I cried when Momma died. But not like now. All them pent up tears inside me from childhood broke out. Between that newfound forgiveness Samuel said I had and now this . . . they was little hope for anything but tears . . . bittersweet tears.

"Oh, sweet Mercy. You cry." Samuel pulled me close as Isabella and Terrance wrapped Maddie in a blanket.

"God, is this Your way of punishing me?" And just about the time them words left my mouth, that baby boy cried again.

When daylight come we found a letter Maddie had left telling the preacher and Terrance she wanted to be taken home.

By midday, Asher Whaley and Ben Stetson come up the mountain to help Samuel and Terrance abide to Maddie's final wishes. The winter mist, cold as it was, quickly turned to a light snow. The only thing of Angel buried on Thunder Mountain was a memory. We all agreed Maddie deserved to be home, so the men carried her ashes back across the mountain to Wadalow Mountain and buried them in a shallow grave next to Angel. Her momma and daddy just to the side.

It seemed all my past was gone. All those ties that bind were cut. I guessed it was the good Lord's way of helping me let go. Move on with the newness He'd give me. I supposed I should be grateful. But for me, right now, I just needed to mourn. Cry. Release the ghosts. Give that baby boy a name. It was time to move on.

I picked up the child with his tiny fist crammed in his mouth to suckle. "Addison Roller. That's your name."

THIRTY-NINE

EVEN THOUGH THE MOUNTAIN was cold, winter offered a special sort of beauty. I couldn't complain much. We managed to stay warm.

The trees hung heavy with a soft wet snow. Ice reached into the edge of the river like fingers grabbing at the rushing water. Limbs cracked and dropped to the ground. Despite the bright morning sun, it wasn't enough to warm the ground. I blew a deep breath into the air; the steam hung close to my face before it slowly eased upward.

I wrapped my arms tight around me and stepped onto the riverbank. Addison wiggled in the sling tied tight against my chest. His warm breath seeped through my dress. I figured if I looked hard enough into the water I could see my sin the preacher had buried under the wash.

Little Addison would have to know Momma, so I tried to remember good things. Anything good. There were few moments. I stared into the water, my eyes blurred with tears. Maddie had managed to remind me of a lot of good times. Things that had to be uncovered. Things that had to have the shroud pulled back. Laughter, summer nights, bustin' bottles. Happiness.

One memory pressed in. I must have been ten. Christmas had come and Momma and me loaded onto the wagon for the trip to the church. The Pastor had spent the day carrying his Bible, flipping through the pages and preaching his Christmas sermon out behind the cabin.

A fine snow coated the ground. Momma sat me between her and the Pastor. Today the Pastor allowed it. Most times, my place was in the back of the wagon. But for some reason, today was different. Maybe the Christmas spirit had actually caught hold of them. Who knows? But I remember how

warm it was between them. I sat perfectly still, afraid the moment would
end.

"Wrap this blanket around you, Mercy. You'll be warmer between
me and the Pastor." Momma pressed the blanket tight around me and
tucked the ends under my legs. "Put your hands under your arms. It'll
keep your fingers warm." I sat there bound tight in the quilt. Happy for
once.

The Pastor climbed onto the metal step of the wagon. He dusted the
snow from the seat and plastered himself close to me. "You ladies look
beautiful today."

Me and Momma was speechless. I couldn't ever remember the Pastor
calling us ladies, much less telling us we looked beautiful. I was afraid to
say anything. Afraid I'd pay a price.

Slouch groaned and leaned into the yoke. The wagon snapped and the
wheels cried as they began to spin.

Within moments I heard, "Silent Night, Holy Night." Momma
hummed, giving an occasional word between hums. I'd almost forgotten.
I wondered if this would be enough of a morsel to feed Addison. Would
it be enough to keep the sadness away? There were so few moments I
could share. Even his birth was filled with bitterness.

My feet slipped as I climbed the boulders. Each step left a mark of
where I'd been. Scooping away the snow, I sat on a huge rock that jutted
into the river. There's nothin' colder than the frosty bite of a cold rock.
As I stared over the water, I realized the river never stops. Even when
ice coats it. Beneath the icy tomb, the water rushes. Just like life, it kept
moving. I guess this was the river's way of teaching me a lesson.

Move on. Move on.

"We won't be long here, Addison. Just let me sit for a minute and we'll
go back to the shack." I rubbed his back through my coat.

I had things to think through. Things I needed to work through.
What options did I have?

My feelings for the preacher had grown. As much as I hated the
thought of loving someone, it was a fact I'd soon have to face. I'd kept
tinkering with the idea of leaving the homestead in the spring, but it was
a hard thing to consider. Samuel was growing attached to little Addison

and I'd be less than honest if I denied that at times, I imagined us a family. The three of us.

The cold cracked my lips. "Where do I begin? Me? I need to start over and I ain't sure how. Why is it so hard for you to answer this question? Is it because you're a river with your path done cut? Maybe it don't matter to you. Maybe it shouldn't matter to me."

I heard a whistle over the sound of the water as Samuel slipped and slid his way to where I was. Dry branches and icy leaves crackled as Samuel ducked under a low-hanging limb.

"Ain't you cold? And I ain't even gonna ask about Addison," he whispered. Dusting away the snow, he sat next to me.

"Preacher, that's the problem. I'm cold through and through. I look at this little baby and I know he's the child of someone I hated. I'm struggling to get past that."

"You will. Once you start to hold that little feller, you'll grow to love him like you've never loved before."

"I have few recollections of good memories. How can I answer the questions he is sure to ask me some day about the Pastor and Momma when I can't answer them for myself? How can I raise this boy with gentleness and not anger and bitterness? I don't know how." Sobs rang across the water.

"You're learnin' to love, Mercy." Addison began to whine. "This little one will teach you that . . . and . . . well, I would like to help teach you that too."

Samuel turned my chin toward him and kissed me. My eyes closed and nothing but sweet thoughts filled my senses. Tender moments. Warm moments. Times I was loved and had forgotten. My heart opened and feelings I'd not had since Thomas seeped through the cracks. This man cared about me. He loved me.

Samuel helped me stand and offered me his hand to lead me across the rocks. As we trekked back to the shack, he didn't let go, and I savored the warmth of our palms touching.

Samuel poured a cup of warm milk into the leather pouch and handed it to me. He smiled as I cuddled Addison. His nose wrinkled. "Shew. Seems like the boy needs a change." A smile tipped the edges of my mouth.

I rocked Addison and kissed his head. After he finished eating, I walked and patted him until he burped.

I lay across my bed and snuggled him against me. My fingers tinkered with the tiny part in his hair.

"I don't know how I'll mange this. I just don't know how."

The fear that gripped my heart closed over me like a casket lid. I held tight to the baby and began to shake. Addison took a deep breath and dropped off to sleep. Peaceful. Comfortable bundled close to me. The fear that swallowed me spit me out. I'd found a second person who could calm me. Little Addison.

When I woke up, hours had passed. I rolled over and pulled the quilt up to my chin. There in the corner by the fire, sat Samuel in the pine rocker from the porch. His feet propped on a bucket. He pushed with his legs and moved it to and fro. He'd taken Addison and cradled him in his arms. Samuel's head teetered to one side as he fought sleep himself. As hard as he worked to stay awake, his eyes fluttered. I eased out of the bed and glanced around the room.

The braided rug Isabella had beat clean in the spring lay covering the spot where Momma's blood had stained the floor. Terrance had built me a new bed, and though the ticking on the mattress held straw instead of down, I knew they'd all worked hard to make the shack a happier, homier place. A place . . . to be called home.

To one side of the room was a wooden box piled with blankets. I laid one across Samuel. He roused and I took Addison, and tucked him into bed.

"Amazing," I said to the baby. "You got no idea of the turmoil that went on in this very shack."

"I call that somethin' you might not want to remember." Samuel shoved his hands into his pockets.

"Preacher. It's a baby. He won't remember nothin'."

"Exactly. He won't recollect a thing. And that is what I call mercy."

I'd often wondered why Momma named me Mercy. What possessed her to give me a name that would haunt me to the grave? But maybe her intentions was good. Maybe something terrible happened when I was born and she saw, like I now saw in Addison, God gave me the mercy so I'd not remember.

Maybe there was something to God Almighty. Maybe, there was something to mercy. Maybe Samuel was right. Until I accepted the gift that was given to me, I could never really know mercy. I glanced at the baby.

"Looks like it's me and you. Somehow we'll manage together."

I always managed, even when things was not in my favor. I never wanted Addison to know about the horrors I'd experienced at the hands of our daddy, but at the same time, he needed to know how he came to be left in my care. I'd manage. Somehow I would . . . just like me an Momma did—by the grace of God.

I remember how hard the winters grew on Wadalow Mountain. Winds whipped through that basin like nobody's brother. It howled and beat at the door, but we kept a good fire built and hot soup stewing in the pot.

The Pastor made it a habit to keep a chill in the cabin. He'd insist on warm water to wash hisself in, but he'd never let me and Momma have any.

"Pastor," Momma said. "My fingers and toes is froze solid. Can't I boil some water for me and Mercy to bathe in?"

"That's the vanity of a woman seeping through. And vanity is from the devil. Now let's go outside to the trough and I'll show you how we rid you of that sin." He snatched me off the chair and flung me under his arm. Momma run behind him pleading for him not to take his vengeance out on me.

"Please, Pastor. I didn't do nothing. I didn't do nothing." I cried. But my tears did nothing but make him more determined. He stood me in the snow, the dead of winter bearing down, ripped my dress off me, and doused my naked body in the cold water of the horse trough.

"Now here." He threw a bar of lye soap at me. "Wash yourself. And don't forget your hair. Wash all of you. Then rinse. And if you ain't got ever spot clean I'll make you sit there until you get it."

Momma cried as she tried to help me, but the Pastor shoved her away. My skin was numb, but I knew better than to rush. The Pastor would just toss me in again. I sat in the trough of water, pieces of ice floatin' around my waist, and I scrubbed. I laid back and wet my head then rubbed the soap hard into my scalp. Momma pleaded.

"Pastor, she can't bend her fingers. Pastor, please."

The Pastor stood, hands pressed against his mouth blowing warm air into his fists. "You scrub the vanity out, Mercy. Show your momma how you are cleansed from *her* sin."

"Yes, sir." I bit my lip to stop it from shaking.

It wasn't enough to be frozen, numb, and blue, but I was nearly fourteen and naked in front of the Pastor. When he meant to take from me, he took everything. That day, I washed what vanity I might have had away in the horse trough. I climbed out and walked to the cabin.

My feet throbbed like I was stepping on nails, but I walked slow. Showin' the Pastor any sign of weakness would have been my death. I didn't have a stitch of clothes on and when I heard Momma's voice gurgle under the water in the trough, I didn't dare turn around. I'd done been cleansed. I couldn't bear to see her cleansed by the Pastor.

I didn't want to think of the Lord. Didn't want to consider that they was comfort to be found, but Momma would always repeat the Psalms, *Deliver me out of the mire, and let me not sink: let me be delivered from them that hate me, and out of the deep waters.* I found myself repeating the words too. "If you're any God at all, deliver me."

My toes turned a blackish-blue and I wondered for days if they'd done froze and died. I made sure the Pastor had warm water every morning so he could shave, and I never once asked to bathe myself. I didn't ask where Momma was either. I knew that answer too. She was barred shut in that cellar. My best guess was, she was dead and hardened by the winter wind.

"Them times is gone. Right, Lord? Long gone."

I knew I had the closest thing to a family I'd ever had right here on Thunder Mountain. I wanted this memory to be my last one of my past. No more trips to hell. No more haunting in my head. Only good things ahead for me and Addison.

"I'll forgive. I have to for Addison's sake."

Right then, right there, my burden lifted. The hard memories of the past blurred and the tenderness of a family coated over the top like a lamb's soft pelt. That was the moment I'd waited for. The time when God did something miraculous.

I felt compassion. And more so, I understood it. Maddie was gone. The Pastor. Momma. I kept tellin' myself they was all gone. It was over. Done with. I reckon as that sweet little youngin grasped my lips with his tiny fingers, I understood what it meant to be needed again. Loved once more. This child didn't know squat about me or the horrors of my past. All he'd know was I cared.

I managed. And I . . . loved him.

FORTY

Spring 1898

SPRING HAD FINALLY worked its way around. The Indian River bulged with swift waters that rolled from the top of the mountain. Tulips popped their yellow heads toward the warmth of the sun. Though there was still a briskness to the air, the scent of the breeze across the mountain was clean.

There was a sense of newness that come to mind. I'd never had anyone rush to drape a cloak around me if I went out to haul in wood, much less take the wood from me and carry it. But Samuel did these things. When I opened my eyes in the mornings, the sweet smell of coffee filled the room. He'd already warmed milk for Addison and he waited like a true gentleman, never crossing over the line from his side of the shack to mine without permission.

Samuel was good to Addison. He carried him with him to the church across the field. If I was busy, I'd hear him sing to the boy.

Addison grew, and every day that passed I pleaded to the good Lord to help me raise this boy to be different. I listened for the Lord to speak to me. Never figured out why He kept silent when I asked Him questions. Somebody with the power to create could at least open His mouth and speak. From time to time I wondered when Addison would show a resemblance to the Pastor. Would I be able to teach him right without taking a stick to him?

In the distance I heard Samuel ring the church bell. When the mountain folk mustered the money to have the liveryman make them a bell, Samuel was beside himself.

"It's a real church now. I can ring the bell and it echoes through the mountains. It calls the folks inside." The preacher was like a kid with his first piece of candy. Samuel rang that bell on and on to make sure everyone heard it. Now that the snows were gone, people could make their way back to the church.

Like always, the coffee hung simmering on the fireplace hook for me. The smell was so heavenly I'd have sworn the Almighty made it Himself. I moseyed to the baby's bed and he was gone. Terror shot through me. Addison was starting to scoot.

I rushed out of the cabin and searched the riverbank. My heart sank. "Oh Lord, where is Addison? Lord, where's my son?" All sorts of horrible thoughts burrowed into my head.

I pulled on my dress and tore across the field to the church. "Samuel, Samuel. The baby is gone. My baby is gone!"

My voice seemed deadened by the ringing of that blasted bell. I burst through the church door. Short of breath and hardly able to talk, I grabbed Samuel from behind.

"Addison . . . is . . . gone," I huffed. "My baby is gone. My son."

People had begun to gather for Sunday service. Mable Stamper stood dusting off her spot on the pew while Harold, her husband, warmed up his harmonica for the singin'. Samuel smiled.

"Well, I wanted you to start to come to church but not like this." He pointed to a corner where a long rope tied to the bell dragged the floor, at the end a huge knot. There sat Addison, gnawing on the end of the rope. I tightened my fists and gritted my teeth. A quiet growl seeped from my mouth.

The preacher lifted Addison into my arms. "Addy, your mother was looking for you. We should have told her you were like the Christ child . . . in your Father's house." Samuel let out a laugh that shook the rafters.

I wanted to slap him. "How dare you take that baby without tellin' me. You scared me to death."

"Mercy, you know I take Addison with me to the church. And this is Sunday. Why would it be any different today?"

I wondered why he made such sense. "Well, you shoulda woke me up."

"You were resting so well. But since you're here, why not stay?"

That was a question I'd not expected. In my head I'd rolled the thoughts of leaving the mountain . . . heading back home to Wadalow Mountain to start a new life. Momma's house was there, everything we'd need to begin again. Though I knew Samuel was asking me to stay for church, I wondered if deep down, he'd want me to stay on Thunder Mountain. And if he did, could I?

I squeezed Addison against me and stared at the six pews stair-stepped through the room. "Are them pews sanded down fine? I don't want no splinters."

"They are. Terrance planed them hisself. And Ruby Morris put the coat of white paint over them. They're real nice."

"What about your preachin'? You a yeller?"

Samuel laughed. "Mr. Colson, Mercy here wants to know if I'm a yeller when I preach the Word."

"Let me see now, Preacher. Are you a yeller." Bart rubbed his chin. "Not that I can say. You make your point stern, but I can't say you is a yeller. Now this young lady . . . she did a pretty good job of yelling."

I felt my face grow warm.

"She can let out a yelp every now and again." Samuel grinned real big. His attempt to tease me was only serving to aggravate.

I'd not been in a church building since the morning Stanley repented. Best I recalled, I'd sworn I'd never be in one again. Yet, here I was. Another first. Proof the good Lord don't have to say things out loud to get across His plan.

"I guess I ain't got no other worries. I suppose I could stay."

The preacher escorted me to the front pew. "One other thing, Mercy."

"What?"

"We ain't a congregation what shouts and jumps over pews."

"You think you're a real hoot, don't you? Alright, I'm sorry I yelled at you."

"You're forgiven. You know I'd never do anything to hurt this baby or you."

Samuel was right. I did know that. I'd gone from a woman never hearing the words "you're forgiven," to a soul who heard it a lot these days. Though I certainly would never hear it from the one person I'd hoped to hear it from—Momma. Getting that sort of thing from people who loved me meant something. Hearing those words come from Samuel was a living example.

"Let's all be seated. Mrs. Morris, will you lead us in a verse of, 'There Shall Be Showers of Blessing'?" Harold blew into that harmonica and made such a sweet sound. I never imagined a song could touch my heart so.

The church instantly filled with voices that melded together perfectly. Harmony meshed the men and women like butter on hot bread. Perfect.

Samuel preached about the goodness of the Lord and how He was the good shepherd.

"The Lord is our shepherd. I shall not want," he read from Psalm 23. "Imagine that. When you are in the Lord, you shall not want. You don't need to want because the Lord sees to it you are filled. You may not be rich, but you are filled with joy and happiness."

I'd never heard Samuel preach. Leastways not to anyone other than me, and he could sure preach me a sermon when I went to feeling sorry for myself. All this time, I'd noticed he was handsome and his heart was right. But I guess I never really saw it clear until now. There in front of these people was a man who knew the Word of God and showed us God was a God of mercy, love, and forgiveness. Samuel deserved better than the likes of me.

He showed me by his example, all men of God were not like the Pastor.

"He maketh me lie down in green pastures. He restoreth my soul." The words sank deep into my heart. Addison played with the belt around my waist. And as Samuel preached, he smiled at us.

"When we are troubled the Lord will lift us from the mire of those who hate us and stand us on firm ground." He lifted his hand upward and tears filled his eyes. "God is a God of mercy."

My stomach sank and I felt sick. Samuel reminded me of Momma. Reminded me of the Scripture I'd held tight to when the Pastor behaved like the devil. Reminded me, I was not alone.

Peace fell. A peace I'd never felt before. Peace I'd waited for. I didn't need to fear sitting in the church. I didn't have to worry the Pastor would yank Addison out of my arms and force some horrible punishment on him.

Instead, I was comfortable. Happy. Safe. *Well, Lord,* I thought, *now's as good a time as any to speak.* The windows on the tiny church were pushed open and the spring breeze carried in the scent of fresh pine. The soft tinkling sound of the chimes over the babies' graves rang across the meadow. Chills climbed my arms.

When the service was over, Samuel introduced me to every member . . . even though I already knew them. I suppose what warmed my heart most was he called me "Addison's mother." He didn't say momma or sister. He said, "Meet Mercy Roller. She's Addison's *mother.*

Mother . . . that was a name that called for respect. Better than momma.

Addison would grow to know I was his sister, but that I loved him and raised him as his *mother.* He would call me Mother by Samuel's teaching. For some reason, I knew this baby and I would clash from time to time. How could we not? We were family. But I had to trust the good Lord would help me discern between being Addison's sister and his mother.

I walked away from the church that day and hesitated at the crosses by the foot of the mountain. My Angel, and Braden. Momma.

Funny. A cemetery ain't something you hope to see grow. I blew a kiss toward Angel and brushed my fingers through the tin chimes. Sweet memories of the babies floated through my head. Times were changin' and so was my heart.

FORTY-ONE

Summer 1898

SPRING HEADED INTO summer and Addison was pulling up and standing. I let him take my fingers and he'd walk on his tiptoes toward the river. He'd look up at me with a grin that made me want to squeeze him. I leaned down and twisted him toward my face.

"Little man, it won't be long before you'll be walkin' on your own. I believe you're about the smartest little boy I've ever known."

No one ever praised me. Never took time to notice the little things I did. But I made sure I noticed Addison. I worked hard to make sure the praise came from the right spot in my heart. I wanted it to be genuine because I'd not had any as a child.

The birds circled above and the smell of lilac filled my senses. I sat on a rock and dangled my feet in the chilly waters of the Indian River. Addison balanced on the tops of my feet and I gently bounced him, soaking his feet to the ankles. The wind sang bass while the river sang the melody and between the two, I realized how the good Lord spoke to me.

I looked up the mountain where the river tipped and poured toward the valley and I asked the same question I'd asked for over a year.

"Where do you begin?"

Then I heard something speak to my heart. Odd thing was, I'd heard it all along. I just didn't know that was what it was. That still, soft voice seemed to always be muddled by the roar of chaos around the Pastor, first in his life and then in his death. But today, the good Lord whispered to my heart.

I understood he'd taken a young girl who was broken. One who'd murdered and hated. One who'd despised Him. Then He quietly healed her from the inside out. Maybe this happened when Samuel baptized me in the river. I guess it kept on when I took Addison to raise. Opened my arms to this gift. The ghosts of the past were banished. In my arms was the opportunity to start over. I could right the wrongs that had been done.

Would my quest ever be satisfied? Ever time I climbed the mountain in search of the river's start, I'd come within sight of an answer and it would vanish.

"So this is it? This is where it begins—where life starts over? That it, Lord?"

There was a rustle in the weeds behind me. Samuel stood in the shadow of the willow trees. I caught a glimpse of him from the corner of my eye.

"Are you spyin' on me?"

"Maybe."

"You don't trust me by the river? Especially with the baby?"

"Naw. I trust you. I guess I just wonder what goes on inside that head of yours."

I sat the baby on my knee and dried his feet. "What goes on in my head is private."

Samuel sat by me. "Ain't you figured it out yet?" He pulled me close.

"Figured what?"

"You keep asking where the river begins. Ain't you figured it out yet?"

I stared at Samuel. "Well I guess I ain't so smart as you are. But I'm comin' to some conclusions," I said. He took Addison and bobbed him up into the air. Drool dripped from Addison's toothless mouth.

"Awe, I can't explain the Almighty. Who can? But I try to put Him in terms I can get ahold of. So I imagine the river began with tears. The tears cried for mankind when they first sinned. God Almighty dragged His toe across the earth He'd formed and left a gulley that needed to be filled. He sat atop that mountain and looked over His creation knowing what lay ahead. He'd have to send His own Son. Make His own sacrifice in order to give us salvation. Then God being God did what was necessary to save us from ourselves. Something important to bring us back into His arms. I figure through it all, He must have cried Hisself a river . . . a river of mercy filled by the redeeming blood of His own child."

That was it. The answer I'd searched for all along. I'd carried it with me the whole time, tied deep in the meaning of my name, buried in the song of the river. Mercy. It was all about mercy. Redemption. It was all about what I'd sought to find and never really understood. Like the curtain in the temple, my blindness was torn and I saw straight through to the holy of holies.

Those were the words I needed to hear, needed to understand. No matter how hard things got, the river still ripped over its rocks, swirling and twirling . . . never ending. It took a journey for me to cut through the mess and find what never changed. I guessed God had been speaking to me all along and I was too deaf, too stubborn, to hear.

"Momma taught me a Scripture, Samuel."

"I've learned you know a lot of God's Word."

"She quoted it all the time. Every time the Pastor was evil I'd hear her whisper the words."

"Well, the good Lord's Word can be a drink of water in the desert," Samuel said.

"When we are troubled the Lord will lift us from the mire of those who hate us."

"The Psalms," Samuel said. "And what have you learned from them words?"

"I learned I've been saved."

I drew Addison into my chest and squeezed. "*Mercy* drops round us are falling but for the showers we plead." I'd pleaded over and over for peace. And now I was showered with love.

Why then, did I have this longing to leave? Maybe it was a need to stand on my own. To grasp hold of something besides fear and hate. Maybe I needed to go back to the house where it all happened and face the demons. I cared for Samuel, but I wasn't ready to love a man. Didn't trust myself to be a fair woman or wife, and I couldn't continue to hide behind the love of Isabella.

The chimes carried a sweet melody across the field, telling me I needed to leave.

Forty-Two

Time heals. Or so they say on the mountain.

I reckon now that the good Lord has ahold of my life, he'll continue to heal me. I didn't get broke overnight and I suppose I wouldn't be nailed back together in an instant either. I'd waited for years to hear the good Lord speak to me. It took me a while to figure He had a firm hold on me all along. When my life quieted enough, I got so I could feel Him in my heart.

There was a hankering in my soul. A thirst I couldn't quench. I knew my time was done on Thunder Mountain. I needed to say good-bye, take Addison, and head across the mountain—go home. I had no reason to go, but then I really had no purpose in staying either. A body understands when their time to move along comes. Samuel seemed content a single man and though he was wonderful to me, he never spoke of us being a family.

"You're leaving? What in tarnation has possessed you to pack up and leave?" Terrance stomped his foot against the ground and commenced to pitch a fit. "I don't get it, Mercy. I just don't get it."

"I'm brokenhearted. Just brokenhearted," Isabella said. "Are you sure, Mercy? I've never had anyone I felt like I could call sister 'cept you. What will I do? What will the girls do without you and Addison?" She teared up.

Isabella was right. She and I had a connection that only sisters seem to muster. She knew my thoughts before I could speak them and she loved me unconditionally. Isabella was, by all due rights, my family.

"Are you telling me you knew about this, Isabella?" Terrance snapped. She dropped her head and stared at the ground.

"I wasn't sure."

I piped up. "Me and Isabella had one talk, months ago. But I never said I was leaving out loud. I wasn't sure until the other day."

"The twins will be lost without Addison. They won't have anyone to play with." She might have been right, but youngins are resilient. They bounce back. I did.

The real shock was Samuel. He'd moped the biggest part of the morning while we packed what few belongings I'd gathered into the wagon. I wondered if he'd say anything before I left. I longed for him to say something. Anything to make me stay. Something to convince me he wanted me as part of his life.

"Mercy, if you leave, then I reckon I'll have to follow."

"You can't leave here, Preacher. You have a church to care for. Folks who love you." I smiled. "Besides, you'll be rid of your thorn in the flesh."

"A thorn that has pricked my soul." He drew with his foot in the dirt. "And so do you. You got folks here who love you. Folks that call you their family." Samuel pointed at the Johnson family. "You helped make this family."

"That's right, Mercy." Isabella brushed away her tears. "Please don't go."

"My time here is done. I need to find out what the Lord aims to make of my life. I need to hear His voice. You know, that voice Samuel preaches on all the time." A soft breeze grabbed my hair and twisted it. Ting, ting. The chimes over the babies' graves sang.

"And just where you plan to go?" Samuel stepped closer. "Who's gonna help with Addison? Who's gonna be a man for that boy to fashion his life after?"

"I need to go home. Back to Momma's house, my house, and let go of the past. Set in a new future. Free from the evils of my childhood."

I wanted Samuel to want me. Not just Addison.

"Samuel, there's a home waitin' for me. If I do nothin' more than close it up tight, I still have a home." I tied what few belongings I had in the back of a borrowed wagon then pulled the rope taut. Slouch snorted and slung her head from side to side, batting flies.

I glanced over the house, the shack, and the field. On the north end of the homestead stood the barn. The mountain folk had pulled together and rebuilt it after the storm. With Samuel and Terrance working side by side, there was hardly a sign of the black cloud day that hit and tore up jack. And now Terrance had managed to finish the back side of the house so the girls had a place to call their own.

And the two-room shack built by so much love . . . my home here. Addison's home. Samuel's home. A family's home. But we still wasn't a family and I had come to understand I needed to be more than just three people. I needed to be a family.

"You're hell-bent on leaving, aren't you?" Terrance leaned against me and kissed my cheek. "Stubborn woman." Clang. Clang. The wind pricked the chimes and they echoed across the field. I'd miss hearing them. They seemed to ring loudest when I felt the worst.

"I mighta stayed had it not been for that blamed ole empty sleeve dangling off your shoulder." I kissed him back and chuckled.

Samuel took my hand. "Is there nothing I can do to get you to stay?"

There was, but it had to be something Samuel thought about. It couldn't be me telling him. It had to come from his heart.

My eyes filled with tears. "Don't make this harder than it already is. I hate good-byes."

"Then don't say it." Samuel slipped his hand behind my neck and pulled me into his lips. For a moment I was lost in his tender touch. Addison grunted from being squeezed between us.

Say it. Say it.

But he didn't.

I didn't think leaving would be this hard. Samuel was right. These people had become my family, Addison's family. They loved us, laughed with us, mourned with us. I wasn't sure why I was leaving except it felt like I should. Almost like I'd overstayed my welcome. I felt this calling. An unexplained feeling that drew me back to the place I'd come from.

Lord, I thought. *Am I running from a ready-made family? Can't you just answer one question point blank?*

A breeze twisted strands of hair around my face. A deer and her fawn stepped on the pathway ahead. Samuel kissed me a second time, then helped me onto the wagon. Tears fell as he loved on Addison and said his good-bye. Clang. Clang.

When we are troubled the Lord will lift us from the mire of those who hate us and stand us on firm ground.

"What will it take?" he asked. I turned my head and slapped the reins across Slouch's back. She jumped and pulled the wagon forward. Addison bent his tiny fingers up and down to wave bye-bye and me . . . I commenced to cry.

The wagon bounced along the path toward the mountain road. And from the distance I heard someone shout.

"Mercy. Lord have mercy. Mercy, wait. Don't go, Mercy."

My name again. This time it was just a name. It held no special meaning. No guilt. No burning. Ting. Clang. Clang. Clang. This time someone called my name because they wanted me to stay.

I knew Samuel's voice, and though it shook as he ran after us, it was his next words that made me hesitate.

"Mercy. Marry me. Please, Mercy. Marry me. Don't go."

I smacked the reins against Slouch and urged her on. Did I really hear those words or was the wind playing tricks on me? If I looked back, would it be a mistake? The sun warmed my cheeks, but still I felt chilled. Clang, clang. Ting, clang, ting. Clang. The chimes sang across the field. Their song carried on the fluffy edges of clouds.

Samuel's words echoed in my mind.

"Mercy, marry me. Please, Mercy. Marry me." My thoughts muddled together as the clang of the chimes grew louder. I didn't deserve someone like Samuel, yet it was someone like him I'd longed for. Each ting of the chimes dug deep into my heart.

It occurred to me ever since Samuel put them chimes over the babies' graves, they seemed to jingle when I needed reassurance. When I hurt, they clanged. When I questioned, they tingled. When I asked the river where it began, they sang. Momma would have said I was slow as molasses not to figure it out. "Out of the mire. On to firm ground." Clang, clang, clang. Did I dare turn around and look back?

I pulled the reins tight and Slouch came to a halt. She flipped her tail, disgusted she'd worked to pull the wagon then was held up. The chimes' melody followed me on the mountain breeze and I heard the whisper of God in their song.

Mercy. Wait. Meerrrcccyyyy.

I sat facing away from the farm. Listening. Pondering. Was God speaking? I slowly eased myself around on the wagon seat and there in the distance was Samuel, on his knees. His hands clasped tight against his chin and I knew the good Lord had let me hear his plea.

Now I had a reason to stay. Now I understood the ground I was on *was* firm . . . solid. It was me who wore the blinders. It was me who didn't see the amazing ways I'd been protected. I could have been dead a hundred times over, buried in the cold ground and never once understood. But all along the Lord was nudging me.

I fought Him. Wrestled Him. Tried to run, tried to blame, and no matter what I did, the good Lord showed me mercy. Covered me in it.

The chimes continued to ring their song on the breeze. Affirmation after affirmation flooded over me, and the yoke that was so heavy eased.

I lifted my hand toward the sky. "I'm much obliged for Your mercy, Sir."

It was like the weight of a fallen oak was lifted off my shoulders and I caught the first full breath of air that I'd had in years. I closed my eyes and allowed the warm breeze to fill my lungs.

"What do you think, Addison?"

The baby giggled. I turned the wagon back around. Samuel ran toward us, threw his leg over the step plate and planted himself firmly next to me. He threaded his fingers through mine and pulled me tight into his grasp. Never in all my life had I felt so loved. Never had I felt so deserving. Never had I wanted anything more than this.

The sound of the Indian River bubbled in the distance. Its roar over the boulders sighed. I'd called out hundreds of times to know where the river began. I'd followed the river, made this quest, and found two things. Two things I never thought I'd ever know.

Mercy.

And Mercy Roller.

Acknowledgments

Dreams are just reality in rest—or that's what I've always imagined. From childhood, my dreams held were in rest—waiting to be freed from the chains that bound me to a lack of self-confidence. Never believing I could actually be a writer.

I remember sitting at my mother's Royal typewriter, clicking away at the keys. Typing the names of the books on our shelves and changing the author's name to my own. God instilled in me, years ago, a passion for written words. He gifted me with an imagination to spin tales and birth characters. How do you properly thank God? My best guess is by giving the work back—completed. Shined so bright that when the words are read, they sing. This book is a gift to me from a loving God, who knew long in advance of its publication it would be written. He smiled over me when He observed me typing on that Royal and He chuckled when I changed the author's name to my own. I am blessed. So thank you to the loving God who saw deep within me and granted a child's dreams from rest to reality.

A special thank you to my sons Chase, Cameron, Trevor, and Justin, who have suffered through the writer's life with me. If for nothing more than the example, they have seen since childhood that dreams really do come true, but they are not free. Rather they come with the price of hard work, determination, and fervent prayer. We've learned this together.

To my husband, Tim, who for the entirety of our marriage has said, "You will have a book. You will." He's spent countless hours reading and rereading words that were not ready for print and when the right ones finally came, he smiled with pride. There are few like him and not one

261

other person I'd dare to compare to him, for he too is a dream that came from rest to reality.

To my agent, Diana Flegal, who didn't cut me loose when I was one of the few who still remained unsuccessful. Thank you. To Eddie Jones, Yvonne Lehman, and Ann Tatlock—folks who have groomed my skills, believed in me, and stood by me when failure seemed to be my best friend. To my editor, Dawn Anderson, who loves Mercy and her journey as much as I do, and for her gift to make the words shine.

And to my niece, Erin Frady Thomas, a special thank you. Her undying belief and her blatant honesty when the story didn't gel, helped me craft a work that teaches true redemption. Erin's excitement and faith in me and this story gave me the inspiration that helped me form the perfect storm. Without her pushing me to think past what is normal, this work would not be complete.

Finally, I've been told when you write a story and it seems so believable that folks ask you if it was based on your own life, then you have "hit the nail on the head." The story of Mercy Roller is her own. My childhood was normal and basically uneventful. My parents, wonderful. They encouraged me to be the best I could be and to always, always seek after Christ, even when it was hard. I couldn't have been blessed with a sweeter childhood.

My life has not been perfect. I've made bad choices at times that brought me pain—who hasn't?—but nothing compared to the character of this story, though I would be less than honest to say my own hurts and disappointments through the years have not fueled the inspiration. A dear writer friend once told me that when I wrote it was as though I stood at a distance, drawing the story, never letting myself truly be a part of it. "You've got to find the wound in your own heart then pick the scab until it bleeds. That's when you'll pour onto the page the compelling words that rip at a reader's heart." Thanks, Eddie. Those were the words I've worked to understand.

My prayer: That women who suffer from sexual, physical, and mental abuse will dig deep into their hearts for God-given strength. I pray they will take hold, allow God to pull them up. I wish for them to stand tall, and find the courage to step away. Freedom is but one frightening step